SARAH'S LEGACY TESTED

Book Three

DAISY BEILER TOWNSEND

Other Books
by
Daisy Beiler Townsend

Homespun Faith

Sarah's Legacy Series

Sarah's Legacy
Sarah's Legacy Shared

Dedication

This book is dedicated to my precious son, Robb Townsend, who has maintained his faith in God through many tests.

Acknowledgements

I want to thank my husband, Donn, for all the ways he supports my writing ministry. I couldn't do it without you.

Thanks to my readers who push me to keep writing! I thank God for all the precious friends I've made through my writing ministry. You are gifts from God.

Ongoing thanks to the American Christian Fiction Writers Scribes who walked with me through the critique process of Sarah's Legacy Tested. Continuing gratitude to Laurie Germaine who critiqued every chapter of the first book of the Sarah's Legacy series. I learned so much. Thanks also to Don McNair, whom I've never met, but whose book *Editor-Proof Your Writing* taught me so much.

Thanks again to my faithful prayer partners who continue to encourage me and pray for me: Angelyn Trumbull, Bonnie Prugh, Cherri McAnallen, DeVonne White, MaryElla Young, and Stacey Pardoe.

Great appreciation to my beta readers, Angelyn Trumbull, Rebekah Crane, and Stacey Pardoe who have read all the previous books in this series and give me input before publication.

I want to continue to express gratitude to Isabel Dye, the wife of George Dye, without whom these books would not have been written.

Disclaimer

Sarah's Legacy Tested was inspired by the Thomas and Sarah Davis family and the Robert and Margaret Dye family. They lived at 259 Broad Street (now 81 Broad Street) in Sandy Lake, Pennsylvania, in the late 1800's and early 1900's—our home from 1988 to 2008. You will also encounter other professionals and residents who lived in Sandy Lake and Stoneboro during that era.

In spite of the fact that the Davis's and the Dye's, and several other characters were real people, and that some of the events in this book actually happened, the characters I've created and the story I've written are a work of fiction.

PROLOGUE

Broad Street
Sandy Lake, Pennsylvania
February 7, 1916

A blast of cold air followed by the cheerful whistled notes of *Down by the Old Mill Stream* brought Polly to her feet. She stared at her father, his cheeks rosy from the cold, his face wreathed in smiles. Father hadn't whistled since... Well, since the love of his life had passed away four and a half years ago.

She should be glad her father was whistling, shouldn't she? So why had her heart dropped into the pit of her stomach? "What are you so happy about?"

Father unbuttoned his heavy, wool coat and hung it on the hook by the door. Had his cheeks just reddened?

"No reason. Have you had a good day?"

"So-so." Polly frowned. "Why are you all dressed up?"

"I had a meeting with Uncle George, Mr. Staup and Lydia Wilds in the borough office." Father headed for the kitchen.

"Is that the woman who left her husband a couple years after they got married?"

He stopped and turned around. "Have you been listening to gossip?"

Her cheeks heated. "Everyone talked about it."

"I don't like gossip." Scowling, Father bit his lip. "It seems only fair to give you the facts instead of just the rumors. Rufus Wilds' first wife left him too. Maybe there was a good reason. He divorced her for desertion a few years before he married Lydia."

"Where did you hear that?"

Color crept up Father's neck. "Lydia told me when we rode to Broad Street to appraise the property she'll inherit."

Polly raised an eyebrow. "Doesn't it seem unfair that she'll inherit his property?"

"Lydia said she's entitled to it. Rufus died without a will, and she's the administratrix of his estate. She's very intelligent and knows her rights."

Polly turned away and muttered something under her breath.

"What was that? You know I hate muttering."

"I said, 'Gold diggers usually know their rights.'"

He stared at her. "Florence, you're being unfair. You don't even know Lydia. Whatever happened to *Love always believes the best?*"

Shaking her head, Polly turned away. "I have a bad feeling about her, that's all."

"This isn't like you. You've tried Lydia and convicted her without a judge or a jury."

Polly expelled a long breath. "Maybe you're right, Father. Maybe you're right."

CHAPTER 1

August 6, 1917

Polly wiped the sweat from her brow and slowed her pace just as Savannah Stevens—no, Young—left the grocery store. She should be accustomed to using Savannah's married name by now.

The girls hugged and Savannah drew her into the shaded area under the awning. "I heard you're in charge at your house this week."

"No secrets in this town. Where did you hear that?" Polly pulled out her handkerchief and wiped her forehead again.

"Dorothy told me at work that Lydia Wilds is spending the week with your father and some of his family at the Dye cottage on French Creek."

Polly's jaw dropped. "What?"

"Didn't you know?"

"I knew Father went with my grandparents, Uncle Pete and Aunt Flo, but I didn't know he took Mrs. Wilds."

"Leave it to Dorothy to find out even the best-kept secrets."

Sagging against the building, Polly shook her head. "Why didn't he tell me?"

"It's no secret…" Savannah hesitated.

"It's no secret what?"

"When your father was appraising Rufus Wilds' property, it was no secret you didn't approve of his widow."

Polly straightened and bit her lip. "You're right. I don't understand my feelings toward her."

"Come on. Let's go have a glass of iced tea." Savannah nudged Polly toward Aunt Adda's restaurant. "It'll be my treat."

♠

Savannah guided Polly into the restaurant which wasn't much cooler than outdoors. Would this heat wave never end? They took a table next to the window and the dark-haired, smiling waitress brought them each a glass of water. "I think we'll both have some iced tea." Savannah returned the woman's smile.

Polly stared at the table without blinking for so long that Savannah reached to touch her hand. "Polly, where are you?"

"I can't stop thinking of Father and Mrs. Wilds at the cottage. He must be really serious about her to invite her to go with him for a week."

"It does sound serious, doesn't it?"

"Every time I think of them together, my stomach churns. What's wrong with me?"

"Maybe you're afraid of the unknown." Savannah took a long swallow of her tea. "Your face is flushed, Polly. Drink some tea."

Polly picked up her glass and took a long drink, then another. Gazing out the window, she rubbed her fingers over the cool glass. "The day Father came home from the meeting of the appraisers with Lydia Wilds, he was whistling. It was the first time I'd heard him whistle since Mother died."

Savannah cocked her head. "How long ago was the appraisal?

"A year and a half."

"Hmm… Has your father been whistling ever since?"

"Now and then. But he hasn't mentioned Mrs. Wilds since the appraisal was finished and that was more than a year ago." Polly took another big gulp of tea. "Maybe he's been secretly seeing her all along." She met Savannah's eyes for the first time. "Go ahead and say it."

"Say what?" This conversation was getting stranger and stranger.

"Tell me I'm selfish or I'd want my father to be happy. Tell me I'd *want* him to find someone who made him *want* to whistle again." A tear rolled down Polly's cheek.

"You are one of the most *unselfish* people I know. You've spent the last six years helping your father raise your brothers and sisters. Selfish people don't do that." Savannah reached to take Polly's hand again. "Didn't you tell me you had a bad feeling about Mrs. Wilds?"

Closing her eyes, Polly nodded. "I did have a bad feeling about her. But maybe that's just because I can't bear to think of Father with anyone except Mother. He loved her so much."

"Sometimes it's hard to know where our feelings come from. Maybe I can talk to Garrett's mother about it tonight at Bible study. Or you could come with me."

"I don't think I'm ready to talk to anyone else about this. Maybe you shouldn't either. Father might think we're spreading gossip." Polly drained her glass and got to her feet. "If I was going to hear this from anyone, I'm glad it was from you, Savannah. You love me no matter what."

Savannah stood and hugged her. "You're the best friend I've ever had."

"Not just friends. We're family. By the way, belated happy anniversary."

"Thank you. I wondered if Garrett would remember. You know how men can be."

Polly raised an eyebrow. "Did he?"

"He did. He said five years is special and took me out for dinner."

"That's wonderful."

"I'd better pay the bill and get back to work." Savannah winked and gave a little wave. "Dorothy might have more news for me."

♠

Polly gathered the few items she needed at the grocery store, not stopping to visit with anyone. Her head ached and her stomach still churned. She could stop and talk to Maggie on the way home, but her sister might be busy with little Eugene. Besides, Maggie might be all in favor of Father remarrying since she'd been out of the house for more than two years.

Or there was Grandma Dye who lived across the street from Maggie now. No, she was at the cottage with…

Angry tears slid down Polly's cheeks and she quickened her pace. How embarrassing that Dorothy knew more than she did about her father's relationship with Mrs. Wilds. How would Polly bear it if he decided to marry her?

CHAPTER 2

"Not so many trousers now that Ben and Robert are gone from home."

Aunt Adda's voice startled Polly as she took down the last pair of men's work pants from the clothesline. Her Aunt watched from the road with a smile, arms full of groceries.

"Only George and Father to wash work pants for now." She returned her aunt's smile. "Do you need help getting those groceries home?"

"No, thanks, I'm fine. I don't have far to go. Do you miss your brothers?" Aunt Adda shifted her bags and rubbed her hand across her perspiring forehead.

"More than I expected—especially Ben. He's coming home for the Stoneboro Fair. Can I get you a glass of water? You look warm." Polly picked up her laundry basket.

"Water sounds good. Maybe we can sit on the porch. I can't stay long." Aunt Adda climbed the steps from the road. "Has Ben heard anything from the draft board?"

"Not yet. He registered in June. After we entered the war with Germany, I knew it wouldn't be long until they'd be calling young men to fight." Polly shuddered. "Roaland isn't old enough is he?"

"My oldest is safe for a few more years unless they change the ages. How about Robert?" Aunt Adda plopped down on the porch steps.

"Robert isn't old enough to be drafted, but he shouldn't have to worry since he got married, unless they change the present exemptions." Polly set her laundry basket on the porch.

"Oh, that's right. He's working at Goodyear in Akron, isn't he?"

Polly nodded and headed for the door to get her aunt a drink. "That's how he met his wife—she's from Akron."

She opened the screen door, entered the house, then let it slam behind her. Ironic that three of her younger siblings lived independent lives, while she…no, she wouldn't think about that. She'd made a promise to her mother on her deathbed that she would help raise her younger brothers and sisters…a promise she intended to keep.

♠

After Aunt Adda left and Polly put away the clean clothes, she stood undecided in the upstairs hall. It was too hot to think about housework or baking. Her neighbor, Blanche Davis, had finished her washing early today and offered to take Polly's younger sisters to the lake in Stoneboro, along with her teenage son, Billy. Surely they'd be okay. Beth was almost fourteen, Elsie and Twila, ten and eight.

This might be a good time to write her thoughts to the Lord. She found it helped to journal her prayers. She ambled into her room and pulled out her dark blue journal and Chartreuse, her green fountain pen. Plopping down on the bed she now shared only with Beth, she leaned against the headboard. When her thoughts stopped racing, she picked up her pen. Then laid it down again.

Flipping back through the pages, she found her entry on February seven last year

Dear Jesus, Today Father whistled for the first time since Mother died. I had such mixed feelings. I should have been happy but I wasn't. Turned out he'd been at a meeting with Lydia Wilds and some other men, doing an appraisal of her deceased husband's property. He'd gotten all dressed up while I was at the grocery store. Why do I have such a bad feeling about her? I thought she was way too eager to get Mr. Wilds' house for herself, even though they'd been separated a long time. Father says I'm being unfair.

Polly looked at the date again and sighed. A year and a half had elapsed with no mention of Mrs. Wilds. She had thought she'd worried for no reason. She picked up her pen and flipped to a clean page.

August 6, 1917 Heavenly Father, I don't know what to say to you. I feel so betrayed that Father would invite Lydia Wilds to go with him to the cottage without telling me. Even though I told him I had a bad feeling about her. Of course, he said I was being unfair. Am I

being unfair? Am I feeling this way because I never wanted Father to bring another woman into Mother's house?

She dropped her pen as thunder pealed and lightning flashed. She'd been so engrossed in her problems she hadn't noticed the approaching storm. The girls might be home sooner than she expected. The storm sent shivers through her, as if it forecasted their future. Sighing, Polly reached to pick up her Bible from the bedside table. She opened it to Reverend Lawrence's text which she'd marked the day before—Philippians 4:6-7.

"Be careful for nothing; but in everything by prayer and supplication with thanksgiving let your requests be made known unto God. And the peace of God, which passeth all understanding, shall keep your hearts and minds through Christ Jesus."

Their pastor had said "careful" meant anxious or worried in this context. They shouldn't be anxious or worried about *anything.* Instead, they should talk to God about *everything,* telling Him what they wanted, while thanking Him for all He'd already done. Then God would guard their hearts and minds with His peace. She read the verses again and again, taking deep breaths to calm the rapid beating of her heart.

Finally, she picked up her pen, blowing on the small puddle of green ink that had leaked onto the paper.

Father, I am anxious and worried. I'm anxious and worried about my father getting involved with someone I don't trust. Maybe I'd be anxious and worried no matter who he got involved with. I'm thankful you've taken good care of us since Mother died, and I don't want that to change. My honest request would be that Father never get married again, but that feels like a selfish petition. Maybe I shouldn't ask you for anything until I'm ready to surrender my will.

I can't expect you to give me your peace when I'm not willing to accept your answer, whatever it is. You taught your disciples to pray, "Thy kingdom come, Thy will be done on earth as it is in heaven." But I'm not ready to pray that way.

The door downstairs crashed open and Twila and Elsie shouted her name in unison. "Polly. Polly. Where are you?"

Maybe Blanche had left ahead of the storm. "Coming." She

blew on the lines she'd written, closed her journal and dropped it in her undergarments' drawer—a habit she'd formed with Sarah's diary when she was hiding it from her mother.

By the time she reached the staircase, Elsie and Twila were halfway up the steps, both talking at once.

"So many people at the lake on a Monday. I thought everyone would be at home doing laundry." Elsie, who had taken over being the "enforcer" from her older brother, George, shared her opinion loudly. Polly still held to the traditional laundry on Monday but couldn't understand why it mattered.

"Billy wouldn't leave Beth alone. Just pestered her all the time." Twila's cheeks were rosy and her brown eyes earnest as she relayed this information.

"Where is Beth?"

"She went to the kitchen for a drink." Twila turned to skip down the stairs.

"Why do you think Billy wouldn't leave Beth alone?" Elsie's braids bounced as she followed her younger sister.

"Who knows why boys do what they do." Polly hurried to keep up. "Maybe that's his way of showing he likes her."

"You mean like he wants to court her?" Elsie's voice squeaked at the end. "Beth's too young for that."

"She'll be fourteen soon and Bill is almost sixteen. Boys might begin to notice what a pretty young lady she is."

Elsie and Twila both turned to stare at Polly. "How old are you, Polly?" Twila's brown eyes widened.

"I'll be twenty-six next month. Why?"

After a moment of silence, Twila lowered her voice. "When will boys start noticing you?"

Polly had no answer. She hadn't met anyone who appealed to her since William Sider. Apparently, the feeling hadn't been mutual. He'd moved to Ohio soon after Savannah and Garrett married. To be honest, she hoped if she never married, her father wouldn't either. But she had no control over her father's choices.

CHAPTER 3

Garrett Young parked his Model T in front of his father's insurance office, gathered his papers in one arm and opened the car door with the other. Selling insurance had many advantages over traveling to Mercer every day to sell clothing for Mr. Black.

It was nice to see Savannah off and on throughout the day when he came to the office to do paperwork. His father owned the building and had turned the second floor into spacious living quarters for them five years ago. Since the Furniture Undertaker business was also closed at night, they didn't have to tiptoe or be annoyed by the noise of others.

He went into the building and then opened the inner door to the insurance office. Dorothy typed industriously and didn't look up. Garrett breathed a sigh of relief and headed down the hall to the office he shared with other agents. Any time he could get by Dorothy without learning the latest gossip was a good day. He wasn't sure why Pa didn't fire her.

Stopping outside Savannah's door, he knocked lightly and went in. His bride of five years was just as beautiful as she had been on their wedding day, and he never tired of feasting his eyes on her. How had he been so blessed to have this exceptional woman as his wife?

Savannah's eyes brightened and she rose to meet him halfway. "Was it a good afternoon? Did you make a sale?"

"It was good." He pulled his grandfather's watch out of his pocket to check the time. Almost closing time. He pulled Savannah close for a kiss—this one more than the peck on the cheek he usually settled for during office hours. "Mr. Miller decided insuring his house was a wise investment."

"Good. Your father will be pleased. He says you could sell ice to an Eskimo."

Garrett grinned at one of Pa's favorite sayings. He added one of his own. "The apple doesn't fall far from the tree. I've learned a lot from my father. How was your day?"

Her smile dimmed a bit. "Do you remember Dorothy saying Bob Dye took Lydia Wilds to the Dye cottage with some other members of his family?"

"I heard her. How in the world does Dorothy know everything that goes on in this town?"

"I wish I knew. Polly got really upset when I mentioned it to her. She didn't know."

"That's strange." Garrett stepped back and shuffled his papers. "Why wouldn't her father tell her?"

"Maybe because he knows Polly doesn't approve of her." Savannah covered her typewriter and put away her steno pad and pen.

"I didn't know Polly didn't approve. Let's talk about it more at supper so we aren't late for our meetings tonight."

Savannah joined him at the door to her office.

"I'll drop you off at Ma's after dinner and then head over to Jackson Center to meet with Pastor Jim. I'll try not to stay too late so I can pick you up when I get back."

"I can walk home. It's good exercise after sitting all day."

"I'd rather you wouldn't. Ever since George Burns kidnapped you—

"That was a long time ago, and he's in jail. Does Reverend Caldwell still visit him?"

"He wants you to call him Pastor Jim. Actually, believe it or not, he says George has been coming to the prison chapel services for some time now. Pastor Jim always says there's nothing too difficult for God. I'll see you upstairs after I finish up."

♠

Savannah reached the outer office as Dorothy stood to get her coat. She glanced at Savannah. "Did I tell you I heard—"

"Stop. Don't. say. another. word." The intensity of her words took even her by surprise. Dorothy froze.

"What's wrong with you?" Dorothy's blue eyes frosted in spite of the heat.

"There's nothing wrong with me. I've listened to your gossip for the last time. I've asked you before to stop. If you ignore me this time, I'm going to complain to Mr. Young."

"Well, look at who's turning into little goody two shoes. I wouldn't think someone with *your* past should be too critical of other people." Dorothy glared at Savannah.

"I know how it feels to have people gossip about me. I hate it and yet, I find myself repeating things you tell me. Today I repeated something and hurt one of my friends."

"I can't believe *you're* condemning me for passing along harmless information." Dorothy opened her desk drawer, threw in her pencils and pens and slammed it so hard the desk shook. "I think I should have a talk with Mr. Young about how *you're* treating *me*."

"I'm sure my father would be happy to talk with you, Dorothy."

She spun around to find Garrett standing behind them, his eyes a steely blue.

Dorothy's cheeks flushed. As she flounced toward the door, she threw one word over her shoulder. "Nepotism."

CHAPTER 4

Savannah leaned over to kiss her husband before getting out of the car. She loved coming to see Garrett's mother even more since she was part of the family.

"Tell Ma I'll come in for a few minutes when I come back to pick you up."

"She'll be happy to hear that. She misses you. Tell Reverend Caldwell I said hello."

Closing the door, Savannah started across the yard. The storm had only cooled things off for a little while and the air was still oppressive. Perhaps the dark clouds held more rain that would cool the air tomorrow.

Mother Young stood smiling in the doorway as Savannah approached. Garrett's mother was the first woman to accept her and believe in her despite her past wicked lifestyle. Even now Savannah choked up with emotion at the grace Garrett's mother had extended.

"Savannah, so good to see you." The plump, rosy-cheeked woman opened her arms wide.

"It's good to see you too. Is the heat bothering you?" Savannah kissed her cheek.

"Some. I try to do my baking early in the morning but I still have to cook our meals."

From long-established habit, Savannah sat in her usual spot at the kitchen table, while Mother sat across from her. Although Garrett called his parents Ma and Pa, Mother and Father were the names that came naturally to Savannah's lips. They seemed to delight in her using those names.

Savannah pulled her Bible out of her bag and Mother opened the worn one she always used. She lifted her gaze to Savannah. "Is there anything special you'd like to talk about?"

"I don't know if I should bring it up…"

"You can tell or ask me anything, you know. No subject is taboo." Mother's kind eyes sparkled.

Nodding, Savannah repositioned herself in her chair. "It's just that it has to do with work. I don't want to put you in the middle of something you'd rather not be involved in."

"If you need to talk about it, I want to listen. I won't even tell Father if you'd rather I didn't."

"Thank you." Savannah sighed. "It's just that I'm so angry at Dorothy. I didn't even know how angry I was until I exploded in the office at closing time."

Mother nodded. "That sometimes happens when we've repressed anger or refused to admit it's there."

"I hated it when Dorothy spread gossip about me. But today I repeated something to Polly that Dorothy told me. Turned out Polly didn't know, and she was very upset. I felt so bad."

Savannah went on to tell Mother how her anger had erupted later and how she and Dorothy had exchanged threats. "It seems childish to tattle to Father. Dorothy and I should be able to settle it ourselves."

Mother sat silent for a moment, smoothing her fingers over the cover of her Bible. At last she glanced at Savannah. "The book of Proverbs has a lot to say about people who gossip. We're told to avoid them, but that's difficult when you work with one."

"Dorothy says someone who's done the things I've done shouldn't be upset about a little thing like gossip."

"Jesus' brother, James, says our religion is worthless if we don't keep a tight rein on our tongues. He also compares the damage we do with them to a spark causing a forest fire. God doesn't have a grading system for sins."

"I don't understand why Father hired her. Her secretarial skills aren't that good."

"Probably for the same reason he hired you." Mother touched Savannah's hand gently to lessen the sting of her words. Savannah's cheeks heated none the less. "I asked him to hire her."

Mother paused, then continued. "Dorothy's father passed away a few years ago. As leader of the Ladies Aid Society at church, I knew of their dire circumstances. She's an only child and her mother is in poor health."

A tear rolled down Savannah's cheek. "I'm sorry, Mother. I'm in no position to condemn Father for hiring Dorothy. I'm sure many people criticized him for hiring me with my sordid past and complete lack of skills."

Mother didn't comment but absentmindedly patted Savannah's hand. "Maybe we could start a Bible study at the office one day a week at lunchtime and invite Dorothy. I don't think Father would mind. He's much more open to spiritual things than he used to be." Mother's eyes shone.

"I don't know if Dorothy will attend if I come. She's never liked me and after today…"

"We'll pray about it and I'll talk to Father."

♠

Garrett pulled into the parking lot at the Jackson Center Presbyterian Church where he often met Pastor Jim. His friend was walking across the parking lot towards the church. He smiled and saluted as Garrett opened the car door.

"Hot enough for you?"

Garrett grinned. It was the standard greeting these days. He was thankful not to be living in the city where the heat was causing much suffering and even death. "It's supposed to be cooler tomorrow. We keep hoping."

They walked up the steps. Garrett appreciated the church allowing them to meet there. Sometimes others joined them for a season, but he had remained constant. When anyone asked about the length of his stay in the group, he told them perhaps it was because he needed it most.

After their usual relaxed time of camaraderie, Pastor Jim opened with prayer. When he finished, he gazed at Garrett for a long moment. "So what are your plans for the future? You've finished every course available for lay leaders."

"I've learned so much. I owe you such a debt of gratitude."

Pastor Jim shook his head. "My life would have been very lonely without you. Itinerant preachers are a rare breed these days, but that's what God called me to be. Thank you for accepting the invitation to be my Timothy."

"Are you cutting me loose?"

"No, I count on you to preach when I have invitations at two churches the same day. Still, I want you to know you have my approval if you want to branch out in other directions."

"I enjoy the opportunities to preach, and I sometimes miss traveling with you like I used to do. Savannah and I wanted to establish a church home." He swallowed hard. "We thought by now we'd have a little one to add to the cradle roll, but that hasn't happened."

"How is Savannah doing with that?"

"She has her ups and downs. I remind her that she's the best gift God ever gave me. I'll never be disappointed in her even if we don't have children. Sometimes she thinks God is punishing her for her past."

"False guilt is one of Satan's shiniest weapons." Pastor Jim tilted back his chair.

"I know. Sometimes I fight that battle, too. "

"Remember, as far as the east is from the west, so far has He removed our transgressions from us."

Garrett picked up his Bible. "Where is that found?"

"Psalms 103:12."

"Thanks." He turned to the book of Psalms. "I'll pray about branching out in other directions, but I'm just not sure I'll ever be ready."

CHAPTER 5

Bob Dye stepped out the front door of the brown-shingled cottage they'd been coming to since he was a boy. The air smelled fresh and clean after the thunder showers the day before and the temperature was cooler. The trip to the cottage had been a spur-of-the-moment one. His soon to be seventy-six-year-old father wanted to escape the heat and had invited him to come along. Temperatures weren't usually oppressive in northwestern Pennsylvania but the past week had been an exception.

He headed downstream, following the path beside French Creek. Had the storm cooled temperatures in Sandy Lake as well? A twinge of guilt plagued him. If not, Florence and the children would still be suffering. The cottage couldn't hold all of them, but even if it could...

If he were honest, he wouldn't have invited Lydia if Florence had come. He'd kept his relationship with the widow very low-key and quiet because of his daughter's outspoken distrust of her. But how much longer could he do that? Lydia lived less than half a mile from their house on Broad Street. It was a miracle someone hadn't seen his horse and buggy there already and passed the information along to Florence. If he went through with his plan to buy an automobile, it would attract even more attention.

Sighing, he dropped down on a large rock beside the creek. It was a bit damp from yesterday's rain but weariness overwhelmed him. Why was he so tired? Surely he should have more energy than this at forty-eight years of age. Maybe his secret relationship with Lydia was weighing him down.

Margaret used to say, "There's nothing covered that shall not be revealed; and hid that shall not be made known." She'd often quoted Scripture, especially if she thought the children were being dishonest. He hadn't actually lied to Florence, but neither had he been honest.

He picked up a rock to toss into the water. No one could fault him for wanting a wife. Margaret had been gone six years. She would want him to be happy. He shifted uneasily on the rock. Why did he always find himself squirming when Margaret and Lydia both came to mind?

Understanding himself had never come easily. He'd always counted on Margaret's help. If she were here, this puzzle wouldn't exist. He groaned and stood up. He missed her so much. Could anyone ever fill the role she'd had in his life?

♠

Charlotte Dye was bustling around the small, sunny kitchen when Lydia Wilds walked in, every strand of her bleached blonde hair in place. *Stop it, Charlotte.* It wasn't like her to be catty about her son's friends.

"Good morning, Lydia. Did you sleep well?"

"So-so. How about you?"

"The cooler temperatures here in the woods by the creek helped. Even my husband slept better last night."

Lydia looked around the kitchen. "Will breakfast be ready soon? I like to eat as soon as I get up."

Charlotte bit her lip. It was hard not to compare Lydia with Margaret who had always helped with everything. "It will be a few minutes." Lydia turned to leave the kitchen. "You could set the table."

"I want to find your son. Maybe your daughter-in-law could help you." Lydia waved her fingers with delicately painted nails as she exited the room. The screen door slammed a moment later.

When Bob had said he'd be bringing Lydia on this trip, Charlotte was surprised. She didn't know her well and hadn't known she and her son were friends. Although she was trying to have an open mind, no one would ever measure up to Margaret.

♠

Bob turned into the path to the cottage when Lydia stepped out the front door. She smiled and his pulse quickened as it always did when she looked at him that way. When he was with her, he was sure they could overcome any obstacles in their path, whatever they might be.

He beamed at her, everything else fading in importance to the desire to make her as happy as she made him. "Good morning, Lydia." Her name tasted sweet to his tongue.

"Good morning. Did you sleep well?" She slipped her arm through his and snuggled against him.

"I did. Probably because I knew you were near by." He touched her cheek. "You look lovely as always." Inviting Lydia to come on this trip seemed to have taken them to a different level where touching was acceptable.

"Thank you. You're so sweet."

"You're the one who's sweet. Let's take a walk. I don't want to go inside yet."

They headed down the path arm in arm. How could something be wrong that felt so right? Florence had never been a good judge of character. Years ago, she'd defended Garrett even when everyone knew what a deceiver he'd been. If only there was some way to prove to her that she was wrong about Lydia.

♠

Polly rolled over and squinted at the sun glinting from the window pane. It had been a long, hot week. The temperatures had cooled somewhat last night, and she couldn't put off picking the tomatoes any longer. She would enlist the help of her sisters which wouldn't please them. They were all big enough to help with the picking and Beth could also help make tomato juice. It would be a hot job. George would probably be glad his work at the garage kept him from having to do *women's work*.

Which day had Father said he'd come home—tomorrow or Sunday? Grimacing, she swung her legs to the floor and stood. All week, she'd practiced what to say to him when he returned but nothing seemed right. She was torn between wanting to act like an adult and wanting to throw a tantrum. *A bit old for tantrums aren't you, Miss Dye?*

Selecting her coolest, oldest brown cotton work dress with one hand from where it hung on a nail, she opened her dresser drawer and gathered undergarments with the other. Beth could sleep for a few more minutes while she dressed and made breakfast. These were the times she missed Maggie most. Despite her constant reading, her sister had been a big help.

What could she do about Lydia Wilds? Like her tongue returning repeatedly to the rough edge of a tooth, she kept returning to her problem. If only there was some way to prove to Father he was wrong about Mrs. Wilds.

CHAPTER 6

A row of quart jars filled with canned tomato juice filled one end of the dining room table. The fruit of their labors yesterday. Pride at their accomplishment and weariness at how much work remained battled for first place. Polly sighed. It was only the beginning. Many green tomatoes hung on the somewhat wilted plants in the garden. Tonight after the sun went down, they would carry buckets of water to revive them.

George could help. Her brother sat at the other end of the table finishing his second plateful of corn on the cob and tomatoes. He usually ate supper later than the rest of the family because of his odd hours at the garage.

"George, did you know—" Did she really want to get into a discussion with him about Father taking Mrs. Wilds to the cottage? If anything George was even more protective of their mother's memory than she was.

"What?" George peered at her, waiting for her to finish her sentence.

"Never mind. I think I'm going to take a walk. I need to get out of the house for awhile. I'm going to sneak out the back door so Twila doesn't beg to go with me."

"Okay. Enjoy your walk."

Polly gently opened the door and slipped out into the pleasant summer evening. She got along much better with George since he'd allowed Elsie to replace him as the enforcer. It was good to still have one brother at home. She hoped the war would be over before he was old enough to be drafted. The draft had cast a pall over everything.

Since the United States entered the war in April and passed the Selective Service act in May, those subjects hijacked every conversation. The first registration day had been two months ago on

June 5 for men ages twenty one to thirty one. She'd read in The Evening Record that the numbers of those being drafted would be drawn in lots of 100,000. This would be done three times at one- to two-week intervals. She shivered in spite of the warmth of the evening.

No one knew how long the war would go on. No one knew how many young men would be lost. The reality of this made her attitude toward Mrs. Wilds seem petty. Maybe instead of battling Father, she should look for someone with whom to fall in love. What if she waited too long and all the young men were gone and life passed her by?

Even Kitt Potter had married Homer Harper last year and moved to Painesville, Ohio. Polly missed her friend even though Kitt came to visit her mother often. Recently, she had come home to give birth to a sickly baby girl. Kitt and little Betty were staying in Sandy Lake with her mother and older sister, Bess, to continue under the care of Dr. Cooley.

Maybe it was time to pay them another visit. Polly stopped her aimless dawdling and headed toward the Potter place. A few minutes of brisk walking and climbing stairs up the steep bank brought her to the front door. She tapped lightly in case Betty was sleeping.

Bess answered the door carrying Betty wrapped in a warm blanket. Sweat broke out on Polly's forehead. Poor baby to be wrapped up in this heat.

"Hi Polly." Bess greeted her with a warm smile. "Won't you come in? Would you like to hold Betty while I get Kitt?"

"Oh, no thank you." Polly flushed at Bess's surprised look. "I'm really out of practice—it's been ten years since Twila was a baby."

As Bess headed for the steps to get Kitt, she called back over her shoulder. "Don't you think you should get back in practice?"

"Why?" What was Bess trying to say?

"Someday soon you'll get married and have children of your own."

Polly blinked. In all her debating about getting married, she had never given a thought to having children. Weariness crept over her. How could she start all over again, raising another family?

She tilted her head. "Well, I might get married, but I don't know about having children."

Bess opened the door and called Kitt, then turned back to Polly. "I can't imagine not wanting to have a family."

"I've been raising children for six years, and I'm not finished yet." She had made a promise to Mother. Looking for a man to marry wasn't an option. What had she been thinking?

"Maybe your father will remarry."

Polly grew still. "Have you heard something about my father?" Footsteps on the stairs drew her attention before Kitt entered the room.

Her friend hugged her and pulled her toward the brocade loveseat. "Can I get you a cold drink?"

"No, I'm fine. I just asked Bess if she'd heard something about my father."

Bess and Kitt exchanged glances. They both started to speak at once, and then stopped. At last Bess nodded at Kitt and left the room with Betty cradled in her arms. Still Kitt said nothing.

"Kitt, what do you know that you're not telling me?"

"It's just that I was sure you knew…" Kitt stopped again.

"Knew what?"

"That your father took Lydia Wilds to the Dye cottage for a week with some of the rest of his family."

Polly leapt to her feet. "Who told you that?"

Kitt frowned. "I think it was Dorothy from Harold Young's insurance office."

Slumping down on the loveseat, Polly's head drooped. "Everyone in Sandy Lake knew except me."

CHAPTER 7

Bob sat up and stretched. The sun hadn't come up yet, but he'd awakened early all week just as he did to go to the mine. Today was their last day at the cottage. His mother always liked to get things cleaned up on Saturday and be back in town for church on Sunday.

Not that he and Lydia couldn't stay an extra day but that wouldn't do her reputation any good. Especially if Dorothy, the town crier, got wind of it. His brother, Pete, and his wife, Flo, would also be going home today so they couldn't count on them for chaperones. He chuckled, thinking of his younger brother in that role. Pete would delight in telling him what to do.

Part of the reason he didn't want to go home was that there would be no more long walks with Lydia, no more holding hands, no more stealing kisses. Life stretched ahead, gray and bleak. He could visit her occasionally but her twenty-year-old daughter, Colleen, was often home in the evenings. They couldn't walk far without passing his house or other interested pedestrians.

If only Florence would find a beau who wanted to marry her, he and Lydia could be married without Florence feeling displaced. Lydia could help raise his younger daughters who were still at home. He smiled to himself at the fairy tale picture. Of course, they would live happily ever after.

He swung his legs over the side of the bed and stood. In a few minutes, he was dressed and ready to wait for Lydia on the porch. Last night, he had pleaded with her to get up early for a walk before cottage clean up began.

An hour later, he was still waiting. Perhaps Lydia hadn't seen the alarm clock on the bedside table in her room. His mother was in the kitchen making breakfast, in full view of Lydia's bedroom door. He couldn't very well go in to awaken her. Regardless of his age, his usually mild-mannered mother wouldn't hesitate to rebuke him if she saw him opening that door.

Flo's voice floated out from the kitchen, greeting his mother. She was a pleasant woman, a good wife to his brother and an excellent mother. He envied them their happy marriage.

"Good morning, Bob."

He turned toward the door. Flo was smiling through the screen. "Morning, Flo. Where's Pete?"

"He got up very early to get some fishing in before clean-up time. Did you get up early to fish, too?"

"Not exactly." Bob didn't want to explain. He'd sensed tension between Lydia and Flo this week. It wouldn't help matters if he told Flo Lydia hadn't gotten up to walk with him.

"Waiting for Lydia?" Flo's eyes gleamed. "Good luck."

"What do you mean?"

"Just that Lydia doesn't strike me as an early riser."

"She said she used to get up in the middle of the night when she was taking in laundry. She doesn't have to do that since her daughter got a job as a stenographer."

"Is Lydia looking for a replacement?"

Bob frowned. "I don't know what you're talking about."

"Eventually Colleen will get married, and Lydia will need someone else to take care of her."

"I don't like what you're implying."

Flo gave him a long, steady look. "I'm sorry if I spoke out of turn, Bob. I just don't want you to get hurt."

♠

Bob glanced around the table as he buttered another piece of bread. His mother and Flo had made eggs, bacon, and fried potatoes for this last special breakfast. Lydia had arrived just in time to sit down and eat with the family. She looked wonderful as always. How did she manage to look so well-dressed? Colleen couldn't make that much money at the milk company. Of course, they didn't pay rent since they'd inherited Rufus's house.

As he ate his last bite of bread, Lydia leaned toward him, her lips brushing his ear. "Let's take a walk."

He looked toward his mother but before he could open his mouth, Lydia leaned in again. "The cottage isn't really dirty—I'm sure your mother and Flo can handle it."

Bob hesitated. His mother and Flo had been doing most of the work all week. He had always helped Margaret clean the cottage when they'd come with his parents. But he couldn't expect Lydia to do things just because Margaret had. He scooted back his chair and got to his feet.

"We'll be back soon." He didn't quite meet his mother's eyes as he turned to follow Lydia.

When they reached the path, she turned to the right instead of the left. "Let's go the other direction today."

Bob followed her into the dense woods. The path was narrow, and he was forced to put his arm around Lydia so they could walk side by side. The feel of her against him and the fragrance of her lily of the valley perfume was intoxicating. When the cottage was no longer in sight, he stopped and faced her.

"Lydia, I don't want to go home and go back to being neighbors. I want to marry you and live together as husband and wife."

She stroked his cheek. "That sounds wonderful. You could move in with Colleen and me. I don't think she'd mind."

"Move in with—no, you don't understand. I want you to live with me." Even as he said the words, Florence's face inserted itself between him and Lydia. *What had he done?*

"Live with you? Oh no, I couldn't do that. Your house is full of children, and I've already raised my children. Besides, I heard your oldest daughter doesn't approve of me. I don't think it would work for me to live there. And I wouldn't want my daughter to live alone." Lydia wrapped her arms around him, stood on tiptoe and planted a soft kiss on his lips. "No, you'll have to live with me."

CHAPTER 8

Polly gazed through the screen door. She didn't know whether to plan on Father for supper or not. In the past Father and Mother always came home from the cottage on Saturday night, but who knew what Mrs. Wilds would want to do. Father would probably do whatever she wanted.

She went back to the kitchen and threw a few pieces of wood into the cook stove. Macaroni and cheese might be a good meal for her and the girls. George planned to go to the races with friends and would eat on the way. Must be nice to be so carefree.

After setting a pot of water on the stove, she pulled a chunk of cheddar cheese from the ice box and began to chop it into small pieces. What had Father and Lydia been eating at the cottage? Polly had cooked for the girls and George all week as usual, but emptiness permeated the house in Father's absence, especially at mealtime.

Polly dumped some macaroni into the water when it boiled. Beth had taken Twila and Elsie for a walk a few minutes ago which added to her present sense of isolation. Visualizing Father and Mrs. Wilds together didn't help.

Hoof beats in front of the house drew Polly into the living room. Father was home. Polly dropped to her knees beside the davenport. She had a few minutes while he took care of his horse. He never put Jasper in the barn without feeding and watering him.

What should I say, Jesus? What should I do?

The quiet in the room was deafening—her heartbeat the only sound. Time stood still until at last footsteps on the porch prompted her to stand. Father passed the window and opened the screen door.

When he caught sight of Polly standing like a chunk of concrete beside the daven, his eyebrows raised. "Hello, Florence. Is everything okay? I rarely see you standing still."

Of all the questions Father could have asked, this might have been the worst. She couldn't lie. What could she say? *The children are all fine.* That much was true, unless you counted her as one of the children.

When Polly didn't answer, Father asked, "Where is everyone?"

"Beth took the girls for a walk." She couldn't bring herself to meet his eyes. "George went to the races."

Father crossed the room, stopped in front of her and tilted her chin to turn her gaze in his direction. "Florence, tell me what's wrong."

Polly licked her lips. What was the Bible verse she'd read this morning? *Let everyone be swift to hear, slow to speak, and slow to wrath...* She'd calmed down some since Savannah told her what Father had done, but she still couldn't think about Mrs. Wilds at the cottage without clenching her teeth. At last she lifted her gaze and met her father's.

"Why did you invite Lydia Wilds to go to the cottage without telling me?"

Father took a step back, his eyebrows rising. Whatever he'd been expecting her to say, apparently it wasn't this. "Who told you?"

"That's not important. Apparently, half of Sandy Lake knew."

At last, Father sank down on the davenport. He buried his head in his hands for a moment, then looked at her. "I'm sorry, Florence. I didn't tell you because I knew you'd be upset. I've been seeing Lydia occasionally ever since I helped with appraising Rufus's house. You made it clear you didn't approve of her."

"Savannah and Bess both knew you'd taken her. I was so embarrassed when they discovered I didn't." Polly's cheeks burned. She clenched and unclenched her fists.

"I'm truly sorry. I guess I knew it would be only a matter of time until you found out. Can you forgive me?"

She took two quick steps away from the davenport. "Don't ask me that."

Father's mouth gaped. "Why not?"

"Because the Bible says I have to forgive you, but I'm not ready to forgive you yet."

Father shook his head. "Leave it to you, Florence, to be completely honest. You put me to shame."

"I want to know the truth." Polly faced her father. "Taking Mrs. Wilds to the cottage for a week sounds like you're serious about her. Are you?"

"I like Lydia very much. I don't know that I can say I love her, not the kind of love I had for your mother. But I like her and I'm lonely. Being with her this week at the cottage...it was wonderful."

Polly's shoulders slumped. "I see."

"I asked her to marry me."

Leaping to her feet, Polly glared at him. "How could you do that without giving me any warning or time to prepare?"

Father took her hand and pulled her down beside him. "I'm sorry, Florence. I didn't plan this. Honest I didn't. After being with her all week, I just couldn't bear the thought of not seeing her every day."

Tears rolled down Polly's cheeks. "If you get married, I'll have to find another place to live."

"Lydia doesn't want to live here. She wants me to live with her."

"Just you? Leave your family and go live with her? I can't believe you'd even consider that." Polly was on her feet again, shaking with repressed rage. So much for being slow to anger.

"Wait, Florence..." Her father reached for her hand again, but she pulled away and ran into the kitchen. The macaroni had boiled dry. It was ruined like everything else.

CHAPTER 9

Polly sat in the quiet sanctuary as the organ played "Tis So Sweet to Trust in Jesus." A tear rolled down her cheek. She certainly wasn't trusting Jesus with her father and Mrs. Wilds. How she hated situations where she had no control. She swiped at her tears with a quick gesture.

Twila missed nothing. "Why are you crying, Polly?"

Glancing around, Polly put a finger to her lips. They needed to discuss whispering.

Elsie, on her other side, leaned in. "Are you crying?"

Father, further down the pew, peered at her. Polly turned her head toward the center aisle to block his view of her face. The back door of the church opened, and she turned further to see who was arriving. Reverend Caldwell. What a long time since he'd preached in their church. She had been angry at God that day, too.

Taking a deep breath, she acknowledged it. She was not only angry at Father, she was angry with God. God, who could have kept her father from being chosen to appraise Rufus Wilds' house, who could have kept him from being attracted to Mr. Wilds' widow. Why was God allowing this painful situation when they'd been doing so well?

Do we dare to believe that sometimes suffering is God's good gift to produce qualities we wouldn't develop any other way? Polly closed her eyes against the words Reverend Caldwell had spoken the last time he preached here.

How difficult it had been for her to trust a God who didn't make eliminating pain His priority. But ultimately, the words of Scripture penned in Sarah's diary after the loss of her baby had become Polly's own: *Lord, to whom else shall we go?*

She closed her eyes and repeated the words inwardly. When Twila grasped her fingers, Polly opened her eyes to smile reassuringly. The hymn ended and Pastor Lawrence introduced Reverend Caldwell.

What a broad-shouldered, handsome young man he was. Strange, she hadn't noticed last time. She'd fancied herself to be in love with Garrett back then.

Reverend Caldwell stood and walked to the pulpit. "Good morning, my friends." His smile warmed Polly's soul. Was he looking straight at her? "I'd like to ask the organist if she'll play the last stanza of that song, hymn number 471. The words fit well with my message this morning."

Polly pulled a hymnbook from the rack and turned to the printed words.

Yes, 'tis sweet to trust in Jesus, Just from sin and self to cease
Just from Jesus simply taking Life and rest, and joy and peaceJesus,
Jesus, how I trust Him! How I've proved Him o'er and o'er
Jesus, Jesus, precious Jesus! Oh, for grace to trust Him more!

When the congregation finished singing, Reverend Caldwell gazed at them. "What is it that stands in the way of people trusting Jesus? It may be many things but most of them are rooted in self. We're afraid if we put our trust in Him, we'll lose our ability to control our own lives, to make our own plans, to have our own way."

Squirming, Polly recalled what she'd written in her diary. *You taught your disciples to pray, "Thy kingdom come, Thy will be done on earth as it is in heaven." But I'm not ready to pray that prayer.* Was her unwillingness to pray that prayer rooted in what Reverend Caldwell called self?

"Most of us recognize the need to stop sinning, but we're often blind to the role self plays in our relationship with Christ. Luke 9:23 says if we want to follow Jesus, we must deny ourselves, give up the right to have our own way, so we can follow Him.

"Some folks think we can make a one-time decision to deny ourselves, but I believe it takes many decisions. I believe Self, capital S, has many thrones in our lives and has to be denied each time a battle rages."

Before her mother died, Polly had repented of putting Mother in the place of God. It was the beginning of a real relationship with God through Jesus Christ. Polly sighed. She hadn't recognized that she herself continued to rule and reign in many areas. What had the young pastor just said? "Self has to be denied each time a battle rages."

Being a Christian wasn't easy. How she longed to talk to her mother about this new challenge of denying herself. However, if her mother were still here, she wouldn't have to fight this particular battle.

Twila poked her with one small, sharp elbow. Folks were standing. Polly had missed the rest of Reverend Caldwell's message. Had he noticed? She tucked a few fly-away red locks behind her ear, stood and joined in singing the Doxology. Reverend Caldwell and Reverend Lawrence walked to the rear of the sanctuary to shake folks' hands.

Very aware of Father a few steps behind her, Polly pushed through the crowd. She wasn't ready to talk with him until she'd had a chance to process this message. She spoke automatically to anyone who spoke to her but engaged with no one, beating a hasty retreat toward the door.

Pastor Lawrence reached for her hand when she would have slipped by him. "Good morning, Polly. Have you met Reverend Caldwell?"

Polly avoided the young preacher's eyes as she shook her pastor's hand. "I don't believe so. He had to leave immediately last time he was here."

Reverend Caldwell leaned toward her. It was impossible to avoid his warm, dark eyes any longer. "I'm pleased to meet you, Polly." He took her hand. "I believe we have some mutual friends, Savannah and Garrett Young."

Withdrawing her hand, Polly nodded. "We're friends."

"Savannah told me how much you and your family helped her when she lost everything in the fire."

"We were blessed to have her with us until she and Garrett married. She's like a sister to me."

"Perhaps you could join us sometime when I get together with them?" Reverend Caldwell leaned toward her again. "I travel so much I haven't taken time to make a lot of friends near my age."

Warmth crept up Polly's neck and ears as she glanced at the crowd waiting to shake hands. Father was at her elbow. She opened her lips but no answer came.

CHAPTER 10

Twila and Elsie skipped in front of Bob as he walked briskly to keep up with them. Florence had made it clear she wanted to be alone after church, and George's long legs put him far out in front of the rest of the family.

Glancing back at his eldest daughter trailing behind them, Bob sighed. Why had she reacted that way to Reverend Caldwell's suggestion of spending time with him and her friends? Was she afraid of sending him mixed messages when she had no intention of marrying? Florence seemed to think keeping her promise to Margaret eliminated any possibility of marriage.

Bob had tried several times to tell her he hadn't made any plans to marry Lydia but she was as skittish as a wild barn cat since they talked on Saturday evening.

Reverend Caldwell's message had raised a lot of questions for him. How could he know if Self ruled him or the Lord? He'd never heard a message quite like the one this morning. Why hadn't he worked harder at building a relationship with God instead of relying so much on Margaret? She always spoke up if she thought he was getting off track. Now that she was gone, it was like walking in the woods without a compass.

♠

After Sunday dinner, Polly curled up on the bed. Beth was downstairs reading to the girls giving Polly the room to herself, a rare opportunity to write in her journal. It was the only time she minded sharing a room. She could have had Ben's room when he got a job in Oil City, but she thought he might come home more often if his room was still available.

She picked up Chartreuse, opened her journal, and wrote the date.

August 12, 1917 Reverend Caldwell preached at our church today, Father. It's the second time he's preached about something so relevant to the trials in my life. Mother would say it's the Holy Spirit guiding him. He gave me a lot to think about, even though it stung. I've never heard a message about being ruled by Self.

Polly picked up her Bible from the bedside stand, then reached for Mother's concordance. Turning to verses about self, she found the one Reverend Caldwell had mentioned. Luke 9:23. "If any man will come after me, let him deny himself, and take up his cross daily, and follow me."

Does denying myself mean doing what everyone else wants me to do or does it mean choosing your will instead of mine?

She nibbled on the cap of her pen. Surely God didn't want her to be a mindless doormat, having no will of her own. Denying herself and taking up her cross daily must mean doing what God wanted her to do. Panic built in her chest. How could she pray "Thy Kingdom come, Thy will be done" when she didn't know what God wanted?

Underneath her anger lay a lot of fear. She took deep breaths and began to draw circles and squares to release her emotions. Her pulse rate slowed. Her brain fog lifted. She began to write.

Mother's kitchen is now my kitchen. Mother's house is now my house. How could I adjust to someone else being in charge? Regardless of my anger at Father, it would be easier if he lived at the widow's house than if she lived here. Maybe that's your plan, God.

Still, how did they know God wanted Father to marry Mrs. Wilds at all?

Heavy footsteps on the stairs…Only Father made that much noise on the steps since Robert moved out. The footsteps stopped by her door. A light tap. Was she ready to talk to him?

Did she have a choice?

"Come in."

The door opened slightly and Father leaned in. "Can we talk?"

Polly beckoned and patted a spot on the edge of the bed. "I'm sorry I've been so difficult. I haven't acted much like a grown up."

"Maybe I haven't either. I'm afraid I've let feelings rule me this week, or as Reverend Caldwell says, Self."

"Me too. I have no idea what God wants you to do. Maybe I just don't want you to mess up my safe little world." Polly folded her arms across her chest, then deliberately unfolded them. Father wasn't the enemy.

"I don't know what God wants me to do either." Father shifted on the bed. "I'm afraid I haven't even asked Him. Mother was usually the one who prayed about God's plans."

Polly was silent, staring into space. Mother was gone and they had to find a way to get along without her, had to find a way to deepen their own relationships with God.

Father cleared his throat. "Florence, I've been trying to tell you, I haven't made any definite plans with Lydia. I promise I won't make any plans with her until you and I come to some agreement about the future. I'm a grown man with a family to consider, and I can't make decisions based on a whim."

Polly sat up straight. "Before Mother died, she told me we can learn to be guided by the Holy Spirit rather than by following our own desires and schemes."

Father stared into space, nodding. "So when Self is on the throne, we follow our own desires and schemes. When Christ is on the throne, the Holy Spirit can guide us in the way He wants us to go."

"Maybe. Mother and I never talked about Self being in control, but it sounds a lot like being ruled by our own desires and schemes. Don't you think?" Polly leaned toward her father.

"I do. Mother was the expert on spiritual things. I miss her so much, but maybe God knew I was too lazy to learn as long as I could depend on her."

"That's the same problem Sarah Davis's family had."

Father frowned. "Who is Sarah Davis?"

"She and her husband, Thomas, were the original owners of our house. The whole family depended on her instead of the Lord." Polly gazed into Father's eyes. "God used her diary to show me I needed my own relationship with Him."

"How did you get her diary?"

"I thought I told you." She rubbed her forehead. "It was under a floorboard in the back bedroom where you and mother slept. I gave it to Savannah before the boarding house fire.”

Father paused, pressing his fingertips together. “Do you know what happened to the family after Sarah died?”

“They fell apart. Two of the children ended up at Warren State Hospital.” Polly closed her eyes for a moment against the memory. “Such a sad story. Our neighbor, Blanche Davis, told me. She’s their grandson’s wife.”

Staring into space, Father stood. “I’m glad you have your own relationship with the Lord. I asked Him to be my Savior years ago, but now I need to figure out how to abdicate the throne.”

CHAPTER 11

Polly paid for her groceries and glanced at her list again. It was so easy to miss something when Twila and Elsie came along to market.

"Let's stop to see Maggie and baby Eugene. *Please, Polly...*"

How could she say no to Twila when she pleaded with those sparkling brown eyes? The week had dragged by with nothing to break the monotony. Her sister, Maggie, would probably be home on a Friday morning.

"All right. We have a little time before I need to punch down the bread dough. If Eugene is asleep, we won't stay."

They waited for a couple of horses and an automobile to pass before crossing the intersection of Lake and Main Streets. Maggie's home, located so close to the intersection, made it a popular place to stop on a hot day. Actually, it was a popular place to stop any day. Twila, Elsie and Beth loved Eugene and missed their big sister. Polly missed her too. She liked to play with Eugene and then give him back to Maggie when she was ready to go home.

Maggie's face erupted in smiles when she opened the door, her plump baby in her arms. "Come in. I'm so happy to see you. I get lonely sometimes."

"It's harder to get lost in a fictitious world now that you have a baby, isn't it?" Polly set down her groceries, reached for her nephew and tickled him under his double chin.

"No fair. Let me hold him." Elsie's pretty mouth drew down into a pout.

Polly kissed Eugene's cheek and passed him to Elsie. Her conversation with Bess haunted her. Was there something fundamentally wrong with her because she wasn't sure she wanted children of her own? She brushed her hand over her eyes in an effort to rid herself of the question and sank down beside Maggie on the couch. "Do you ever have time to read?"

"Sometimes when Paul has a shorter day at the mine, he plays with Eugene while I put my feet up with a good book. He knows how much I love to do that."

"He seems like a good father. But if you ever need help during the day, the girls could help you." Polly patted her sister's cheek. "Eugene wouldn't get into mischief with eagle-eyed Elsie watching him."

"Actually, I picked some tomatoes earlier that I need to can. Could the girls stay and entertain him while I work on them?"

"Of course. They'd be delighted. I need to get home and check on my bread or I'd stay and help too."

"Thanks, Polly. You're the best. I don't know how you handled everything when you took over Mother's house."

"You helped a lot—when you weren't reading a book." Polly chuckled and hugged her. Before leaving, she admonished her younger sisters. "Take good care of Eugene while Maggie works on the tomatoes. Then come straight home."

Beth gave a little wave but Elsie and Twila barely glanced at her as she left the house, arms full of groceries. After turning left on Walnut Street, the clip clop of horse's hooves prompted her to move to the side of the road. She glanced back, half expecting to see the Potter's buggy. Instead, Lydia Wilds smiled at her from the small buggy she and her daughter used.

"Hello, you must be Florence Dye. I don't believe we've been introduced."

Polly licked her dry lips. "Hello, Mrs. Wilds. Everyone but my father calls me Polly."

"It looks like you have your arms full. Why don't you jump in and I'll give you a ride home?"

Hesitating, Polly tried to think of a reason to refuse. No excuse presented itself. "All right. Thank you." She went around to the far side of the buggy, set her groceries on the floor, and climbed in.

Usually she had no problem making conversation, but she couldn't think of a thing to say as Mrs. Wilds clucked to her horse. Polly glanced at her sideways and couldn't deny she was an attractive woman—probably somewhat younger than her father, although maybe not as young as she tried to appear.

Scolding herself for her attitude, Polly tried to smile at the woman beside her. "I appreciate you giving me a ride."

"I thought we should get to know each other since we'll soon be related, in a manner of speaking."

Polly drew a deep breath. "Related?"

"When your father and I get married, I'll be your stepmother. I hope we can have a good relationship. Stepmothers often get a bad name, like in Cinderella."

Chewing on her lip, Polly glanced at Mrs. Wilds. "When did you last talk to my father?"

"Last Saturday. That's another reason I offered you a ride. I wanted to make sure he isn't sick. I couldn't imagine why I haven't seen him since we got home from the cottage, now that we're engaged. He was so sad to have our week at the cottage end."

What should she say? She longed to tell this woman her father had changed his mind, but that wasn't exactly true. "He isn't sick. I…I guess he's just been busy." It was a lame excuse but the best Polly could do. Apparently her father hadn't told his "fiancée" about their talk.

Mrs. Wilds stopped her buggy in front of the Dye home. "Tell your father I'd like to see him tonight. Colleen is going out with friends so we'll have some privacy."

Words collected on Polly's tongue, none of them kind. She took a slow, deep breath as she jumped down from the buggy and grabbed her groceries. This was Father's relationship, not hers. She wasn't in control. "I'll tell him. Thanks again for the ride."

She stumbled up the steps and across the porch without a backward glance.

CHAPTER 12

Polly stood in front of the icebox, tapping her toe. What to fix for this unusual meal? Maggie had called to ask if the girls could eat with them and stay overnight. George had plans with friends. Leftovers should suffice for her and Father. They weren't his favorite but he wouldn't complain.

She pulled a container of beef stew from the ice box. A small amount of applesauce and bread with butter and strawberry jam would help round out the meal. After putting the stew in a pan on the stove to warm, she turned to the fresh loaf of bread waiting to be sliced. She bit her lip and concentrated on making uniform slices with Mother's bread knife. Would she ever be as good at this as Mother?

When the last slice was cut, she breathed a sigh of relief and put down the knife. *Do I have to keep my promise to Mrs. Wilds?* The question pounced as soon as she finished concentrating on the size of her slices.

Taking a bread basket from the cupboard, she arranged a few slices of bread and covered it with a napkin. She already knew the answer to her question. Besides, Father needed to tell Mrs. Wilds there wasn't going to be a wedding any time soon.

She took plates, silverware and glasses into the dining room, thinking how odd it was to be setting the table for two. Actually, it was odd for her to be setting the table at all. Usually Beth, Elsie, or Twila did it.

Mrs. Wilds had said her daughter was going out with friends. Polly had met Colleen Wilds, a daughter from Mrs. Wilds' first marriage. She was a couple years younger than Polly. Colleen's mother would probably say Polly and Colleen would be "related" someday. She cringed. It was way too early to be thinking about being *related* to this woman or her family.

The front door slammed. Father's cheery "Anybody home?" reached her in the dining room.

"In here. Supper will be ready by the time you wash up."

He stepped into the dining room and glanced at the table. "Where is everyone?"

"The girls are at Maggie's and George is with friends. It'll be just the two of us."

Polly took two trips to bring the food in from the kitchen, while Father washed up at the sink. At last everything was ready, and they were seated in their usual spots.

"Would you say the blessing, Florence?"

Polly bowed her head. "Heavenly Father, thank you for food and strength to do the work you've given us to do. Amen." Self-consciousness always attacked her when she prayed aloud with adults. Would she ever be able to pray beautiful prayers like the ones that had flowed from Mother's lips?

She filled a bowl with stew for Father, then one for herself. It was so quiet without Twila and Elsie chattering and Beth mothering them. Dread about the conversation she needed to have with Father darkened the room. He stared vacantly into his bowl of stew, seemingly unaware of the silence.

"Father…"

He jumped and dropped his spoon. "I'm sorry. Mother used to say I was woolgathering when I did this." He winked at Polly.

"What were you thinking about? Did you have a hard day at the mines?"

"There's talk that President Wilson might decide to control coal prices until the war is over. The men are worried about how that would affect their wages, of course. But that isn't what I was thinking about."

"What then?" Polly took a slice of bread before passing the basket to her father.

He sighed, a sound that seemed to come from the depth of his soul. "I still haven't talked to Lydia since we got back from the cottage."

"I know. I saw her today."

Eyebrows lifted, Father stared at her as he automatically took a slice of bread. "Where?"

"She gave me a ride when I was walking home from the market. She told me we'd be related soon since she's engaged to you."

Father grabbed a glass of water and took a long swallow. Then another gulp. "I did ask her to marry me but nothing was settled."

"She said she wants to see you tonight. Her daughter is going out with friends."

"I shouldn't have been so hasty. Lydia's going to expect..." His voice trailed off.

As Polly buttered her bread and added a layer of jam, the telephone rang. She went to answer it. Was Father going to allow himself to be controlled by what Mrs. Wilds expected?

Savannah's cheerful voice broke into her dismal mood. "Hi Polly. Reverend Caldwell is coming to have supper with Garrett and me. He mentioned he'd like to get to know you better. Could you come? I'm sorry it's such late notice."

"Thank you for asking, but Father and I are already eating."

"Could you come for dessert? We're having your favorite—peach cobbler. Your father could come, too."

Polly hesitated and glanced at Father. "I think he has plans, but I could probably come after I finish eating and clearing the—"

Shaking his head, Father interrupted. "You can go as soon as you're done eating, Florence. I'll clear away the food. I'm in no hurry."

Surprised at her father's unusual offer of help, she stared at him. Then her eyes twinkled and a giggle escaped her lips. He was stalling.

"Coward."

♠

Bob took his time clearing the table and putting away the food. It wasn't a task he was used to doing. He got a dishcloth from the kitchen and wiped the table. Perhaps he should dry it as well—was that the proper procedure? Where did Florence keep the dish towels? Probably wherever her mother had kept them.

He bit his lip as he returned to the kitchen and began opening drawers. Florence was right. He was a coward. What would he say to Lydia? Her charms that had prompted him to ask her to marry him, how would he resist them now?

A dry dish towel at last. He turned to go back to the dining room when a sharp knock startled him. The outside door stood open, and a flash of green caught his attention as he turned in that direction. Lydia stood on his front porch.

CHAPTER 13

Bob dropped the dish towel on the counter and walked toward the living room. His chest felt tight. He could hardly breathe. How had he gotten himself into this predicament? A grown man should know better.

"Hello Lydia. Florence said you wanted me to come to your house tonight."

"I got tired of waiting. Like they say 'If Mohammed won't come to the mountain, the mountain must come to Mohammed.' So here I am."

Lydia's lily of the valley perfume wafted into the living room as Bob opened the screen door. This was the first time she had been in his house. It didn't seem right. Maybe he should suggest a walk.

"Aren't you going to invite me to sit down?" Lydia headed for the davenport beside Margaret's gray chair. "Come sit with me."

Bob perched on the edge of the daven as far from Lydia as possible and took a deep breath. "Lydia, I need to talk to you."

"That's why I'm here." She scooted closer to him. "We need to make plans for our wedding."

"I don't think this is such a good idea." He clasped his hands in his lap.

"What isn't a good idea?" Lydia leaned closer, trying to make eye contact.

"Us getting married. It wouldn't work for you to live here and I can't leave my children to live with you." He continued to avoid her gaze.

"But getting married was *your* idea."

A quick glance showed Lydia's pink lips pouting.

"I know." Bob floundered to find an explanation. "I shouldn't have invited you to the cottage. It put ideas in my head that weren't realistic."

He stood and began to pace. "I'm so sorry. I asked you to marry me without thinking things through. It was a mistake."

Lydia flounced to her feet. "Are you saying we shouldn't see each other anymore?"

"No, no. I'm not saying that." What *was* he saying? He couldn't bear the thought of not seeing her at all. "We just need to slow things down. Give our families time to adjust to the idea of us being together."

"This is all Florence's idea, isn't it? I'm surprised she even gave you my message." Lydia pushed back the curl that had escaped her carefully arranged blonde hair.

Biting his lip, Bob remained silent. Was it all Florence's idea? At the cottage, he'd been very sure he wanted to marry Lydia. It had only been after his daughter said… well, there had also been Reverend Caldwell's sermon—

"That's what I thought." Lydia's hazel eyes flashed.

"It wasn't only Florence's idea." Bob returned to the davenport and sank down with a deep sigh. "Come sit down."

Lydia took a few steps backward and plopped into Margaret's chair—he needed to stop thinking of it as *Margaret's chair*. It was just a chair, a gray chair. Lydia's lips were closed in a firm line.

"I heard a sermon on Sunday that made me realize I haven't even prayed about whether God wants us to be married."

A sound between a snort and a laugh escaped Lydia's lips. "Do you really think God cares who people marry? Don't you think He has much more important issues on His mind—like the war, for example?"

Bob wrinkled his forehead in a frown. Did he believe God cared who he married? Margaret had believed God cared about things like that, and Reverend Caldwell and Florence probably believed it too. But did he believe it? He groaned out loud. "I don't know, Lydia. I really don't know."

♠

Polly strolled down the road, the breeze lifting her curls that had come loose from the hurried chignon she'd attempted this morning. When had she last spent time on her *own* appearance? Beth helped with the younger children but Polly always braided their hair which left little time for her own toilette.

Why hadn't she re-combed her hair before she left the house? But then, who was she trying to impress? She had no time for a beau. More tomatoes waited to be picked and canned tomorrow. More corn would be ready soon. Her life was too busy fulfilling her promise to Mother to have a beau.

It was a nice evening and she enjoyed walking. No need to take the buggy. Would Father actually clear the table and put the food away? She chuckled. He must be desperate to put off facing Mrs. Wilds. Determined not to worry, she recited Scripture verses as she walked.

Let everyone be swift to hear, slow to speak, and slow to wrath.

If any man will come after me, let him deny himself, and take up his cross daily, and follow me.

What were the words to the last verse of "'Tis So Sweet to Trust in Jesus?" Something like "Just from sin and self to cease…" Easier said than done…

CHAPTER 14

"I'll be right back." Savannah smiled at Garrett and Pastor Jim as he'd asked her to call him. She slid the last of the leftovers in the icebox, and then sped down the stairs to open the door for Polly.

Savannah smiled at her friend. If she'd invited Polly earlier in the day, perhaps Polly would have changed her clothes and combed her hair. With an internal shake, Savannah scolded herself for criticizing. "Come in, Polly. Pastor Jim brought ice so he and Garrett could churn homemade ice cream. You and I can dish up the peach cobbler and relax while they do the honors out back."

While Savannah gathered ingredients for ice cream for Garrett, he and Pastor Jim exchanged greetings with Polly. Then the men trooped down the stairs, and Savannah handed Polly a spoon. "Give us all large servings."

"Smells wonderful." Polly sniffed appreciatively and removed the dish towel protecting the delectable dessert.

"Thank you, Polly. I don't often find time to make desserts even though I love to bake. Mother Young taught me."

"Someday you can teach your daughters how to cook and make desserts."

Savannah drew a deep breath. Folks must wonder why she and Garrett still had no children. She'd spoken to no one but her husband and Mother Young about her fears. A tear slid down her cheeks.

"What's wrong, Savannah?" Polly dropped the serving spoon on the counter. "Let's go sit down. We have plenty of time before the ice cream will be ready."

Polly pulled a clean handkerchief from her pocket and handed it to Savannah as they walked to the walnut, pedestal-style round table. "Did I say something to upset you?"

"No, no, it's not your fault." Savannah plopped into a chair. "It's just that...I want children so much. I don't know why I'm not getting, you know..." Why was it so hard to talk about having babies?

"Have you gone to see Dr. Cooley? He's a wonderful doctor. Maybe he could do something." Polly pulled out a chair and sat down beside her distraught friend.

After a long, hard blow, Savannah swiped at her eyes and wiped her nose. "I hate talking about this…"

"Sometimes it helps to talk even though it's hard."

Savannah stared at the table. "I'm afraid God is punishing me for what I did when I lived above the tavern. Maybe that's why I'm not getting pregnant."

Polly reached to take Savannah's hand. "I don't believe that's the reason. The Bible says if we confess our sins, God forgives us and removes them as far as the east is from the west."

"If God isn't punishing me, why can't I conceive?" So there it was. She'd finally put it into words.

"Look at me, Savannah." Polly gazed into her friend's eyes. "Do you think Sarah Davis's babies died because God was punishing her?"

"No, but she was a godly woman. Why should God punish *her*?"

"Even godly people sometimes think God is punishing them when bad things happen." Polly was silent for a moment. "How much of Sarah's diary did you read before it burned in the fire?"

"It didn't burn in the fire. I took it to work the day the boarding house burned."

Polly's face lit up and she leapt to her feet, knocking over her chair in the process. "Oh thank God." A tear ran down her cheek. "I didn't ask before because I didn't want you to feel bad, but I'm so relieved." She picked up her chair. "It's one of my treasures."

"I'm so sorry. I didn't know you thought it had burned. I've read all of it more than once. I shouldn't have kept it so long."

"It's okay. Did you notice how Sarah responded every time something bad happened?" Polly leaned closer.

Savannah shook her head, trying to remember what she'd read.

"She always ran *to* God instead of blaming Him or thinking He was punishing her."

"I don't think I'm blaming God, exactly." Savannah smoothed

her fingers over the tabletop. "I *deserve* to be punished for the things I did. My own mother wouldn't forgive me. Why should God?"

Savannah's words hung in the air.

At last Polly spoke softly. "Because God isn't like your mother. If you think God is like your mother, you'll always run from Him when trouble comes."

Male voices and laughter floated through the open window. Footsteps on the stairs and Pastor Jim's easy laugh indicated the ice cream was finished. Could Polly be right? How could Savannah be sure God wasn't like her mother? It seemed too good to be true.

♠

Polly scooped good-sized portions of peach cobbler into the Willow Pattern bowls. She and her family had given the ceramic dinnerware to Savannah and Garrett for a wedding gift.

Pastor Jim stood beside her waiting to add a large dip of ice cream to each serving. "Do you cook for your family?"

With a nod, Polly carried the last two bowls of dessert to the table. Pastor Jim followed. "I've cooked for them for over six years since my mother died."

"Garrett told me about that. I'm so sorry." His eyes shone with sympathy.

Polly plopped into a chair. "Thank you. I promised my mother on her deathbed that I'd help Father raise the children if she died. It's a big responsibility." There she'd gotten that out in the open.

"I'm sure it is." Pastor Jim eased himself into a chair across from her.

Silence fell between them while Savannah and Garrett finished washing up the ice cream paddle and mixing container. "I'm sorry I'm not very good company." Polly glanced at Jim.

"Something troubling you?" The pastor's gaze was compassionate.

Polly shrugged. "I'm sure you hear plenty of sob stories in your line of work. I won't tell you mine on your night off."

Before he could answer, Savannah and Garrett rejoined them at the table. The atmosphere lightened and soon good-natured banter filled the room.

"This peach cobbler is scrumptious, Savannah." Garrett smiled at his wife. "Have you ever tasted anything this good, Pastor Jim?"

"You know how the women at the churches where I preach are always trying to outdo each other, but I've never tasted peach cobbler better than this. I wouldn't dare say that to any of them." The pastor grinned.

Polly glanced at him. "Why not?"

"Saying I like their cooking would be akin to a marriage proposal."

Eyebrows raised, Savannah pursed her lips. "Hmmm... Don't you want to get married?"

"I have nothing against marriage. It's just that a woman's baking skills are not my only criteria for choosing. Plus, I don't want to get stuck in the middle of a competition."

"I understand." Garrett nodded. "You'd be surprised how many widows and old maids serve me delectable treats when I arrive for appointments to sell insurance. They want to be sure I know they won first prize for the best apple pie or the best blueberry jam at the Stoneboro Fair."

"Is that right? How come you never mentioned that before?"

Polly couldn't decide if Savannah's question was joking or serious.

"You have nothing to worry about." Garrett leaned across the table to kiss Savannah's cheek. "None of them can hold a candle to your looks or your cooking, Sweetheart. Besides, I always try to make sure they see my wedding ring."

Savannah smiled at the pastor. "Did you hear that, Pastor Jim? A wedding ring might solve all your problems."

The young pastor smiled and shrugged. "Maybe." He rubbed his chin. "Actually, I have a personal favor to ask of you all. Would you call me Jim? I need at least a few friends who treat me like a regular guy."

Habits can be hard to break, but they all agreed to try. For the first time in a long time, the war, the possibility of her brothers being drafted or her father marrying all seemed far away. If Savannah still felt sad, she hid it well. She appeared to be having a good time.

Polly leaned back in her chair and picked up a newspaper from the bookcase behind her. "I haven't even taken time to read the newspaper this week. Let's see what's in the—" She gasped. "Lord, have mercy."

"What is it?" Savannah leaned over to get a better look, while Garrett and Pastor Jim stared at her across the table.

Reading the headline of Monday's paper, Polly's voice was barely above a whisper. "*Infantile Paralysis Outbreak In New Castle.*" She stared at Savannah. "Seven new cases reported in the past four days, a total of fourteen since the first of July—probably more that haven't been reported."

"It's very contagious, isn't it?" Savannah reached for Polly's hand.

She nodded, her gaze on the paper. "One child has died already. The State Health Department has taken charge. They may keep schools closed until cooler weather."

What was that verse she'd memorized? "Be anxious for nothing, but in everything, by prayer and supplication with thanksgiving, let your requests be made to God..."

Father, please keep my little sisters safe from this awful disease. I couldn't bear it if anything happened to them.

How had Sarah gotten through the loss of five of her children? *Only God could get me through the death of a child.* The words from Sarah's diary reverberated in her heart.

CHAPTER 15

"Thank you for inviting me tonight, Savannah." Polly pushed back her chair and stood. Her legs trembled. "I'm sorry I spoiled the fun by reading the newspaper." There was no use trying to regain the lighthearted mood. It was almost eleven o'clock anyway.

Savannah got up and pulled Polly into a hug. "It's okay. You comforted me earlier when I needed it. That's what friends are for. Do you want us to take you home?"

"No need for that." Jim got to his feet, too. "I'll take Polly home."

Polly shook her head. "You don't even know where I—"

"This will give me a chance to see where you live." Jim shook Garrett's hand and gave a little bow in Savannah's direction. "Thank you so much. I can't remember the last time I had so much fun."

Giving a brief nod to Garrett, Polly started toward the stairs. A few minutes ago, she hadn't wanted the evening to end. Now she wanted to go home and call Maggie to make sure the children were okay. She'd heard the dreaded disease often began with flu-like symptoms. She was so deep in thought she stumbled on the first step and would have fallen if Jim hadn't grabbed her arm.

"Thanks. I'm so clumsy." Polly gently released her arm and continued down the stairs.

"Do you want to take some ice cream with you?" Savannah peered after them and shone the light of a lantern as they descended the dimly lit stairs.

"It would melt before I got to Jackson Center." Pastor Jim chuckled.

"There wouldn't be enough for everyone at our house tomorrow. It will be a nice treat for you two." Polly waved as she opened the outer door.

Pastor Jim's roan horse stood patiently at the hitching post. Could she really call this man by his first name? He gave her a hand up into his carriage. "I didn't know you had a buggy. You're usually on horseback."

Jim rubbed his horse's nose, then reached to untie her. "I can make better time riding Delilah. Tonight I wasn't in a hurry and thought you might need a ride home."

"You named your horse Delilah?" Polly couldn't hold back a giggle.

"Don't you like the name?" Jim climbed into the buggy beside her.

She squinted at him, trying to see if he was smiling. *Why would a preacher name his horse Delilah?* "Well, surely you know the story of Samson and Delilah…" Polly's voice trailed off.

"I do. Let's just say this horse has quite a story, too. Every time a stallion came near her, she pretended to like him. Then when he started to get serious, she took off and led him on a merry chase. Her owner gave up on her and sold her to me for a song. I called her Delilah because I like to think that even Delilah wasn't beyond God's redemptive grace."

"Were you right?"

"I've had her for four years." The smile in Jim's voice was apparent. "It's been three years since she's run from another horse."

"What's the secret? What changed her?" Polly allowed herself to relax against the buggy seat.

"I gave her a lot of attention and a lot of love. I always rewarded her good behavior. And I always believed the best of her. I never doubted that eventually she would change." Jim clucked to Delilah, who responded by setting off at a gentle trot.

What if she were to believe the best about Mrs. Wilds? Would it make a difference? Or would it bring disaster on her family?

♠

Polly jumped out of the buggy the moment it stopped. "Thanks for the ride, Jim. I appreciate it. No need for you to get out. Good night."

"Good night, Polly." Jim clucked again to Delilah as Polly ran up the steps.

I'm glad he didn't insist on walking me to the door. It would have felt too much like a date. That wouldn't be fair when I have no intention of marrying. All Savannah's talk about marriage had made her a bit nervous.

The inner door was open into the living room. A small gas lamp flickered on the table beside Mother's chair where Father sat in the dimly lit room.

Pulling the screen door open, Polly walked in. "You didn't need to wait up for me." So many questions she wanted to ask about Father's evening. Had he gone to see Mrs. Wilds? "You look so tired."

Father rubbed his face and tried to smile. It was a feeble attempt. "Did you have a good time?"

"Until I saw Monday's newspaper. Did you know there was an outbreak of infantile paralysis in New Castle?" Polly lowered herself to the davenport. Her nostrils twitched. What did she smell?

"I read it in the Record Argus. I didn't want you to worry." Father glanced at her. "I'm praying it doesn't come here. We won't go anywhere near New Castle."

"But there's nothing to stop those people from coming here. Especially people who haven't been diagnosed. I read that last year there were more than 2,000 cases in Pennsylvania alone." Polly sneezed.

"Gesundheit. What was that verse Mother liked to quote when I worried?" Father wrinkled his brow.

"*Be anxious for nothing, but in everything by prayer and supplication with thanksgiving let your requests be made known to God.* I thought of that verse earlier." Mother would be pleased Polly had managed to memorize some of her favorite verses.

Her nose twitched again and she leaned toward Father. "What do I smell? It's making me sneeze."

"I think it's Lydia's perfume." He glanced at Polly.

Polly sat up straight. "She came here? I thought she wanted you to go to her house."

"I guess she got tired of waiting." Father leaned his head against the back of the chair.

"We don't have to talk about it tonight if you're tired." Despite her words, Polly longed to know what had been said.

"There's not much to tell." Father relayed his conversation with Mrs. Wilds. "She doesn't think God cares who we marry, says He has more important problems—like the war." Closing his eyes, Father rubbed his hands over his face again.

Gazing at him, Polly was silent for a long moment. "Do you believe God cares about things like that?"

Father opened his eyes and stared into space. "I don't know, Florence. I just don't know."

CHAPTER 16

"Thanks for a good dinner." Garrett leaned in to kiss Savannah's cheek and pushed back from the table. "Pastor—uh Jim and I aren't meeting tonight. He needed to visit someone in the hospital. I think I'll come with you to Bible study and spend time with Pa."

"He'll like that." Savannah smiled at her husband and started clearing the table.

Garrett picked up his plate, silverware and tumbler. "Sometimes I miss the days when he was just my father instead of my boss."

Savannah paused and looked at him. "I didn't know you felt that way. Would you rather work somewhere else?"

With a quick shrug, Garrett headed for the kitchen. "I don't know. I like my work and I'm a good salesman—"

Savannah followed. "But?"

"Five years ago, Pastor Jim said he thought in time God might have other work for me to do." Garrett stacked his dishes in the sink.

"I didn't know that. What kind of work?" Savannah glanced at Garrett and began rinsing the dishes.

He shook his head. "He wanted God to tell me Himself when it was time."

"Has God told you?"

Hesitating, Garrett stared at the floor. "Not really. I like preaching when Jim asks me, but I couldn't earn enough to support us being an itinerant pastor like he is." He expelled a long sigh. "Maybe he was wrong."

"You're a very good preacher. You have a gift with words. Let's pray about how God wants you to use it."

♠

Savannah kissed Mother's cheek, then followed Garrett into the living room. Father's eyes lit as he stood to greet them.

"I've come to visit while the ladies have Bible study." Garrett dropped into the armchair across from Father's favorite Thonet rocking chair.

His father smiled at Savannah, then glanced at his son. "You and the Reverend not meeting tonight?"

"Not tonight. He had a hospital visit."

Returning to his chair, Father raised one eyebrow. "I'd think by now you'd have learned everything he could teach you."

Periodically, Father quizzed Garrett about his Monday nights with Pastor Jim. Savannah shrugged and went back to the kitchen where Mother was filling four glasses with iced tea. Savannah reached for two of them. "I'll take these to the men."

Garrett glanced at her as she stepped back into the living room. "Maybe God has work for me to do. I want to be ready."

"What kind of work? You aren't thinking of being an itinerant preacher are you?" Father's voice rumbled.

That too had been an ongoing theme.

"I wouldn't be able to support us." Garrett reached for his iced tea and took a swallow.

Father was too intent on their conversation to notice the glass of tea Savannah held out to him. "What makes you think God has work for you to do?" Father's jaw jutted.

Garrett stared at the floor and was silent. At last he raised his gaze to his father's face. "Reverend Caldwell suggested it."

"I knew it. I knew it. I knew he was filling your head with foolishness." Father glared at Garrett.

Savannah cleared her throat. "I brought you a cold drink."

He reached for his drink but refused to be deterred. "You need to stop meeting with Reverend Caldwell. He takes religion too far."

"I'm a grown man and I have to make my own decisions." Garrett took another long swallow of tea. "I don't want to argue with you. Let's talk about something else."

Savannah slipped from the room. She was proud of Garrett for not yelling back at his father. He'd come a long way.

"What's all the commotion about in there?" Mother rearranged a curl and fastened it with a hair pin.

"Father isn't happy about Reverend Caldwell's influence over Garrett. He wants them to stop meeting." Savannah slipped into her chair across from Mother.

"I thought he'd gotten over that. I was going to ask him this evening about us having a weekly Bible study at noon in the office...this might not be the best time." She fanned herself with her hand. "How are things going with Dorothy?"

Savannah shrugged. "We stay out of each other's way. At least she hasn't tried to spread any gossip lately."

"That's good. Let's keep praying for her. Anything else we should be praying about?"

Leaning over, Savannah untied and removed her shoes and tucked her feet under her. "Do you think God has plans for us? Like what work we do or whether or not we have children?"

"Jeremiah 29:11 says, *For I know the thoughts I think toward you, thoughts of peace, and not of evil, to give you an expected end.* So yes, I think He has plans for us." Mother's face glowed as it always did when she quoted scripture.

"Then let's pray that God will tell Garrett if He has work for him to do. And could we ask Him to give us children?"

Mother's brow furrowed. "We can certainly ask God to tell Garrett if He has work for him to do, and we can ask Him to give you children if that's His plan." Clasping her hands in front of her, Mother gazed at Savannah. "Garrett's father and I waited many years for God to give us a son. It was just God's timing. Some people never have children."

Savannah pressed her hands against her flat abdomen as Mother prayed. What if God didn't choose to give them a child? Could she still trust that He loved her and wasn't punishing her for her past?

CHAPTER 17

"Do you think we could have a special party for my birthday next week?" George squatted on the floor beside Polly where she read to Twila and Elsie in Mother's sitting room.

"What kind of party?" Polly had learned to ask questions before saying yes.

"Maybe invite some of the fellows to come for cake and ice cream? I'll only turn sixteen once."

George rarely asked for favors. "I suppose we could do that. What kind of cake?"

"Chocolate, of course, with cooked maple sugar frosting." George smacked his lips.

"Yum yum…" Twila clapped three times.

"None for you." George's eyes had a teasing gleam.

Before Twila could say a word, Elsie made her usual proclamation. "No fair."

George tapped his toes and made a great show of changing his mind. "Maybe just a small piece for small girls."

Polly jumped in to head off an argument. "What else do you want for your birthday?".

George stared into space. "An automobile. I'd like to have an automobile."

A loud snort escaped Polly's lips. "Father isn't going to buy you a car."

"Probably not, but he's been talking to Garrett about it, getting his recommendations. It'll only be a matter of time until he buys one, so why not now?"

Polly rolled her eyes. "Go on before I change my mind about the party. Oh wait, what day do you want to have it—on Wednesday, your birthday, or on Friday?"

George tilted his head, his light brown hair gleaming in the glow of a gas lamp on the end table. "Friday is usually the best time for parties." He stood to leave. Then turned back. "Did you hear that New Castle schools may delay their opening?"

She put a finger to her lips, but it was too late.

"Will we have to start school before they do?" Elsie's lower lip protruded.

"We need to hope and pray there's no reason for our schools to start late." Polly touched Elsie's nose with a trembling index finger. "And pray for the children in New Castle who are already sick."

Elsie's eyes rounded. "Is that why their school might start late? Because children are sick?"

"That's part of the reason. The illness is very contagious—"

"And it spreads faster in hot weather." George chimed in.

"Is it an epa… epa…" Elsie knew many words but couldn't always pronounce them.

"Epidemic." Polly finished her sister's sentence. "I'm afraid it is. People who have it need to be quarantined."

"What's that mean?" Twila had been silent until now, brown eyes wide.

"Quarantined? It means they need to keep away from other people so no one else catches their disease."

Elsie and Twila stared at Polly. She tried to keep her tone calm and even, so as not to alarm them. With a slight shake of her head at George, she discouraged him from continuing this conversation.

"Can children die from this illness like Mama and our baby brother died?" Elsie had only vague memories of that difficult time. Twila had none at all.

Polly's gaze met George's before she looked into Elsie's eyes. She had hoped that question wouldn't be asked. Still she couldn't lie. She nodded as George quietly left the room. "Children can die from this disease. That's why it's important that everyone follow the rules made by the Health Department."

"When do we have to go back to school?" Twila wasn't eager for vacation to end.

"The week after Labor Day. Bring me the calendar, Twila, and I'll show you."

"Let me do it, Polly. She's not old enough." The girls raced toward the colorful Mercer County State Bank calendar on the sitting room wall.

Polly hid a smile. Although Elsie was the older of the two, Twila had already caught up in height. "Let Twila bring it to me and you can take it back, Elsie."

If only all their problems were that easily solved.

♠

Be anxious for nothing... Be anxious for nothing... Be anxious for nothing...

No matter how she tried, Polly couldn't get free of the cloud that had descended when she heard about the outbreak of infantile paralysis. Her days and nights were troubled the rest of the week.

On Saturday morning, Twila didn't come downstairs with Elsie as she usually did.

"Where's Twila?" Polly stopped slicing bread and hugged Elsie.

"She said she doesn't feel well. Is breakfast almost ready? I smell bacon."

"Almost. Could you set the table while I check on Twila?"

Polly released a breath when Elsie picked up the bowls and silverware and headed for the dining room without an argument. Polly sped from the kitchen, through the living room and up the stairs. *It's probably nothing. She's just a little under the weather.*

She knelt beside her sister's bed and laid a hand on her forehead. Her big brown eyes were closed, her forehead definitely warm. "How do you feel?"

Twila turned her face away and groaned. "I feel sick. I don't want any breakfast."

Beth poked her head into the doorway. "What's wrong with Twila?"

"Bring me the thermometer. She isn't feeling well and I think she has a fever. Maybe I should call Dr. Cooley."

"Already?" Beth's brown eyes widened.

Polly's stomach lurched and rolled. *Oh, God, after six years, I still wallow in indecision at times like these.* She dropped to her knees and rested her forehead on the edge of Twila's bed.

CHAPTER 18

The hours dragged as Polly waited for her father to return from the mine. Twila's temperature hovered between 100 and 101 degrees. Why had Father been needed today of all days?

Every now and then Polly lifted the washcloth from Twila's forehead and dipped it into a basin filled with cool water. Many people believed in piling heavy blankets on a feverish person, but Mother had always insisted on placing wet, cool washcloths on their foreheads instead.

Wishing she could do more, she offered Twila tea or orange juice and toast, in addition to the cold water she'd been drinking. The only response was a listless shake of Twila's head. Late afternoon her sister sat up and covered her mouth, then gagged and swallowed convulsively. Polly leaped to her feet. "I'll be right back."

She dashed down the steps, yanked a small bucket from under the sink, and headed back upstairs. Even though it had been more than six years, it seemed like only yesterday she'd done this for Mother before she died. That dark day was the last thing she wanted to think about.

After dropping to her knees beside Twila's bed, Polly held the bucket under her youngest sister's chin. Her father's voice from the doorway startled her. "What's wrong with Twila?"

"I don't know. She has a fever and feels sick. I thought she was going to vomit. Do you think we should call Dr. Cooley?"

Father took a few steps into the bedroom. "How high is her fever?"

"A little over 100. Up and down most of the day."

Closing his eyes, Father bit his lip. "Let me think about it while I go downstairs and wash."

Polly's shoulders sagged in relief. Father would make the decision.

She glanced at the alarm clock on the girls' bedside table, then went to the top of the stairs and called Beth. It was almost time for supper. Perhaps Beth and Elsie could warm some leftovers.

♠

By the time Father returned, Twila had lain back down with eyes closed, the bucket beside her. Polly joined him in the doorway, speaking in a whisper. "Did you know infantile paralysis often begins with flu-like symptoms?"

Father nodded. "I read it in the newspaper." He stared at his youngest daughter who seemed to be resting quietly. "I understand it's very hard to tell the difference this early. Let's wait until tomorrow. Maybe she'll be better in the morning. I'll sit with her for awhile."

Glancing at her sister, Polly stood undecided. Even though she didn't trust her own decisions, it was hard to leave Twila's side. At last she turned and started toward the steps.

"Maybe I should go get Lydia."

Polly stopped abruptly and turned around. She opened her mouth. *Be swift to hear, slow to speak and slow to wrath.* She clamped her lips together, bowed her head and then raised it again. "Go get Lydia?" She kept her tone low.

"I'd like another opinion about whether to call the doctor. Maybe she knows more than I do about the symptoms of infantile paralysis." Father rubbed his forehead.

"Are you sure you want her to be exposed? Adults can be infected, too."

Father's shoulders slumped. "I guess not. We'll just wait and pray."

♠

Polly and Father took turns sitting with Twila throughout the night. Her fever never rose any higher and she never vomited. Elsie slept with Beth in the other bedroom. When daybreak came, Twila seemed a bit better, her forehead a little cooler. Exhausted, Polly allowed her eyelids to close and dozed off and on. Maybe the family could get their own breakfast today.

A gentle hand on her shoulder woke Polly with a start. "Do you want me to take the family to church or would you rather I stay home with Twila?"

When Polly blinked sleep from her eyes, Father's face came into view. "You go ahead. I'll stay with Twila." Just thinking about getting cleaned up for church required more energy than Polly could muster.

As Father's footsteps clumped down the stairs, she leaned her head against the back of her chair. Her father's words from yesterday returned to her unbidden. "Maybe I should go get Lydia."

The last thing Polly wanted was advice from Mrs. Wilds about the children or anything else. Her motive in mentioning the possibility of her being exposed had not been concern for the woman's wellbeing. It had seemed like the best way of discouraging Father from having her come. She squirmed a bit at her own manipulative behavior.

"Polly."

Twila's voice was barely a whisper, but Polly was instantly alert. "What can I get you, Little One?"

"A drink of cold water, please."

"How about a piece of toast to go with it?" Polly stooped beside the bed to look into Twila's eyes.

"No, thank you. Just water."

Polly stood, picked up Twila's glass, and started toward the hall just as George came from his bedroom. He was dressed for church. "How is she?"

George might tease and badger his little sisters but his concern for Twila was clear. "Maybe a wee bit better. She asked for a drink of cold water. I haven't taken her temperature yet today."

"I'll bring her a drink." George took Twila's glass from Polly's unresisting fingers. "Can I get you a drink too? You look tired."

Blinking back tears at the unexpected kindness, Polly nodded. "Thank you. A drink would be wonderful."

♠

After Twila swallowed some of the water George had brought, her even breathing told Polly she had fallen asleep again. She drank some of her own water, slid further down in her chair and closed her eyes.

Surely it was only seconds later that Father called her name. "Back already?" She blinked in the sunshine that streamed through the window.

"Church is over."

Father wasn't the chatty sort but even for him, that was a short answer.

"What was the sermon about?"

"Reverend Caldwell preached about suffering." Father shifted from one foot to the other.

"Really? He didn't mention he'd be there." Polly's brows puckered.

"I think it was a last minute thing. He asked about you."

Rubbing her eyes, Polly tried to focus. "What did he say about suffering?"

Father sighed and screwed up his forehead. "He said suffering produces perseverance, perseverance produces character…" Father paused. "Oh yes, and character produces hope."

Polly blinked. Jim had preached on something similar a few years ago. Before she could bring it to mind, Father squatted and took her hand. *Uh oh, did he have bad news?*

"What's wrong?" Polly's eyes were wide open now.

A deep sigh escaped Father's lips. "Do you remember the children Twila played with after church last week?"

Polly nodded. "I didn't know them."

"Someone told me their family lives in New Castle." Father's voice dropped an octave. "One of the children developed infantile paralysis this week."

CHAPTER 19

Doc Cooley stood from examining Twila and put away his stethoscope. "It's impossible to tell the difference between influenza and infantile paralysis at this stage. Best to keep her quiet and away from the other children. Give her plenty of fluids and don't force her to eat." He stared into space, his blue eyes thoughtful. "Let's try some Gelsemium. Dr. McCann in Dayton, Ohio, is reporting excellent results in treating influenza with that remedy."

Polly glanced at her father. "I've never heard of it."

He nodded agreement and turned to the doctor. "What is it?"

"It's a homeopathic remedy." He put his stethoscope in his black bag and pulled out a paper packet. "Some medical doctors are skeptical of it. I prefer to let the results speak for themselves." He poured a few white pellets into his hand, bent over and held them out to Twila. "Put these under your tongue and let them dissolve." He smiled into her eyes. "They won't hurt you and they might help."

Obediently, she popped the pills into her mouth and leaned back against the pillows.

"Thanks, Doc. Sorry to call you out on a Sunday." Father shook the doctor's hand. "What do I owe you?"

"You can take care of it next time you come to the office or I'll send you a bill." The kindly doctor patted Polly's shoulder. "Don't borrow trouble, child."

She nodded. "I'll try not to." If only it were that easy.

♠

Father sat with Twila while Polly threw together a light lunch. Everyone liked the new Kraft Processed Cheese which made quick sandwiches. Potato chips, which she could buy at the market, were also a favorite when time was short. She wasn't sure what Mother would think of these short cuts, but today it would have to do.

She took Father a plate and then went across the hall to get her journal. She pulled the dark blue book out of her dresser drawer and picked up Chartreuse. After tucking her pillow under her arm, she headed back across the hall. Sitting beside her sleeping sister would give her time to process her whirling thoughts.

"I'll take over now, Father. You can take a break."

"Aren't you going to eat?"

"I snacked while I cooked." Polly removed her shoes and situated herself on Elsie's bed.

Father patted Twila's cheek. Then he smiled at his oldest daughter, took his plate and left the room. His heavy footsteps thumped down the stairs.

Polly traced the gold lettering on the front of her journal. Soon she'd ask Savannah if she would return Sarah's diary. What a blessing that it hadn't burned. It seemed almost too good to be true.

She opened her journal. *August 26, 1917. Thank you, Father, for Dr. Cooley. He is a blessing to us just as his father was to Sarah Davis even if he couldn't promise me that Twila doesn't have infantile paralysis. Oh Father, please, please let her be all right.*

Polly squeezed her eyes shut with the fervency of her prayer. At last she opened them and began to write.

Father said Rev... Jim asked about me. I hope he knows we can only be friends. I wish I could have heard his message. If I'd had a journal the first time I heard him preach, I could have written down what he said about suffering.

She nibbled the top of her pen and stared into space. Seven or eight years ago, Reverend Caldwell had preached about Jesus not coming immediately to Mary and Martha when their brother died, even though He knew about the death. Then as clearly as though Jim stood in the room, the words he'd spoken came to her and she began to write.

Do we dare to believe that suffering is sometimes God's good gift to produce qualities in us we wouldn't develop any other way?

Polly put down her pen and read what she'd written. She still didn't like pain and suffering but she had to admit it had produced good fruit in her life. She had been forced to mature in order to be a good role model for the younger children. Glancing at Twila's pale face, she bit her lip. *Please, Father, no more losses.*

What had Sarah written in her diary? *Only God could get me through the death of a child.*

♠

Bob stood at the bottom of the stairs, torn between wanting to be alone and needing to be with his children. Their conversation around the dining room table was muted, as it had been since Twila's illness.

"Abdicate the throne." He spoke the words to himself and headed for the dining room. His children needed him more than he needed to be alone.

Elsie's eyes lit as he entered the room. "Sit by me, Papa."

"But this is my seat over here. I thought everyone had to sit in their own seat." He winked at Elsie and slid into Twila's chair.

"Maybe you could sit next to me just until Twila gets better. How long do you think that will be?" The corners of Elsie's mouth drooped.

Bob popped a potato chip into his mouth to give himself time to think. At last he shook his head. "I don't know. Dr. Cooley gave her some medicine which might help if she has influenza."

"Does she have the flu?" The look in Beth's eyes told him she wanted the truth.

He sighed. "I don't know. Even Dr. Cooley says it's too early to tell."

Beth wanted to be a nurse when she grew up. She respected Dr. Cooley's authority. "Papa—"

She was in that in between stage when she sometimes called him Papa and sometimes Father. "Yes?"

"Mother used to pray for us sometimes when we were sick. Do you think we could pray for Twila?"

Polly had stepped into her mother's role and prayed with the children more readily than he did. But Beth's gaze brooked no refusal. George also watched him.

"I'm not very good at praying out loud—"

Beth sighed. "I could pray."

Shame crept over Bob. What was wrong with him? "Thank you, Beth." He smiled at her. "I'm the father, and I need to pray for my daughter."

Smiling at her father, Beth closed her eyes. "Thank you, Papa."

Bob licked his dry lips and closed his eyes. "Heavenly Father, thank you for my children. Thank you for watching over them every day. You know what's wrong with Twila even though we don't. Would you touch her and heal what ever is making her sick? In Jesus' name. Amen."

He opened his eyes and looked around the table. Should he tell them God doesn't always answer prayers the way we want? No, they had already learned that lesson.

♠

A gentle tap on the screen door drew Bob's attention as he pushed back from the dining room table. He hurried to open the door and beamed at the girl who had become like a daughter to him.

"Savannah, come in. We've been missing you. How are you?"

"I'm fine, but Dorothy gave Father Young some disturbing news at work on Friday."

Frowning, Bob motioned for Savannah to sit down on the davenport. "What is she gossiping about now?"

"I don't know whether to call this gossip or not." Savannah shrugged and shook her head. "But since it might affect your family, I wanted to talk to you. She said one of the children from New Castle that visited your church last week has come down with infantile paralysis."

"This time she's right." Bob scrubbed his face with both hands. "They told us in church this morning."

"Did any of you have contact with her?" Savannah's eyes were wide with concern.

"I might as well tell you the whole story. We didn't want to worry you if it wasn't necessary." Bob took a deep breath and told Savannah everything that had happened since Twila became ill the day before, including Dr. Cooley's visit. "Polly is sitting with Twila now."

"How is Polly holding up?"

"It's hard to tell. She always tries to be strong for the rest of us. But Twila is her baby."

Savannah got to her feet. "Could I go up to see her?"

Bob stood as well. "Doc Cooley gave Twila some medicine, but you might be just what the doctor ordered for Polly. Go ahead."

♠

Savannah tread lightly up the stairs in case Twila was sleeping. When she entered Twila and Elsie's room, Polly's eyes were closed, her head resting against the headboard of Elsie's bed. Her journal lay open on her lap.

Whispering Polly's name, Savannah knelt beside her.

Polly's eyelids fluttered open. When she gave a soft cry and sat up, Savannah gathered her friend into her arms. "Oh Savannah, Twila is so sick. What if it's… what if it's…"

As Polly sobbed, Savannah soothed her like a child. "It's okay, Polly. It's okay to cry."

CHAPTER 20

Polly jerked awake as the sun shone through the window. She leaped to her feet—she hadn't meant to fall asleep. The light outlined Twila lying so still that Polly feared the worst. She opened her mouth to call Father, then paused as Twila turned toward her, her chest rising and falling in peaceful sleep. Polly dropped to her knees beside Twila's bed, her legs unable to hold her, face buried in the bedclothes.

"Thank you, thank you, thank you, Father." Her words came out in a whisper, muffled by the quilt. Lifting her head at last and leaning closer, she touched her lips to her sister's forehead. It was cool, not a trace of fever.

As Polly straightened, Twila's eyes fluttered open. The corners of her mouth turned up. "Polly…"

"What, Little One?" Polly's throat was so thick with gratitude, the words were almost indistinguishable.

"I'm hungry." Twila scooted herself into a sitting position. "Can I have something to eat?"

Tears coursed down Polly's cheeks, sobs making it impossible for her to speak. She nodded, kissed Twila's forehead and headed downstairs to tell Father the good news.

♠

Polly opened the oven door, squatted and leaned in to stick a toothpick into George's cake. Not quite done. She closed the door, thankful for the cooler weather the last few days. After grabbing the broom, she swept up the mess she always made when she baked. Had Mother been this messy?

Not that George's friends would notice or care, but Polly had spent the morning cleaning. She'd also made a trip to the market to pick up Ginger Ale, George's favorite soft drink, and more potato chips. With a sigh, she sank into a chair she'd pulled into the kitchen and rested her head on her hand. Parties were a lot of work.

Elsie's high-pitched giggle and Twila's accompanying lower-pitched laughter reminded Polly she'd resolved never to complain about anything after Twila's quick recovery following Dr. Cooley's visit on Sunday. Besides her fever having broken, she ate every bit of the breakfast Polly fixed for her. Beth insisted it was because Papa had prayed.

Thank you, Father. How many times had she breathed that prayer this week? She wasn't proud of how frantic she'd become when it appeared Twila might have infantile paralysis. Her resolve years ago to run *to* God rather than blaming Him had been tested, but she hadn't failed completely.

Mother had said faith is like a muscle. If it's never exercised, it will never grow strong.

Twila rushed into the kitchen. "Something smells good." She sniffed appreciatively.

The *cake*... Polly leaped out of her chair, rushed to the woodstove and flung open the door. She breathed a sigh of relief and grabbed another toothpick. The cake hadn't burned and the toothpick came out clean.

After pulling out the nine-by-twelve pan, she closed the oven door and set the cake on the counter. Next she spread the maple sugar icing on the cake while it was still hot as the recipe instructed. The smell was heavenly.

The hinges of the screen door squeaked and after admonishing Twila not to touch the cake, Polly stepped into the living room to see who had come in. Father stood just inside the door, head tilted and eyes closed as he took in the fragrance that permeated the house.

He opened his eyes and smiled. "Are we having company?"

"Are you implying we only have cake when company comes?" Polly wrinkled her nose.

"Well..." Father didn't disagree.

"I know, I know. Baking isn't my favorite thing. Did you forget we're having George's party tonight?"

"I didn't remember. I should have invited Lydia—maybe we still could." He raised a brow hopefully at Polly.

"Invite Lydia to George's birthday party? Why would you do that?" Polly struggled for composure.

"Just an opportunity for her to get to know you and the children better. I said I'd come see her this evening."

"I don't think George would be pleased if you invite Mrs. Wilds to his party, but it's up to you."

♠

Polly dashed up the steps. The party was set to begin at seven o'clock. That should give her a few minutes to comb her hair and change her dress. Not that George's friends would notice or care about that either. Why was she bothering? If she were honest with herself, it was probably because of the possibility that Father would invite Mrs. Wilds.

She groaned. Who cared what Mrs. Wilds thought? Mother would have cared. Her mother had always done her best to look neat and well-groomed even when there was no special occasion, but especially when guests were coming. Sometimes Polly had complained that Mother cared too much about what others thought.

Now was not the time to analyze her mother or herself. She whipped off her work dress, stained with maple icing, and grabbed a pale green one usually reserved for Sundays. In record time, she put it on and grabbed a comb. One look in the mirror told her she should have allowed more time to get ready. Ringlets had escaped her morning coiffure and clung to her damp forehead.

With a sigh, Polly did her best to calm and restrain her hair into some semblance of order, reminding herself again that it didn't matter.

A loud knock on the screen door brought George and Polly into the upstairs hall. How handsome her well-groomed brother had become. "Do you want to answer the door or shall I? If we don't hurry, Twila or Elsie will take over."

"I'll get it." George ran down the stairs smoothing his hair. Had he invited any girls?

In a moment he was back, a disgusted look on his face. "Did you invite Billy?"

Polly frowned. "I might have mentioned to Blanche that you were having a party."

"I invited Vance since we work together at the garage, but I told him not to tell his brother."

"Why?" She studied George's face. "Blanche probably assumed Billy was invited, too."

"Billy's not my favorite person. I sent him to the sitting room where Beth is entertaining Elsie and Twila." George turned to go back downstairs as another knock vibrated the screen door. "I wish you hadn't mentioned my party to anyone without asking me."

Had Father mentioned inviting Lydia Wilds? Probably not. Polly bit her lip and started down the stairs.

The party seemed to be in full swing, loud laughter and boisterous voices filled the living room. Some of George's friends sprawled on the davenport and others in chairs or on the floor. No girls in sight.

George hadn't wanted any planned games, so Polly spent most of the evening in Mother's sitting room with Beth, Elsie, and Twila and yes, with Billy. He seemed happy to chat with Beth.

George's friends responded politely to Polly's greetings when she passed through to get refreshments, but as she expected, barely noticed her until she started bringing food and beverages. Her brother was a good host, pouring Ginger Ale for his friends and passing around baskets of potato chips.

Polly had just counted out sixteen candles when the screen door squeaked and complete silence fell in the living room. She poked her head in the doorway. Father and Mrs. Wilds stood just inside the screen door. George had dropped a basket of potato chips and made no effort to pick them up.

Father broke the uneasy silence. "George, this is our neighbor, Lydia Wilds. She wanted to wish you a happy birthday."

George bit his lip. He stood unsmiling until the silence became oppressive. "I know who she is."

Polly stood paralyzed in the doorway. Why oh why had Father thought this was a good idea? Someone needed to do something.

Mrs. Wilds gave a high-pitched, tinkling laugh and took a step toward George. "Happy birthday, George. What gift did you want for your birthday this year?"

George glanced at his father, then shook his head. "Just a party with *my friends*."

Had he emphasized the words *my friends*?

Finding her tongue at last, Polly stepped into the living room. "Hello, Mrs. Wilds." She did her best to give a welcoming smile…a grimace was probably more like it. "I'm just about ready to light the candles. Looks like the living room is full, but you can sit at the dining room table if you want."

Back in the kitchen, she shoved candles into the cake in record time and grabbed a box of matches. After striking one on the coarse surface of the box, she lit candles as fast as she could. No sounds of conversation came from the living room. George's friends had apparently taken their cue from his silence. Mrs. Wilds' occasional laugh and muted conversation with Father in the dining room were the only sounds.

At last, she picked up the flaming cake and carried it to the living room, speaking loud enough for those behind the sitting room door to hear. "Time for the birthday cake."

Everyone from the sitting room and the dining room joined them as George's friends smacked their lips. "Make a wish, George." She held out his cake.

He glanced at Father and Mrs. Wilds, then back at the cake. With one mighty whoosh, he blew out all the candles.

"What did you wish George?" Twila and Elsie were jumping up and down, speaking in unison.

George shook his head. "If I tell you, it won't come true. And this is one wish I *really* want to come true."

Father had not yet purchased the automobile George had hoped for, but from the look on George's face as he glanced again at Mrs. Wilds, Polly didn't need to ask what he'd wished.

CHAPTER 21

The sun shone through the bedroom window as Savannah opened her eyes, then blinked a few times. They usually closed the lacy white curtains that hung at each of the windows in their bedroom but last night they hadn't.

Why was Garrett still sound asleep beside her, unbothered by the sunlight? Although he told her stories about sleeping in and being late when he worked for his cousin, Irv, it was rare for him to sleep later than she. He often awoke before their alarm rang.

Savannah glanced at the clock and leaped out of bed. Eight o'clock. "Garrett, wake up. We must have forgotten to set the alarm."

Garrett turned over and opened one sleepy eye. "Good morning to you, too." He grinned and opened his other eye to wink at her. "You need to check the calendar."

"What?" She peered at him, then flopped back into bed. "What was I thinking? I forgot it's Labor Day. Sorry I woke you."

"It's nice to be awakened when we don't have to rush to get ready for work. Do we have plans?" He pulled her into his arms and buried his face in her hair.

"Just a picnic with your parents later." Savannah snuggled closer.

"You smell nice."

Savannah chuckled. "That's because my husband gives me expensive perfume that smells much better than the cheap stuff."

He pulled in a long breath. "Orange blossom?"

"Umm. You're good. I doubt most husbands can identify—" Savannah cringed as an abdominal cramp took her breath away.

Oh no, not again. In spite of her efforts to control it, a sob escaped.

Garrett lifted his face from her hair. "What's wrong?"

She moved away from him and clutched her stomach. "My monthly was a few days late and I thought maybe…" Her body shook with sobs as she swung her legs over the side of the bed.

"Savannah, wait…" Garrett reached for her.

"Not now. I need to take care of…" She hurried into the bathroom.

♠

Garrett sat up and bowed his head. They'd been through this before during the five years since they'd married. Lately, it had become almost a monthly occurrence. Something had to change.

God, isn't there anything I can do? Helplessness permeated him.

He got out of bed and began gathering clothes for the day. Clouds began to blot out the sun reminding him that the forecast was for cool weather and possible showers. Just what they needed—rain to drown out their picnic. He sat on the edge of the bed to pull on his socks just as Savannah reentered the room.

"Come sit with me." Garrett patted the spot beside him.

Savannah opened a bureau drawer and pulled out a handkerchief before plopping down beside him. She wiped tears from her cheeks.

"How can I help?" Garrett tilted her chin toward him.

Blowing her nose, Savannah shook her head. "There's nothing anyone can do. If God doesn't want us to have children, we won't."

Garrett's forehead puckered. "I don't think we can assume God doesn't want us to have children. Maybe we have a problem that can be corrected."

"Polly asked if I'd seen Dr. Cooley. She said he's a wonderful doctor." Savannah sat up a little straighter.

"That's a good idea." The heaviness lifted from Garrett's chest. Maybe there was hope. "We can call to make an appointment—probably not today."

Savannah managed a smile. "No, let's not interrupt Dr. Cooley's holiday. I'll call tomorrow during my lunch break."

♠

Bob shivered as the sun hid behind the clouds that had

gathered since he'd left the house. He needed time to think before the family started their holiday. There'd been an uneasy peace since George's party as Bob wrestled with who was to blame for Lydia's chilly welcome. Polly had warned him George wouldn't be happy if he invited Lydia, so maybe he was to blame for ignoring her warning.

How were his children ever going to get to know Lydia if he couldn't bring her to the house? Not that he'd been particularly comfortable himself when she'd come uninvited. How could he expect his children to adapt to something which still seemed foreign to him?

His steps slowed as Lydia's house came into view. He loved going there, especially when her daughter wasn't home. Maybe that was the answer. Maybe Lydia should invite him and his children to come to her house where their mother's presence wasn't so strongly felt.

With no conscious volition, his feet carried him to Lydia's door. When he raised his hand to knock, the earliness of the hour gave him pause, and he lowered it again. Before he turned away, the door opened. Lydia smiled, hair slightly mussed and a sleepy look in her eyes, dressed in a feminine, pale pink wrapper. What would it be like to wake up every morning to this?

♠

"Polly, Polly."

Groggy and half-asleep, Polly rolled over and opened her eyes. "What is it, Twila?"

"Where's Papa? It's a holiday but he's gone." A frown wrinkled Twila's forehead.

Polly glanced at Beth, still sound asleep. "Shhh. Don't wake Beth. I don't know where he is. Maybe there was an emergency at the mine, but I didn't hear the telephone." Polly covered a large yawn. "Go downstairs and see if he left a note."

Twila scampered down the steps as Polly leaned against the headboard. Maybe Father had gone to get something at the market. Were the stores open on Labor Day?

In a few minutes, Twila was back. "No note."

"Don't worry. If he didn't leave a note, he'll be back soon." She reached to give Twila a hug. "Why don't you crawl into bed with

Beth and me. School will be starting soon so enjoy this while you can."

Twila hesitated. "Maybe Father is at Lydia Wilds' house."

Polly scowled. "Why would you say that?"

"Because I had a dream about them being at her house."

Rolling her eyes, Polly tugged her little sister into bed. "Just because you dreamed it doesn't mean it will happen."

CHAPTER 22

Bob whistled a tuneless song before launching into "Down by the Old Mill Stream" as he ran up the porch steps. The children should be awake by now and ready to hear the plans for the day. Last night he hedged when they tried to pin him down about a picnic. Since they'd wanted a picnic, surely they'd be excited no matter where it was held.

He reached to open the screen door but drew back as it opened toward him. Florence stood in the doorway, a quizzical look in her eye. "Maybe Twila was right."

"What do you mean?" When Florence didn't move, he pulled the door open wider. "Are you going to let me come in?"

Florence stepped back. "Twila dreamed you were at Mrs. Wilds' house."

Bob felt heat creep up his neck. "What makes you think she was right?"

"Because you were whistling. You only whistle when you've been to see Mrs. Wilds."

Pushing past his oldest daughter, Bob came into the house. He rubbed his neck and avoided her eyes. "I didn't plan to go to her house. I just needed time to think about today, so I took a walk."

"You just happened to take a walk down Broad Street toward where Mrs. Wilds' lives?" Florence's gaze hadn't left his face.

"Why is it that when we talk about Lydia, I always feel like a school boy who's in trouble with the teacher?" Bob walked over and dropped down on the davenport, still avoiding Florence's eyes.

She shrugged. "Why do you think?"

Footsteps pounded down the stairs and two girls in white nightgowns pounced on Bob. "There you are, Papa." Twila curled up beside him on the daven. "I dreamed you were at Lydia's—"

"Don't call her Lydia, Twila. That isn't polite." Florence perched on Mother's gray chair.

"Mrs. Wilds seems a bit formal if we're going to be friends."

Bob patted Twila's cheek. "Maybe you could call her Miss Lydia."

"Are we going to be friends?" As usual, Elsie got straight to the point.

"I hope so." Bob pulled her onto his lap, something he didn't often do anymore. "Lydia has invited us to a picnic at her house to celebrate Labor Day. Would you like to go?"

"Oh Papa…" Twila started to bounce on the davenport until she caught a glimpse of Florence's face. Thunder clouds blotted out any rays of sunshine that had been there. "Is Polly coming?"

"What do you think, Florence?" Bob tried to meet her gaze, but she turned away. "She invited all six of us to come."

"I don't know." Florence glanced at the doorway to the stairs as footsteps sprinted down the steps. "Maybe it would be better if George and I stayed home." Florence stood.

"Couldn't you give Lydia a chance?" Bob knew George would be a lost cause if Florence didn't go. He might refuse anyway.

George stepped into the living room, still combing his blondish-brown hair. "Looks like a serious meeting. What's going on?"

Bob filled him in on Lydia's invitation. "I'm sorry I brought her to your party without talking to you first. Can we put that behind us and try again?"

George backed up and plopped onto the downstairs landing. "Why does it always have to be last minute? Why can't you ever give us time to get used to the idea?"

"Would it make a difference?" Bob got to his feet. "Or would it just give you time to come up with an excuse to say no?"

Twila grabbed Bob's arm as he took a step away from the daven. "Maybe George and Polly will change their minds." Her head swiveled back and forth as she looked from George to Florence and then back to him, dark eyes pleading.

♠

"How's Dorothy doing these days?" Mildred Young stood at the table in their sunny kitchen cutting potatoes into small chunks for potato salad.

Harold poured himself a glass of iced tea and sat down across from his wife. "I guess she's doing okay. Why do you ask?"

"Sometimes I worry about her tendency to gossip. Makes life difficult for others in the office." Mildred took mayonnaise from the ice box and put a glob into the red bowl on the table, then added sugar, and vinegar. The tangy smell of the vinegar made her nose twitch.

Her husband sighed and nodded. "She could single-handedly write a gossip column for the paper if they wanted one, which they don't. I've never seen anything like it." He raised an eyebrow at his wife. "You were the one who suggested I hire her."

"I know. She really needed a job, but I feel sort of responsible." Mildred stirred the dressing with a wooden spoon. "What would you think about Savannah, Dorothy and me having a Bible study at noon once a week at the office? Maybe sooner or later, I could address the subject of gossip."

Before he could answer, a light tap on the screen door announced Savannah and Garrett's arrival. Mildred wiped her hands on her apron and met them at the door. She embraced them in one warm hug and drew them into the kitchen.

"What a good idea to have a picnic today. I can't remember whose idea it was…" Mildred chuckled.

"I believe it was yours, Ma." Her son kissed her cheek and returned her smile, but Savannah's face was unusually solemn.

"So it was." Mildred dumped the dressing on the potatoes, diced onions, and sliced hardboiled eggs. "Savannah, are you feeling okay? You look a little pale."

"Not the best today, Mother, but I'll be fine." Savannah didn't quite meet her eyes.

"Maybe you're in the family way." Harold smiled at his daughter-in-law.

Sobs escaped Savannah's lips. She covered her face with both hands and ran out the front door.

CHAPTER 23

Polly slipped out the back door, closing it softly behind her. She needed time to think. Was she being unfair to Father by refusing to consider Mrs. Wilds' invitation? Twila had obviously wanted to go before loyalty to Polly swayed her decision.

She walked behind Blanche's house to avoid being seen by anyone looking out the window at the Dye home, then cut down to Broad Street. Her gaze fixed on the road, she tried to pray. "Heavenly Father…" No words came. What could she say?

What would Mother want her to do? No, the question was what did her heavenly Father want her to do?

Long, shuddering breaths caught her attention. She glanced up. What was that sound? Someone crying?

Head bent, feet dragging, Savannah came toward her, passing the Potter place on her right.

"Savannah, what's wrong?" Polly hurried to her friend's side and wrapped her arms around her. She'd seemed fine a few days ago when Polly had told her Twila didn't have infantile paralysis.

A muffled chuckle prompted her to pull away from Savannah. "I thought you were crying." She peered at her friend.

"I *was* crying. Then I remembered the first day we met. Do you remember? I was running away from Sandy Lake and you had milk and jam in your hair."

Polly giggled. "I remember. We're a pair. Last Sunday I cried in your arms and today it's your turn. Why are you crying?"

"It's a long story." Savannah pulled in another long breath. "You know how I've longed for a child?"

When Polly nodded, Savannah told her about yet another disappointment that morning and Father Young's chance remark about her being in the family way. Polly tried to ignore the nibbling of guilt she experienced every time this subject came up. She asked herself the question she'd asked a hundred times: *Is there something wrong with me that I don't want children?*

"Polly…"

She lifted her gaze to Savannah's. "I'm sorry. It…it must be hard to want something so much and not be able to have it."

Savannah sighed. "I was going to call Dr. Cooley tomorrow to make an appointment. But what if he tells me there's nothing he can do? That we'll never be able to have children? Maybe that would be worse than not knowing. At least now I have hope."

Polly put her arm around her friend. "I don't know what to tell you. Why is it life has so many questions and so few answers?"

♠

After Florence and George left the room, Bob gently released his arm from Twila's grip and took a few more steps away from the daven.

"What's wrong, Papa? Where are Polly and George? I heard your voices down here."

He'd been so deep in thought, he hadn't noticed Beth slip into the room. He glanced at his daughter. She was growing up so fast. When had she become so tall? "I'm not sure where they are. Could you read to Twila and Elsie or take them for a walk? I need some time to think."

"Of course, Papa. I'd be happy to help." Beth pulled Twila close and stretched out a hand to Elsie. "Let's take a walk. School will be starting soon, and we won't have much time for walks."

When had Beth ever told him no when he'd asked her for something? What wonderful children his wife and Florence had raised. He needed to pay more attention to the little ones or he'd wake up one morning to find they'd grown up. Already Twila looked more like ten years old than eight.

With a last searching look at Bob, Beth opened the screen door for herself and the girls and let it close behind her.

Allowing his head to fall forward, Bob walked to Margaret's gray chair and lowered himself into it. Maybe he could absorb some of her wisdom just by sitting in her chair. He closed his eyes. *Wisdom is crying in the streets…*

Where had he heard those words? Ah, of course. When people

did foolish things, Margaret would say, *Wisdom is crying in the streets but they won't listen.* He picked up her Bible that still lay on the small end table beside her chair. That line sounded like Proverbs.

Peace washed over him as he read the first chapter, especially verses twenty and twenty one. *Wisdom crieth without; she uttereth her voice in the streets: she crieth in the chief place of concourse, in the openings of the gates: in the city she uttereth her words..."*

As he sat quietly, memories of Twila's illness washed over him and the realization he'd had of how much his children needed him. How much Florence needed him to be intimately involved with the raising of these children.

The Holy Spirit seemed to be saying, *If you think about it, it's not so hard to figure out what you need to do. Wisdom has been* crying in the streets *all along.*

The truth was his older children weren't ready for him to remarry. Knowing their feelings was part of the reason he'd kept his relationship with Lydia a secret. He and Lydia could be friends, but there would be no more sneaking around. He'd be upfront about their friendship.

He was done pressuring his children to accept her as anything more than his friend. Twila didn't remember her mother and Elsie just barely, so perhaps they could have more easily made the adjustment, but it wasn't fair to the older children.

Unbidden, a question arose that had yet to be answered: *What if Lydia isn't willing to settle for friendship?*

♠

Bob put a note to Beth on the table telling her where he'd be, then headed out the front door. He needed to tell Lydia why they weren't coming for the picnic. He also needed to tell her why they could only be friends. His decision was made, but he feared she would try to change his mind. His feet dragged as he headed for her house.

Self has to be denied each time a battle rages. The words were so clear, he looked around to see who had spoken. Then he remembered. Reverend Caldwell had said those words a few weeks earlier when he preached at their church. What Scripture had he quoted? Luke 9:23?

If we want to follow Jesus, we must deny ourselves, give up the right to have our own way, so we can follow Him.

Bob sighed. How quickly he had forgotten the message he'd heard and his desire to be guided by the Holy Spirit. "Father, why is it so hard for me to abdicate the throne and allow the Holy Spirit to guide me? Probably because I haven't had much practice."

He squared his shoulders, went up the steps to Lydia's house, and knocked. After a short wait, the door opened wide.

Lydia reached for his hand and drew him inside. "I hoped it would be you." She snuggled close and kissed his lips.

CHAPTER 24

Bob instinctively pulled Lydia closer in the dimly lit hallway, then released her so quickly she stumbled and almost fell. Her eyes widened and the come-hither look turned cold.

"Why did you do that?" She took a few steps back.

"I'm sorry, Lydia. We need to talk." In spite of the cooler temperatures, Bob's palms were sweating as they walked into the living room. He sat across from her rather than beside her on the uncomfortable settee she'd inherited along with Rufus Wilds' house.

Lydia said nothing, just stared at him with frosty blue eyes. She wasn't going to make this easy.

He sighed. "Lydia, I like you a lot. If I didn't have children to consider, I'd marry you in a minute." He went on to explain his realization of how much his children needed him when Twila was ill. "I hope we can still be friends, but I'm done insisting my children welcome you as part of our family. The older ones aren't ready for that."

"I knew this was Polly's fault. She's never liked me." There was a bit of a whine in Lydia's voice.

"The situation isn't her fault. She made a promise to my wife to help me raise our children and her top priority is keeping that promise. I owe her a great deal."

"So the truth is your *wife's* wishes and your children come before me." Lydia's eyes flashed. "I'm glad I realized that before it was too late." She sprang to her feet. "I guess there's nothing more to be said."

"Just one more thing. You wanted me to leave my children to live with you, but you weren't willing to leave your daughter to live with us—even though she's not a child. So I suppose one could say you were also putting her before me."

A bit of the fire went out of Lydia's eyes. "I suppose one could say that."

"And when Florence made the promise, it was to the woman who had been my wife for many years. I don't believe it should be a huge offense that I referred to Margaret in that way."

Lydia sank back into the settee. "It's just that..." Her voice trailed off and she seemed to shrink in size.

Bob rose and sat beside her. "It's just what?"

"Everywhere I go, people sing Margaret's praises. If I didn't know better, I'd think she walked on water. How can I ever compete with that?"

"It's not a competition, Lydia. I'm sure you have talents and abilities too. I'm sorry if you've ever felt I was comparing you to Margaret." Bob was tempted to take her in his arms, but resisted.

Lydia sat silent for a long time until her daughter's voice floated down the stairs. "Mother, I need you."

She blew out a long breath, and then stood. "I don't know, Bob. I don't know if we can go back to just being friends. I don't know if there's any future for us. Maybe we need to take a break to find out what we really want."

Lydia walked into the hallway and opened the door. "Good bye, Bob. We'll probably see each other around town."

♠

Savannah hugged her friend when they reached the Young's house. "Thanks for walking me back. Would you like to come in to say hello?"

Polly hesitated. "No, I'd better not. I don't want to interfere with your family plans." She groaned as she turned toward Main Street.

"What's wrong? I didn't even ask why you were out walking alone on Labor Day." Savannah took a step toward Polly.

"Father wants us to go to a picnic at Lydia Wilds' house."

"Oh, Polly." Savannah grabbed her hand. "I know how you feel about Mrs. Wilds, but maybe it'll be easier going to her house than having her come to yours."

Polly closed her eyes and mumbled something under her breath.

Savannah leaned toward her. "What was that?"

With a sigh, Polly lifted her head and stared at her friend. "I don't like her. I don't think that will change whether she's at our house or I'm at hers." She clasped her hands in front of her. "Why don't I like her? Why don't I trust her?"

"I don't know what to tell you." A smile tugged at her lips as she patted Polly's arm. "Why is it life has so many questions and so few answers?"

With a backward glance at her troubled friend, Savannah climbed the front steps and opened the kitchen door. The fragrance of baked beans wafted out and Garrett was immediately by her side. "Are you all right? I wanted to follow you, but sometimes you want to be alone."

"I crossed paths with Polly, so we walked together and comforted each other. I'm better now."

Father Young rose from the dining room table where his wife was setting out plates. "I'm sorry if I upset you. Me and my big mouth."

"You didn't mean any harm." Savannah managed a smile. "I've wanted a baby for a long time, so what you said hit a tender spot."

"Garrett thought it might be something like that." Father cleared his throat. "Babies often don't come on our time table. Our son didn't."

When his father reached to rumple Garrett's well-combed hair, he ducked. "Just one of the things I didn't do on your time table." He grinned at his father, then stepped to Savannah's side. "Savannah is going to call Dr. Cooley tomorrow to make an appointment. Maybe we have a problem that can be corrected."

Savannah shook her head. "I don't think I'll call him. I've changed my mind."

Garrett's forehead puckered. "Why?"

When Savannah explained her concern, Garrett looked at his mother. "Ma, talk to her."

His mother shook her head. "This is something you and Savannah need to settle. I can't tell her what to do."

CHAPTER 25

Polly kicked a pebble thoughtfully down Mill Street. "What do you want me to do, Father?" She quieted her heart and waited as she walked.

What had Jim said a few weeks ago about being ruled by Self? Something about Self having many thrones in our lives. She squirmed. "I don't want to be selfish, Lord, not caring at all what my father wants or needs."

Self has many thrones in our lives and has to be denied each time a battle rages.

She sighed. There was certainly a battle raging now, both for her and for her brother, George. Did denying herself mean agreeing to go to Mrs. Wilds' picnic? Or at least being willing?

"Lord Jesus, I'll do whatever you say. It's up to you. I'm willing to deny myself, take up my cross and follow you to the picnic if that's what you want me to do."

♠

Bob trudged down Lydia's front porch steps. He hesitated at the bottom. Instead of heading for home, he turned right. He needed some time to pull himself together before he faced his children. Even though he'd done the right thing, there was no way he could go home and act happy.

He left the road and found his way to the creek that flowed merrily without a care in the world. After dropping down beside it, he leaned against the scratchy bark of a huge oak tree, breathed in the woodsy aroma of moss and ferns, and closed his eyes.

"Why…" He swallowed. "Why does doing the right thing feel so wrong?"

"What did you say?"

Bob leapt to his feet and almost slipped down the gentle slope into the brook. His red-haired daughter grabbed his arm and pulled him back.

"What…what are you doing here?" Bob's voice came out scratchy and hoarse.

"I saw your note to Beth and came looking for you. When you headed for the creek, I thought maybe we could talk. But if you want to be alone…"

"It's all right." Bob plopped down beside the brook again, glanced at Florence and patted the vine-covered ground beside him.

She sank down and spread her skirt around her. "Are you all right? It sounded like you were talking to someone."

He shook his head. "Not really. Well, maybe God."

Florence gave a quick nod. "Sounded like you said, 'Why does doing the right thing feel so wrong?'"

Stealing a quick glance at her, Bob closed his eyes again. "Yes."

After a long silence, Florence touched his hand. "What did you do that feels wrong?"

His eyes fluttered open. "It doesn't really matter how it *feels*. I know it was right." He sat up straight. "I told Lydia we can only be friends. I won't pressure my children to be part of her life or to have her be part of ours."

"Even though you want to marry her?"

Bob sighed. "I've been selfish, just wanting my own way, regardless of the consequences to my children. The Holy Spirit has been reminding me about denying myself, abdicating the throne."

"That's what He's been saying to me, too. I thought He wanted me to be willing to go to Lydia's picnic."

Bob picked up a few pebbles and tossed them, one by one, into the creek. "I'm no expert at this, but do you think God wants us to be willing to do whatever He wants whether it's what we want or not? To surrender our will, deny ourselves?"

"Maybe you're right." Florence rubbed her forehead. "Maybe we can't really follow Jesus until we've surrendered our will."

"Abdicated the throne." Bob gazed at the water flowing downstream. "The water has no trouble flowing as long as nothing hinders the flow." He cleared his throat. He was still awkward at discussing spiritual things with his daughter.

Florence smiled. "The same way we have no trouble following Jesus unless our un-surrendered will gets in the way?"

"Something like that."

"Mother would be so proud of you. She'd probably say the Holy Spirit will make a philosopher of you yet." Florence stood and smoothed the wrinkles from her skirts. "So what does Lydia think about just being friends?"

Bob groaned, and then told his daughter about his conversation with Lydia. "In the end, she said maybe we need to take a break until we decide what we want."

His daughter stepped back a few paces. "Are you okay with that?" She leaned in and reached out a hand as he got to his feet.

"I will be. God is on the throne and He'll see me through."

♠

Guilt washed over Polly at the lightness of her heart as she and her father left the brook and headed for home. In spite of his sadness, a huge weight had been lifted from her shoulders.

Thank you, Father.

Could it be God was making a way to keep her promise to her mother?

PART 2

CHAPTER 26
September 27, 1918

"Polly, can we ride the train to the Fair tonight?" Twila batted her eyelashes over her dark brown eyes as she usually did when she wanted something. Who had taught her that?

Smiling at her youngest sister, Polly tugged gently on her ponytail and continued stirring tonight's supper—fragrant left-over vegetable soup. "Maybe. Yesterday and today Uncle Sam has scheduled special trains on the New York Central and is giving a special rate for people going to the Stoneboro Fair."

"Who is Uncle Sam? Where does he live?" Twila furrowed her brow.

"Everyone knows we don't have an Uncle Sam." Elsie, who had just flounced into the kitchen, joined the discussion. "It's a nickname for the United States."

Twila glared at her sister and opened her mouth. Heading off an argument, Polly grabbed some bowls and spoons and handed them to the girls. "Would you set the table, please? If we want to make the train, we'll have to hurry."

Easily distracted, Twila grabbed the bowls while Elsie picked up the spoons. "Can we get something to eat at the Fair?" Batting those eyelashes again.

Unable to hide her smile, Polly nodded. "If Papa says it's okay."

Right on cue, the front door banged and Twila dashed to greet her father with Polly close behind. "Papa, can we have money to ride the train and get something to eat at the Fair?"

"Hello to you, too." Father chuckled. "Let me wash up. If supper is ready, we'll talk about it while we eat."

"It's almost ready." Polly headed back to the kitchen to bring in the soup while her sisters set the table without argument.

She called for Beth and as soon as she came to the table, they bowed their heads while Father said a brief blessing. He had barely said amen when Twila started again. "Can we, Papa?"

"If Polly doesn't mind taking you, it's okay with me." Father glanced at his oldest daughter.

"Why don't you come with us?" Elsie peered at her father, then picked up a piece of homemade bread and buttered it.

Father cleared his throat. "I asked Lydia to go to the Fair with me tonight. She's excited to ride in our new car."

Sometimes Lydia accepted Father's invitations and sometimes she didn't. He'd been true to his word about not forcing them to accept her as part of the family, so Polly tried not to interfere. She bit her tongue to keep from suggesting that Lydia might accept Father's invitations more frequently now that he had a car.

"I wanted to take the car to the Fair tonight."

Polly glanced up to see her brother, George, standing at the foot of the table. "I didn't hear you come in from work, George. Come sit down and have some dinner."

Was there a girl he wanted to impress with the car?

Even as he sat down, George continued to look at his father with wide, puppy-dog eyes. "Some of my friends are taking their father's cars."

"Not a good idea." Father emphasized his words by a strong shake of his head

George groaned as Father finished chewing his bite of bread. "Why not?"

"I heard that more than 30,000 people attended the Fair yesterday, and there were a thousand more cars than ever before. Probably not a good time for you to be driving."

"Then why are you taking the car? You're not an experienced driver yet either." Disappointment sharpened George's tone.

Father sighed. "You're probably right. But I already promised Lydia I'd take her to the Fair by car. I don't want to disappoint her."

After taking a big bite of soup, George spoke under his breath.

Before Father could question George's mumbling, a habit he despised, Polly spoke up. "The girls and I are riding the train to the Fair. You could go with us. Beth can come too."

"I don't want to go to the Fair with my little sisters." George pushed his chair back with a loud screech and left the table.

♠

"Hurry, girls, or we'll miss the train." Polly shooed her sisters out the door and down the stairs to Broad Street. "Beth, would you grab Elsie's hand so she can keep up?"

Elsie scowled. "I don't need anyone to hold my hand."

"You're right. I keep forgetting how grown up you are. Eleven your last birthday."

Twila tugged her hand out of Polly's. "I don't need anyone to hold my hand either."

Polly didn't remind her that it had been she who'd held Polly's hand, not the other way around. Her little sister liked the benefits of being the youngest when it suited her purposes.

"What's Jim doing this evening?" Beth puffed a bit at the pace they were keeping.

"Reverend Caldwell to you. I don't know what he's doing. I told you we're just friends."

"I thought he might take you to the Fair, or do ministers think going to the Fair is too worldly?"

"What's worldly?" Twila peered at her big sisters as though they spoke a foreign language.

Polly blew an errant strand of hair out of her eyes, then tucked it behind her ear. How to explain *worldly* to a nine-year-old? "Maybe the opposite of spiritual."

"What's—"

"I hear the train whistle. Let's run." Polly cut off her sister's question. In spite of their disclaimers, she grabbed Twila's hand while Beth grasped Elsie's as they raced down Main Street.

The girls would be so disappointed if they missed the train and the Fair.

CHAPTER 27

As soon as Polly and her sisters reached station, Polly dashed to the window to buy tickets. The other passengers were already boarding. Why hadn't she gotten an earlier start?

Grasping a handful of tickets, Polly tried to herd her group toward the steps to the empty platform while Twila stood on tiptoe waving to a friend. "Hurry. Hurry."

What if they closed the doors? A tall, slender young man in a New York Central uniform bounded up the steps ahead of them, stood beside the door, and motioned to her. "Take your time, ma'am. We won't be leavin' without ya."

Those were undoubtedly the sweetest words she'd ever heard, but they rushed anyway, her cheeks on fire. How embarrassing that they'd delayed the train's departure. Beth entered first, then Polly stumbled in an effort to get herself, Twila and Elsie through the doorway at the same time. She would have fallen if the dark-haired employee hadn't caught her from behind.

He lifted her over the threshold as though she weighed less than nothing. "There now, it's safe that ya are."

When Polly regained her balance and turned, she found herself gazing into the deepest brown eyes she'd ever seen. She gulped, every word of thanks leaving her.

"I didn't recognize ya at first, Lass, but it's the daughter of Robert Dye you're bein', isn't it?"

"You know me?" Polly's voice returned with a bit of a squeak at the end.

"We've not been introduced, but I worked for your father in the mines before startin' on the railroad. Will Reiser at your service, ma'am." He gave a mock half bow that made her smile.

"Polly Dye, or perhaps you've heard my father call me Florence."

"Aye, that I have." Will's eyes twinkled. "Not your favorite name?"

"No. No, it's not." Polly tore her gaze from Will's. "These are my sisters, Twila, Elsie, and Beth."

Will's smile warmed Polly to the core as he gave another half bow to the girls. "Well now, it's a lucky man Robert Dye is to have so many beautiful ladies in his household."

Before they could speak further, the conductor's voice boomed. "All aboard. All aboard."

"Let's find ya seats and then it's returnin' to my work I must be." Will guided Polly down the aisle. Her sisters followed close behind until they found four seats together.

He started to leave, then turned back. "What word are ya havin' from your brother, Ben? He was drafted a few months back wasn't he?"

She nodded. "He hasn't finished his training. We're hoping the war will be over before he's sent overseas."

"I'll be hopin' the same."

Polly reached out to touch his arm. "Thank you, Will. Thank you so much for saving me from falling and holding the train for us."

Was the warmth that made her tingle coming from his arm or from her fingers?

♠

Bob closed the front door, ran down the steps, and cranked the shiny black Model T sitting in front of their house. A trace of guilt still mixed with the excitement that bubbled up every time he approached his automobile. "Sorry, Margaret."

His wife hadn't liked… He corrected himself. *Margaret* hadn't liked automobiles. Lydia clammed up every time he slipped and referred to Margaret as his wife. After seven years, one would think it shouldn't be such a hard habit to break.

The automobile roared to life, and Bob leaped into the front seat. Letting out the clutch with only a few jerks, he eased the car onto Broad Street and drove the short distance to Lydia's house. She was standing on her front porch dressed in what must have been her best clothes. Where in the world had she gotten those Mary Jane slippers with lots of beading that matched the beading on the low-cut bodice of her dress? Bob glanced at his casual pants and shirt. He swallowed. Would Lydia complain about how he was dressed?

He eased the car into her driveway and yanked on the emergency brake. She came down the steps and he met her halfway to the car. "You look lovely." Lydia's beauty made it hard to give up the idea of marrying her.

"Thank you." Her gaze skimmed over him, taking in his dark brown slacks and beige shirt. She didn't comment on his appearance. He breathed easier as he opened the passenger door.

"How do you like your new Model T?' Lydia gazed at his vehicle with something like adoration. Why had she never looked at him that way?

He took a deep breath. "I believe Henry Ford is quoted as saying, 'The horse is done.' That says it all."

Lydia continued to stare into the automobile's interior but made no move to enter. Bob took her arm." Aren't you going to get in?"

Instead of answering, Lydia turned and leaned in to place a warm kiss on his lips. "I want to drive."

Bob gasped and stumbled back a few steps. He found himself repeating the excuses he'd given George at supper—too many people and too many cars at the Fair.

Lydia snuggled closer. "I heard that in 1885 Karl Benz's wife, Betsy, borrowed her husband's car and went on a sixty-five mile journey with her sons to see their grandmother. If she could do that, I'm sure I can drive to the Fair."

His heart pounded and his mouth went dry. Why was it so hard to say no to Lydia? At last his shoulders slumped. "All right. I guess I can teach you to drive."

"I don't think I'll need any lessons." Lydia pulled away and stood straight and tall.

Bob blew out his breath and walked with her to open the driver's door. "The car is still running, so we won't have to crank it. I'll tell you what to do when I get in."

When Bob opened the passenger's door, Lydia already had her hand on the lever that controlled the parking brake. "Wait. Wait, until I get in."

The car rolled backward before he'd finished closing the door as Lydia worked the floor pedals. His mouth fell open. "How did you know what to do?"

Lydia avoided his eyes. "I have other friends who have automobiles."

He pressed his lips together to avoid saying something he'd regret. After all, he'd been the one to say they could only be friends. He had no right to complain if Lydia had other friends who allowed her to drive their cars. Maybe they were women. Choking back a snort, he turned his head to watch the road.

CHAPTER 28

Lydia made an abrupt stop when she turned the corner onto Chestnut Street. A long line of automobiles waited to enter the Fairgrounds. She came within a hair of hitting the bumper of the car ahead of her.

Bob gasped and then tried to cover it with a cough. "If you'd rather not wait in this line of cars, I can give you money to pay your way in to the Fair. You could wait for me at the new grandstand. The Rocky Grove Band is playing tonight. I thought you'd enjoy that." Bob held his breath.

"All right. I hate waiting." Lydia pulled on the parking brake as Bob went around the Model T to open the door for her. She stepped onto the running board, then down to the road.

Bob jumped into the car before she could change her mind. "I'll see you soon. You can find us seats in the grandstand if you want."

The line of cars weren't breaking any speed records and Bob's patience was wearing thin as he crept along. At last he entered the Fairgrounds and turned left on a narrow, dirt road. When he neared the top of the hill and started to turn toward a parking space on his left, an automobile crested the hill and shot toward him. Making no effort to stop or slow down, it collided with the right corner of his front bumper before he could even find the brake.

Bob groaned, opened his door and stumbled out. A man in a cheaply made suit and a woman in a flashy red dress had already exited the other car. The woman gripped her neck, complaining in a shrill voice that it was probably broken.

Broken? How could her neck be broken? Both cars had sustained some damage, but the impact hadn't been sufficient to break someone's neck, had it?

The man in the truck behind Bob shouted out his window.

"Get out of the way. You're holding up the line."

Several people honked their horns.

A security guard arrived, red-faced and flustered. He wrote down their names and a description of the accident on a notepad, and then asked both drivers to move their cars. Mr. Collins insisted his car was damaged too badly to drive, but finally complied.

At last both cars had been removed to parking spaces and the guard took their names and statements. Bob's mouth fell open as he listened to the story the other driver and his passenger told. "That's not what happened. I wasn't driving fast. They were speeding and made no effort to stop when they saw I was turning."

When the guard closed his tablet, Mr. Collins glared at him. "So what are you going to do about this?"

"I don't know. I can't sort out who's to blame."

"I know who's to blame." Mrs. Collins squinted in Bob's direction. "He'll have to pay for the damages to our car and pay for our pain and suffering."

The security guard squirmed. "You'll have to get a lawyer if that's what you want."

Even in the midst of his own fears, Bob couldn't help feeling sorry for the hapless security guard. He held out his hand to him. "Thank you for your efforts."

As Bob walked back to his car, Mr. Collins pointed a finger at him. "You'll be hearing from us."

"This isn't over." Mrs. Collins took a few steps in his direction.

♠

"Where in the world have you been?" Lydia's face was the brightest shade of red Bob had ever seen. "Is this the way you treat all your girl friends? Invite them to the Fair and then abandon them?"

Bob stared at the ground for a moment, then met her gaze. "I don't have any other girl friends." He gulped. "I'm sorry you've had to wait so long. I had a bit of an accident."

"An accident? With the car?"

When Bob nodded, she stamped her foot. "And you thought it wouldn't be safe for *me* to drive your car. That's the reason you suggested I get out, isn't it?" Lydia's face turned even a brighter shade of red if that were possible. "You didn't trust me to drive your car on the Fairgrounds."

He couldn't deny her words. He hadn't trusted her. "I'm sorry, Lydia. You're absolutely right. Maybe if I'd let you drive, this wouldn't have happened." The words were bitter on his tongue.

Stretching out his hand, he spoke in a gentle tone. "You look overheated. Can I get you something to drink?"

Lydia ignored his hand but turned toward the concession stands. "We've already missed half of the band's program, might as well miss some more."

Bob followed her, shoulders drooping. *What's wrong with me, Lord? Why can't I do anything right?*

♠

As Polly and her sisters came in the door, she stopped and stared at her father sitting, head bowed, in Mother's chair. "Father, I didn't expect you to be home yet."

He lifted his head but his shoulders still slumped. "I had an accident with the car. The evening was ruined."

"Did you ruin the car, too?" Elsie had her hands on her hips, staring at her father.

"That's not the important thing, Elsie. Were you or Mrs. Wilds hurt?" Polly knelt beside Father.

"No, the accident happened at the Fairgrounds. Lydia had already gotten out of the car. But the woman in the other car says she's hurt. The couple claims the accident was my fault and I'll have to pay."

"Oh Papa." Polly lapsed into her girlhood name for her father. "What will you do?"

"We'll probably have to go to court."

"If they sue you, maybe you can get your friend, Mr. Cochran, to defend you." Polly touched her father's arm. "He's a lawyer, isn't he?"

"He's a very good lawyer. We'll just have to wait and see what happens. There is some damage to my car, too." Father rubbed his forehead. "Lydia thinks if I'd let her drive, the accident wouldn't have happened."

Polly jumped to her feet. "Why would you let Lydia drive your car?"

Her father shook his head. "It's a long story. Did you girls have a nice evening?"

Twila's face lit up. "We got to see all the animals. I wish we lived on a farm so we could have more animals."

"I've been involved with the mines for too long. I don't think this old dog can learn new tricks." Father sighed. "How about you, Florence? Did you have a good time?"

"Other than almost missing the train." Polly's cheeks warmed at the memory of Will Reiser lifting her into the train. "Do you remember Will Reiser?"

"He worked for me before he became a brakeman for New York Central. I was sorry to lose him. Why do you ask?"

"I almost fell getting on the train and Will helped me." Polly fanned herself. "I loved his accent. Irish, I think?"

Something changed in her father's expression as he took in her words and flushed cheeks. "He's Irish, Austrian... and Catholic."

CHAPTER 29

Polly tossed and turned until long past midnight, torn between the afterglow of meeting a man who moved her as no man ever had, and the look in her father's eyes when he told her Will was Catholic. Her parents had never specifically told her that Presbyterians and Catholics shouldn't marry, but it was well-known that such marriages were often fraught with irreconcilable differences. Not to mention, frowned on by many in both denominations.

And what about her promise to Mother to help Father raise her younger brothers and sisters? Was she so fickle that her promise could be so easily forgotten because she was attracted to a man she'd just met? How could it be that after only one meeting with Will, she sensed longings for intimacy deeper than ever before?

She groaned. How many times would she fight this battle? She had celebrated her twenty-seventh birthday this month with no doubts that raising her younger sisters was her top priority, sure that nothing could change that. Although she and Jim had become good friends, Polly had impressed on him at every opportunity that they were *only* friends. Even Savannah had finally stopped dropping broad hints about Jim's need for a wife.

Occasionally, Polly had sensed that the itinerant pastor wanted more than friendship but was waiting for some sign she shared his desire. A sign that never came.

At last she climbed out of bed, careful not to disturb Beth. She picked up Chartreuse and her journal which she no longer bothered to hide. When had she stopped writing in her journal? Life for the past year had been less turbulent since Father had given up pushing them to accept Mrs. Wilds. She'd felt less need to write private thoughts, less need to talk to the Lord.

Polly tiptoed down the stairs, lighted the lamp on the table, and dropped into the cozy depth of her mother's chair. She blew a film of dust from her journal. Was that how her soul looked after a year with few trials?

She smiled, remembering how she'd fought against the pain and suffering God had permitted in her life in the past. Glancing at her last journal entry, she noted the date: August 26, 1917. Words she'd written that day leapt from the page.

Do we dare to believe that suffering is sometimes God's good gift to produce qualities in us we wouldn't develop any other way?

Those were Jim's words when he had still been "Reverend Caldwell" to her. They were the words that had changed her thinking about the reason God allowed pain and suffering, the words that reminded her of how she'd clung to God when they thought Twila might have infantile paralysis.

Polly picked up Chartreuse and dated her journal page.

September 28, 1918 Lord, I'm so confused. Am I crazy to refuse a relationship with a man who has such spiritual depths while allowing myself to be drawn to a man I barely know? A man who is Catholic?

♠

Polly had no answers to the questions she'd scrawled in her journal the night before. Her head ached as she tried to solve the puzzle of her feelings toward Will. She answered Twila and Elsie's endless questions all day with absentminded nods or shakes of her head, hoping she wasn't making any ridiculous promises she wouldn't be able to keep.

When Jim called to invite her to go to the Fair with him that night, she cut the conversation short with an abrupt refusal. "I'm not in the mood."

Head still pounding, she asked Beth to take the girls for a walk to enjoy the fine fall weather while it lasted.

Alone at last, Polly focused on her dilemma. Should she look for an opportunity to see Will again? Otherwise, how would she know if her strong feelings for him were real? Her head stopped throbbing as she came up with a plan. She would ask Beth and Father to watch Twila and Elsie tonight so she could ride the train alone to the Fair. No guarantees Will would be there, of course, but it was worth a try.

Polly hummed a happy tune as she finished sweeping and

started dinner. She laughed aloud as she recognized the tune: *Down by the old mill stream where I first met you, With your eyes of blue, dressed in gingham too…*

I'm as bad as Papa. Much as I hate hearing him whistle that tune, the words fit Lydia better than they fit Will.

Slicing cheese and buttering bread, she made quick work of getting dinner ready. She stared at the contents of canned goods in the cupboard, then pulled out a jar of applesauce. The meal would be a bit skimpy. Father should be home from the mines soon, and she didn't want to waste any time.

"Why are you humming, Polly?"

She glanced into her baby sister's brown eyes. "Am I humming?"

"You're humming that tune Papa whistles when he's going to see Mrs. Wilds."

Hunching her shoulders, then lowering them, Polly tilted her head as she opened the jar of applesauce. "I don't know. I guess I'm feeling happy."

"Is it because of that man who helped us get on the train last night?" Twila was much too perceptive for her years.

"Why would you think that?" Polly spooned applesauce into a bowl.

Twila shrugged. "Sometimes I just know things."

Polly turned the toasted cheese sandwiches in the cast iron skillet, then handed a stack of plates to Twila. "Set the table, please. Then go call Elsie and Beth."

"But Papa isn't even home yet." Twila's forehead puckered into a frown.

"He'll be here soon. I have plans for tonight, so I want to get an early start."

"What kind of plans?" Twila jiggled from one foot to the other.

"Enough questions. Just do as I asked, please."

With a drawn-out, long-suffering sigh, Twila dragged her feet as she obeyed.

♠

"Are Kitt or Savannah going with you to the Fair?" Father's eyes were filled with questions as Polly opened the screen door.

She shook her head, choosing not to speak.

Taking a few steps toward the door, Father tried again. "Are you meeting Reverend Caldwell there?"

Polly smoothed her hand over her emerald green dress that her mirror told her brought out the color of her eyes. "Can't I go anywhere alone just once without answering a barrage of questions?"

As if on cue, Twila and Elsie dashed into the room, coming to a screeching halt when they saw Polly at the door. "Where are you going, Polly?" Their voices were in perfect unison.

She groaned. "Out. I'm going out." She stepped through the open door and let it slam. Completely ignoring the little voices clambering behind her, she strode across the porch and down the steps.

In spite of her efforts to make better time tonight, she would still be cutting it close to get to the train. Her Sunday shoes pinched, unused to being worn for what amounted to a foot race.

As she passed the Potter's house, Kitt stepped out on the porch holding baby Betty. "Polly, where are you going?"

Ordinarily, she'd be delighted for a chance to talk to Kitt. They saw so little of each other now that Kitt was a mother and, technically, lived in Painesville, Ohio. Today, Polly didn't even slow down. "I'm going to the Fair. Gotta hurry. Have to get to the train."

Kitt raised her voice. "Maybe Bess could keep Betty and I could go with you."

"Not tonight, Kitt. Maybe next year." Next year... What would next year hold?

CHAPTER 30

Polly ran the last few blocks to the station, thankful she didn't have Twila and Elsie to drag along tonight. Once again, the platform was crowded with people most likely going to the Fair. She dashed to the line at the ticket window.

As she waited, she kept glancing over her shoulder looking for someone in a New York Central uniform. Disappointment surrounded her like a cloak when Will had not appeared by the time she climbed the platform steps and approached the train. A tear slid down her cheek as she stepped through the doorway where he'd helped her the night before.

Silly goose. What made you think he'd be here waiting for you? He didn't even know you were coming.

As she looked around to find a seat, a voice with a familiar lilt spoke her name.

"Polly." Will got up from his aisle seat a few rows back.

She looked into the warm, brown eyes that had haunted her since the night before.

"Good evening, Lass. Are you here alone?"

Unable to speak because of the unexpected lump in her throat, Polly nodded and took a few steps in his direction.

As the train moved out of the station, he stepped into the aisle "Would you care to sit here with me?" He grabbed the seat ahead of him as the train lurched, then grasped her elbow to steady her.

Polly smiled and nodded again. He'd think she'd lost her ability to speak. As they settled into their seats, her voice returned. "You're not wearing your uniform."

If Will thought it was a stupid, inane thing to say, he gave no indication. "I have this evening and tomorrow off, so I'm going to the Fair. Then I'll spend tonight and tomorrow with my mother."

"Where does she live?"

"On Chestnut Street in Stoneboro. I board in Franklin when

I'm workin'."

Polly reached across Will to hand her ticket to the conductor, very aware of his nearness and the fresh scent of Ivory soap. She couldn't stop smiling. "Thank you so much for helping us last evening. I could have been hurt."

"It was a pleasure, to be sure, helpin' a lovely lass like yourself."

The words flowed from his lips like poetry and heat rose into her neck and cheeks. They rode for a few minutes in silence as she struggled to contain her flushed face and breathe normally. The train whistle sounded. The short ride from Sandy Lake to Stoneboro was almost over. She never wanted it to end.

Will cleared his throat. "Polly..." He hesitated. "Would you be thinkin' me forward if I asked ya to accompany me to the Fair? I know we just met last night... although I feel like I've known ya much longer..."

"I feel that way too." She hugged herself, almost unable to believe this was happening. "I'd love to spend the evening with you."

As the train pulled into the station, Will stood and stepped back to allow her to go first. His hand warmed the small of her back, and then moved to cup her elbow as he guided her from the train.

They joined the throngs of people crowding off the platform and heading up Franklin Avenue. A festive spirit was in the air. Friends called to each other in boisterous voices.

"Let's step aside for a few minutes until this mob thins out." As they stepped off the road, Will continued to shield Polly by keeping himself between her and the crowds. She had never felt so protected and secure. Her heart beat a contented rhythm.

At last they joined a few stragglers and headed for the Fairgrounds. Will tucked her hand through his arm. When they reached Chestnut Street, he pointed out the house where he lived with his mother when not staying in his room in Franklin. His brothers, John and George, lived near her on the same street.

"George and Dora have five children; John and Nelly seven." Will smiled. "I love children."

Polly gulped. Will loved children. It was well known that

Catholics didn't believe in any form of birth control. How could she have forgotten?

"What's wrong?" Will peered at Polly. "Your face is pale."

"Nothing." Polly pasted a smile on her lips. Her stomach churned. She withdrew her hand from the crook of Will's arm and walked faster.

Out of the corner of her eye, Polly glimpsed a puzzled frown marring Will's brow.

After he paid for their tickets at the entry gate, he pulled her aside. "Polly, what's the matter? Did ya change your mind? Don't ya want to be with me tonight?"

She bit her lip, thoughts churning. What could she say? It was too soon to talk about whether she and Will agreed on having a family. They'd just met, for goodness' sake.

Taking a deep breath, she smiled. She wouldn't let this ruin her magical evening. Polly took Will's hand and gripped his fingers. "I'm sorry. It's nothing for you to worry about. Let's just enjoy the evening."

"Hello, Polly."

She glanced up in surprise. Jim Caldwell stood by the ticket vendor, one eyebrow slightly raised. "I thought you weren't in the mood for the Fair tonight."

Polly dropped Will's hand. Her ears burned at being found out. "I…I changed my mind." She hesitated, then glanced at Will. "This is Will Reiser. We met on the train." All of that was true but it still seemed dishonest somehow.

The two men shook hands. An awkward silence fell, and Jim turned away. "I'd better go. I promised the Jackson Center Presbyterian Church I'd help at their concession stand."

Will watched him go. "A friend of yours?"

Polly sighed. How had things gotten so complicated? "He's an itinerant pastor who preaches at our church some times."

♠

Despite the rocky beginning, the evening turned out to be as magical as Polly had hoped. As they rode carnival rides, inspected and discussed the many exhibits, as well as the prize-winning vegetables and baked goods, it was as though someone had lifted her burdens and made her young, carefree and lighthearted. When Will reached to take her hand, she clasped his willingly, not caring who might see.

The shrill whistle of the last passenger train pulling into the Stoneboro station jolted Polly out of her dream world. "Oh dear, I'm going to miss my train." She let go of Will's hand and ran toward the nearest exit.

He caught up with her effortlessly. "Whoa, slow down, Lass. I'll borrow me mam's horse and buggy to take you home. That'll give us a wee bit more time."

Tilting her head to look at him, Polly lost herself in the warmth of his deep brown eyes. The intensity in their depths took her breath away. Would he kiss her?

"Polly…"

For the second time that evening, Jim Caldwell's voice brought her back to reality. She gulped and turned away from Will.

"The last train is leaving for Sandy Lake. Do you need a ride home?"

CHAPTER 31

The sounds of the Fair echoed around Polly as she tried to smile at Jim. "Thank you, but Will offered to take me home." The frown in Jim's eyes showed concern. He probably thought she had just met Jim for the first time on the train. "He used to work for my father."

Jim's forehead smoothed, although something else lingered in his eyes. "I see. Well, then… I'll see you some time."

As he headed for the area where horses and buggies waited, she called after him. "Thanks again, Jim." He lifted a hand but didn't slow his pace.

Will gazed after him. "He seems a bit put out." He raised a brow.

"Jim and I have…have spent time together with mutual friends. We're not courting." She didn't mention her promise to her mother as she usually did when explaining why she didn't have a beau.

Nodding once or twice, Will reached for her hand again and headed for the Chestnut Street exit. "It's just sure I want to be, Lass. I'm not the sort to be coming between two people who…who have an understanding."

"The only understanding Jim and I have is that we're friends." That was as honest an answer as Polly could give. It seemed to satisfy Will and they walked hand in hand in companionable silence to the small house where his mother lived, catching a whiff of "Fair Food" now and then.

As they neared the house just outside the Fair entry, Polly glanced at Will. "Does your father work away from home?"

"Me father passed some years back. It's just me and Mam now."

He tapped lightly on the door, then held it open for Polly to precede him. The fragrance of Irish stew wafted out and a plump, blue-eyed woman bustled into the room. She stopped short at the sight of Polly. Her sizeable green apron covered most of her brown work dress.

"Who have we here then, Son?" She gathered the apron in two work-worn hands and rolled it over them.

So that's where Will got his delightful accent.

He hugged his mother and kissed her cheek, before drawing Polly forward. "You'll be remembering Robert Dye, me boss at the mines, Mam? Polly is his daughter."

"Aye." His mother paused, looking from one to the other, a small frown puckering her shiny forehead. "How long have ya been knowin' each other?"

Polly gave her warmest smile. "We met last evening on the train, Mrs. Reiser." It was clear she was trying to determine the extent of their relationship without asking outright.

"And again tonight. Mayhap it was a bit forward of me, but I invited her to accompany me to the Fair. I was right taken with her, Mam." Will's eyes crinkled in a forthright grin.

Mrs. Reiser unwrapped and rewrapped her arms several times in rapid succession, obviously agitated.

Before she could speak, Polly jumped into the conversation again. "I'm sorry. It's all my fault. We lost track of time, and I missed the last passenger train to Sandy Lake. I could call my father to come get me."

"Mam doesn't much care for telephones, but there's no need to call your father. I'll go hitch up Sally and take ya home." Will headed out the back door.

When the door closed, panic built in Polly's chest and her mouth went dry. She glanced at Mrs. Reiser again who bit her lip and avoided meeting Polly's eyes. What could she say to break the awkward silence?

Mrs. Reiser heaved a deep sigh. "You'll be understandin' it's nothing personal. I'm sure you're a right fine lass. It's just that..."

"I'm not Catholic." Polly spoke the words softy, looking into Mrs. Reiser's anxious blue eyes.

♠

Will took Polly's hand to help her into his mother's buggy. She settled in beside him, and he tucked a light quilt around her against the chill of late September. She closed her eyes against his nearness, her heart pounding.

Why did life have to be so confusing? She finally found someone she liked a lot, only to discover he was Catholic. Not that she cared if he was Catholic, but their parents obviously cared. Also, he undoubtedly would want children. A huge sigh escaped her lips.

When she opened her eyes, she found Will studying her.

"What is it, Lass? Did me mam say something to upset ya?"

"I thought we could have this one night without worrying about…about…" Polly's voice trailed away.

"About me being Catholic and you being Presbyterian?"

She nodded. "Why does it matter? We both worship the same God, don't we?"

"That we do. And it could be worse. At least in this land, the Catholics and the Presbyterians aren't shedding blood over their differences." Will sat back, gathered the reins and clucked softly to Sally. "Up until now I've abided by Mam's wishes, courting only Catholic girls. But I got a feelin' in me bones that will change."

♠

Polly turned the door knob with as little noise as possible. The lamp light shone through the window. Father must be up. He jerked awake as soon as the door clicked shut.

"Florence, I was so worried about you. I heard the last passenger train go through Sandy Lake quite awhile ago. Where have you been?" He rubbed his bloodshot eyes.

"Nothing to worry about, Father. I missed the last train so Will Reiser brought me home in his mother's buggy." Polly tucked a few strands of fly-away hair behind her ear.

Gloom settled over her father's features, the corners of his mouth turned down. "Florence—"

"Will and I are just friends. We only met last night. Like I said, nothing to worry about." Polly started for the stairs.

"But—"

"Please, Papa, not tonight. Don't say anything else to ruin this one magical evening."

C-HAPTER 32

Savannah sat on the edge of the tub in the dark bathroom, buried her face in her hands, then grabbed a washcloth to muffle her sobs. Too late. Garrett's footsteps in the hall and his light rap on the door told her he was awake. How many times had she hidden her crying since the day he'd first asked her to call Dr. Cooley?

"Savannah, are you okay? You've been in there a long time."

She had tried so hard not to worry him since she'd refused to make an appointment. What a coward, she chided herself, plain and simple.

"I'm okay." She choked out the words.

"If you're okay, why are you crying? Open the door." Garrett's voice had an edge, he wasn't going away.

Trying to remove traces of tears with the damp washcloth, Savannah stood and leaned over to twist the knob.

Garrett stepped into the small bathroom. He turned on the light and reached for her. "What's wrong?" His touch was gentle although his tone was gruff.

She dissolved against him, sobs shaking her entire body. At first, he simply held her, soothing her. But then he stiffened and leaned back so he could see her face. "It's the baby thing again, isn't it?"

Closing her eyes to avoid his piercing gaze, Savannah nodded. "I can't help it."

"Have you been doing this every month? And hiding it from me?"

She nodded again. "I didn't want you to worry. It was my decision not to call the doctor."

Garrett sighed. He took her hand, guided her into their bedroom and pulled her down beside him on the bed.

♠

Closing his eyes, Garrett cried out silently. *A year ago I said something has to change, but here we are again. What can I do, Father?*

An inspiration seized Garrett as he and Savannah sat side by side on the colorful quilt that covered their bed. He straightened his spine. "Savannah, we don't know why we haven't had a child. My parents didn't have children for years, so perhaps the problem is with me, something hereditary. I'm going to call Dr. Cooley tomorrow and make an appointment to see him."

Savannah stared at him, openmouthed. Why hadn't he done this a year ago? There was no reason to assume the issue was Savannah's, no reason to assume she should be the one to see Dr. Cooley. He stood and pulled her up beside him. "Let's go back to bed and try to get some sleep. I think Jim is preaching at our church in the morning. That's always a treat." He kissed her forehead and leaned over to blow out the lamp.

"Garrett." Savannah tugged him back. "I'll go see Dr. Cooley, too. This time I won't change my mind. I promise."

Garrett pulled her close and kissed her lips. "We'll face this together, Darling. Whether good news or bad."

♠

Savannah's hand nestled snuggly in Garrett's as they sat beside his parents in the same uncomfortable pew where they sat every Sunday. It wasn't unusual for one's posterior to get pinched if someone shifted positions. Was it essential that church benches be uncomfortable?

The organ played softly as Jim left his seat after the offering. He walked to the pulpit, Bible clutched in his left hand. Each time he preached at their church, she learned something new. What a fine pastor and loyal friend.

Warmth glowed in his eyes as his gaze rested briefly on Garrett and Savannah, then passed on. Savannah's senses heightened, as though the Holy Spirit whispered, *"Listen, Savannah. Listen. I have something important to say."* She tilted her head and focused her attention.

"One of the most amazing things about the Bible is that the Holy Spirit can take a familiar Scripture and use it to teach us something altogether different than we've learned from it before. At times He may show us we've attached a meaning that doesn't line up with His."

Pastor Jim paused and opened his Bible. "I'd like to talk to you today about Philippians four, verses six and seven, a familiar Scripture to most of us. Unfortunately, I often hear verse six quoted alone, although without verse seven, the thought is incomplete."

Be careful for nothing... He stopped and looked at the congregation. "Careful, as used in this context, means anxious. He continued to read, his deep, rich tones lending beauty to the words. *...but in every thing by prayer and supplication with thanksgiving let your requests be made known unto God.*

"It's easy to look at verse six and decide that after I've given my requests to God, I don't need to worry because He's going to answer my prayers, give me what I asked for.

"But if we read verse seven, we find that isn't what we're promised. *And the peace of God, which passeth all understanding, shall keep your hearts and minds through Christ Jesus."*

We're promised in verse seven that as we surrender our requests to God, He'll give us His *peace*, peace that passes all understanding, peace that is beyond anything we can imagine.

"Sometimes we want something so desperately that when we ask God for it, we're unable to receive His peace because we can't bear to consider the possibility that God may not give us what we want."

Quiet permeated the sanctuary. Jim's eyes roved over the congregation.

"I believe true supplication with thanksgiving implies humbly surrendering the deepest desires of our hearts to God. When we let our requests be made known to God in that way, His peace will permeate our beings." He looked around the room. "Peace that passes all understanding.

"We may mourn and grieve when the answer to our prayers is no, but that peace will be an anchor for our souls."

Tears rolled down Savannah's cheeks as she gripped Garrett's fingers and their eyes met. What was God preparing them for?

Chapter 33

Savannah and Garrett had just finished eating Sunday lunch when the telephone rang. It so seldom rang on Sundays. They looked at each other with eyebrows raised. With a shrug, Garrett lifted the receiver from their wooden wall phone.

"Hello." Garrett's immediate smile eased any worry Savannah had. "Just a minute. Let me check with my wife."

Savannah never tired of Garrett calling her "my wife."

He covered the receiver and raised an eyebrow in her direction. "Jim has something to discuss with us. Do you mind if he comes over before he goes back to Jackson Center?"

"Not at all. We should've invited him and Polly to come for lunch."

"I think he ate lunch with the Board." Garrett uncovered the receiver. "She said that would be fine. We'll be waiting for you."

He hung up, stretched and yawned. "What do you think Jim wants to talk with us about?"

Filling the white enamel dishpan with hot water from her copper tea kettle, Savannah began methodically washing tumblers, silverware, and ceramic plates. She bit her lip, and considered Garrett's question. "I don't know." She winked at him. "Maybe you're in trouble with the Church Board or maybe they want to offer you a job."

Garrett pulled an embroidered dish towel from the hook under the sink. He didn't always dry the dishes but it was a good time to chat. "One extreme or the other. Isn't there anything in between?" He grinned.

She shrugged. "What do *you* think he wants to talk about?"

"We'll know soon. Jim should be here any minute. I think he called from Reverend Lawrence's telephone."

Sure enough, before the last dish was dried and put away, the clip clopping of a horse's hooves came down Maple Street to the hitching post behind the Furniture/Undertaker's building. Garrett put down his dish towel and clattered down the stairs to greet their friend.

Savannah gave the counter one last swipe and called a greeting to Jim as they appeared at the top of the stairs. "Can I get you something to drink?"

"No thanks. I'm too full to drink even a swallow of water. Why does everyone think they have to outdo themselves cooking for preachers?" Jim patted his slender waist.

She laughed. "Maybe they think you need fattening up. Although I don't believe Polly ever joined in the competition."

Had she imagined it or had Jim's smile faded when she mentioned her friend's name? When he made no comment, she headed for the small sitting room area, choosing not to pursue that subject. "Come and sit down, Jim."

Garrett and Jim followed, her husband perching beside her on the turquoise loveseat, and Jim seating himself in one of the matching wing chairs. He held a folder from which he pulled a sheet of paper. He glanced at it, cleared his throat, and then looked at Garrett. "Do you remember when you and I started meeting five or six years ago, I told you I thought God might have some other kind of work for you to do?"

Garrett tilted back his chair. "You wanted God to tell me Himself."

Jim nodded. "Has God ever spoken to you about doing something other than selling insurance?" His penetrating gaze lingered even after Garrett bowed his head and stared at the floor.

At last Garrett looked up. "I can't distinguish between what God says and my own thoughts."

"One of the ways God speaks to us is through our thoughts. What have you been thinking?"

Savannah held her breath. More than a year ago, Garrett's father had become very upset when his son had suggested God might have other work for him to do. Her husband hadn't mentioned it since.

"I love preaching. I sense the presence of God when I preach, and people tell me the Holy Spirit speaks to them through my preaching. So, I've thought maybe…" His voice trailed away.

"You've thought maybe God is calling you to preach?" Jim finished Garrett's sentence.

"Maybe." Garrett's answer was so soft Savannah could barely hear it.

Jim drummed his fingers on the arm of his chair. "Did you know the pastor of your church will be retiring in a year or two?"

Savannah and Garrett both shook their heads.

"It's not widely known yet. The Board wants to be prepared. They'd like you to consider coming on as an assistant pastor now to prepare for that time."

Garrett scooted closer to the edge of the loveseat. "But I haven't gone to seminary or had any official training."

"The Board is aware of that. They're also aware that you've been receiving one-on-one training with me as my Timothy for many years. It's unusual but they would accept that in lieu of seminary, while asking that you take some specific courses in the next year or two as you prepare for ordination."

Jim handed Garrett the top sheet of paper he'd been holding. "This is the financial arrangement they're offering for the present time. If all goes well and you're hired full time when Reverend Lawrence retires, you would receive a raise and more compensation."

Garrett repositioned himself so he could look into Savannah's eyes. "What do you think?"

Before she could answer, Jim held up his hand. "You don't need to tell me today. Take time to think and pray. The Board would like an answer in a few weeks."

Savannah took a deep breath and tried to quiet her heart. Her pulse raced. Between the anticipated visit with Dr. Cooley and the news Jim had just delivered, she couldn't form a sensible sentence. What did God want them to do?

CHAPTER 34

Polly stared at the telephone hanging on their dining room wall as though she could induce it to ring. Why hadn't Will called? Not that he'd made any specific promises about calling but after he'd said he wouldn't abide by his mother's wishes anymore about dating only Catholics, she'd assumed she would hear from him. But a week had passed with no communication.

Perhaps he'd been busy with work. She didn't know his schedule. Sighing, she turned away from the telephone just as it erupted with one long peal and two short ones, the signal that the call on the party line was for them. She grabbed the receiver and spoke into the mouthpiece. "Hello."

"Polly, so glad you're home. Garrett and I need some help passing the time until our appointment with Dr. Cooley to get our test results on Monday."

Savannah's pleasant tones grated on Polly's ears, simply because it wasn't Will's voice. She tried to hide her frustration. "What did you have in mind?"

"We're inviting the only friends we've told about our problem—you and Jim—for dinner tonight."

Polly could barely restrain a groan. Exactly what she didn't want…another awkward situation with Jim. She hadn't told Savannah about her 'date' last week with Will. Was it a date?

"Polly, are you still there?"

Savannah's voice drew her back to the present. How could she say no to her friend who hardly ever asked for anything? But how could she say yes?

"Umm… Have you already invited Jim?"

"Yes, he's coming."

Polly closed her eyes. "Then maybe you should invite one of your other girl friends. Isn't there someone else you could ask?"

"You mean someone like Dorothy, the town crier at the office?

I don't think so. We're trying to keep this private. Did you and Jim have a fight?"

"Not really. I don't want to explain now—someone might be listening in." Polly drew a deep breath. "It could be awkward but I guess I can come."

As she hung up the receiver, her father walked in. "An important telephone call?"

Polly shrugged. "Savannah wants Jim and me to come for dinner tonight. I can fix something for you and the children before I leave."

"I invited Lydia to go out for dinner, but she hasn't given me an answer."

"Probably because you haven't gotten the car fixed yet." As soon as the words were out, Polly clamped her teeth together. Why couldn't she keep her mouth closed?

Father said nothing for a moment. Then he shook his head. "I don't think she's forgiven me for ruining our evening at the Fair."

Gritting her teeth and swallowing sarcastic words, Polly turned toward the kitchen just as the telephone rang again. She grabbed the receiver and couldn't restrain a smile when Will's melodic voice reached her ear…a smile that quickly disappeared when he asked if she was free this evening.

"I'm sorry. I already made plans for tonight. My best friend needs me."

Father raised a questioning eyebrow as he sank into a chair. She avoided his eyes as she tried to come up with another plan. "Do you have to work tomorrow? Maybe we could meet after church."

Polly's shoulders slumped. "Oh, I see. Maybe some other time. Thanks for calling." She put the receiver back in place.

"Who was that?"

She suspected her father had already guessed who it was. "Will Reiser."

The brown of her father's eyes deepened. "I thought you were going to have just one magical evening with him."

"I don't want to discuss this with you. Will and I are just friends." She'd never had a friend who made her heart race like he did.

♠

Polly hurried down the road. If only she could arrive at Savannah and Garrett's apartment before Jim so she wouldn't have to talk to him alone. Her breath came in gasps as she trotted down Main Street. At the sound of horse's hooves, she glanced up to see Delilah pulling Jim's buggy and turning onto Maple Street just ahead of her. She groaned and slowed down. Maybe he wouldn't wait for her but would go up to the apartment.

When she turned the corner behind the Undertaker/Furniture building, Jim was standing by the door. "Hello Polly."

Jim's kind smile and gentle voice were unchanged. Was he going to act like nothing had happened? If they were only friends as she'd been saying, perhaps he was right. She drew a deep breath while all her defensive words disintegrated. "Hi Jim."

He rapped on the door, then opened it. Savannah was waiting at the top of the stairs. "Come on up. I've missed you both. We really need our friends right now." She leaned in to give Polly a hug as she neared the top of the stairs.

The evening passed quickly as they ate and played Dutch Blitz and Chinese Checkers. Jim's manner toward her remained unchanged, and Polly began to relax. Maybe this hadn't been a mistake after all. Garrett and Savannah shared some of their misgivings about their test results and filled Polly in on Garrett's opportunity at the Episcopal Methodist Church.

"You two have a lot to consider, don't you?" Polly looked from Garrett to Savannah. "I'll be praying for you as you get your results and make this decision."

What about the decision you have to make? She pushed away the unwelcome thought and glanced at Jim. *Oh no, he always takes me home from these evenings.* She checked the wall clock above Savannah's dining room table. Maybe if she left early, Jim wouldn't feel the need to offer her a ride.

She pushed back her chair and stood. "Thank you for a lovely evening. The food and the company were good as usual."

"We haven't had dessert yet, Polly. I made your favorite— peach cobbler." Savannah smacked her lips.

Polly smiled in Jim's direction and reached for her sweater she'd tossed on the loveseat. "Jim can eat my share."

He immediately stood. "I should be going too. I have an early service in Jackson Center tomorrow. I'll give you a ride home, Polly."

"Oh that's not necessary. It's a nice evening for a walk." She held her breath.

He glanced out the window, then back at her. "It's getting dark. I'd feel much better if I took you home."

Polly groaned inwardly but kept a smile pasted on her lips. She hugged Savannah and thanked her again for dinner while Garrett and Jim exchanged a hearty handshake and a bit of conversation.

Heart pounding, head throbbing, Polly headed down the stairs. At the very least, she owed Jim an apology for going to the Fair with Will after telling him she wasn't in the mood. But that might open the door to a discussion she'd rather not have.

She stepped into the cool, October air and walked over to smooth Delilah's velvety nose. What had Jim told her about Delilah? That every time a stallion took in interest in her, she'd take off and lead him on a merry chase... Was Jim comparing her behavior to Delilah's?

The door at the bottom of the stairs opened and closed, and Jim gave her a hand into the carriage. After he untied Delilah and got in beside her, they sat in deafening silence. At last, Jim clucked to Delilah and simultaneously they turned toward each other.

"Jim..."

"Polly..."

Jim chuckled. "You first."

"I owe you an apology." Polly sighed. "I'm sorry I went to the Fair with Will after telling you I wasn't in the mood."

He nodded. "It's okay. I'm just puzzled. You've told me for more than a year that you're not interested in being courted because of your promise to your mother." He paused and cleared his throat. "Now I'm thinking you're just not interested in being courted by me."

Polly hesitated. Before she could answer, a lean, lithe figure stepped out to cross Maple Street as Jim coaxed Delilah to a stop at the corner.

"Polly. It's so happy I am to see ya. On my way back to Franklin, I decided to get off the train here to make one last effort..." Will's voice trailed off. He looked at Jim, then at her. "This is your best friend?"

CHAPTER 35

Savannah opened her eyes, glanced at the autumn leaves outside their bedroom window, then closed them again. If she could go back to sleep, she could postpone this day a bit longer. Today was the day of reckoning. After their appointment with more poking, prodding and tests than she cared to remember and a week of waiting, they would receive the results and Dr. Cooley's opinion about why she hadn't conceived.

She peeked at her husband sprawled beside her on the bed, one arm flung across her body, eyes closed. Was he sleeping or just postponing the day as she was?

As though sensing her gaze, his eyes fluttered open. She opened hers completely, and he drew her nearer and leaned in for a kiss. "Good morning, beautiful wife."

"Good morning, handsome husband."

It was a routine they'd started a few years ago. One she hoped they'd continue for the rest of their lives. Surely seeing one another through loving eyes should maintain the perception of beauty no matter how age might change their outward appearance.

Garrett caressed her cheek. "Are you ready for today?"

Nodding once, she allowed her eyes to close for a moment, then to open again to meet his. "I think so. Since we surrendered our deepest desires to the Lord after Jim's message, I've had more peace than I've had in a long time."

"I hoped you weren't hiding your emotions from me." Garrett sat up and drew her up beside him. "We can't help each other if we aren't honest."

"I know. I still desperately want children. But I want God's will for our lives, whatever that may be, more than I want children. And I want peace. Not the turmoil I've experienced this past year."

Savannah leaned over and pulled a faded burgundy book from her bedside table. "I've been reading Sarah's diary again. The one that belongs to Polly."

Garrett raised an eyebrow. "I thought you were supposed to return that."

"I am. I will. But I can't bring myself to part with it yet." She flipped through the pages of spidery handwriting. "A year ago, Polly asked if I noticed how Sarah responded every time something bad happened."

Tilting his head, Garrett looked puzzled. "How did she respond?"

"She always ran to God instead of blaming Him."

"Ah, I see. Not an easy thing to do, is it?"

"I've heard that even people who claim they don't believe in God, blame Him when something goes wrong." Savannah kissed Garrett's cheek and moved to get out of bed.

He tugged her back. "Let's pray before we go for our doctor appointment."

They clasped hands and bowed their heads. "Father, this is a scary day. We don't know if Dr. Cooley will have good news or bad, but I'm reminded of something I read in the book of Job yesterday. *Shall we receive good at the hand of the Lord, and shall we not receive evil?*

"You've given us so many blessings. Help us not to turn away from you if the news we receive today is bad. Amen."

♠

Nurse Dayton asked Savannah and Garrett to have a seat in the waiting area until Dr. Cooley returned from an early morning house call. They sat side by side on uncomfortable wooden chairs. Savannah's nose itched from a whiff of Lysol that wafted to her nostrils from time to time.

When the nurse disappeared into the doctor's office, Garrett stood and began pacing the small area. Savannah wanted to scream at him to sit down. Every sound was magnified in her ears. Why had she agreed to all these tests? What if… What if… What if Dr. Cooley had discovered one of them had some awful disease?

She stared at the floor. Dr. Cooley's inner office door opened and his nurse's white shoes squeaked as she returned. "I'm sorry about the Lysol smell. We've heard reports of the Spanish Flu in Massachusetts. Trying to keep our facility extra clean."

Savannah focused on Nurse Dayton's words as Garrett dropped into the chair beside her. While she was lost in her own little world of possible diseases, others were fighting a known illness. "Have many people died?"

"Oh yes. Many of the more than six thousand cases died."

The look in Garrett's eyes told her he also thought they needed to keep their personal problem in perspective.

An automobile pulled up behind the doctor's office, a car door slammed, and the back door opened and closed. Nurse Dayton smiled. "Dr. Cooley will see you in a few minutes."

Savannah swallowed convulsively. Garrett's Adam's apple rose and fell. When Dr. Cooley himself opened the door and greeted them, they both stood.

"Come in and have a seat." He smiled. "Sorry to keep you waiting. I had an unexpected call this morning."

As always, the warmth of Dr. Cooley's blue eyes encouraged Savannah. Surely he must have good news for them.

The doctor sat down beside his cluttered roll top desk. He sorted through a pile of folders, picked one up and opened it. Staring at the contents, he cleared his throat. A shiver ran down Savannah's spine. Was Dr. Cooley avoiding eye contact?

At last, he cleared his throat again and stared at a spot just over their heads. "There's no easy way to say this." His voice was so soft, Savannah could barely hear him. "From the tests we've done and my examinations, it's clear that both of you have gonorrhea."

Savannah gasped and Garrett closed his eyes. Dr. Cooley looked from one to the other. "You're familiar with the condition?"

"Yes, but wouldn't we be having symptoms? How can you be sure?" Contracting venereal disease had been one of her greatest fears while entertaining gentlemen in her room above Mr. Burns' tavern. How could this be happening now that she'd been faithful to Garrett for years?

"Unfortunately, sometimes there are no symptoms until it's too late."

"Too late." Garrett jerked up in his seat. "Are we going to die?"

"No, it's not too late for you both to be treated. But it appears too much damage has been done for Savannah ever to conceive. I'm so sorry."

A tear ran down Savanna's nose and dripped, unheeded, onto her rose-colored dress. Dr. Cooley handed her a clean handkerchief from his vest pocket. "I've always avoided gossip as much as possible but..." He stopped and cleared his throat again, looking at Savannah. "Surely you knew this might happen as a result of your former... ah, your former profession?"

Heat flooded Savannah's cheeks and neck. "I knew. But why now?" Savannah's voice croaked.

"As I said, sometimes there are no symptoms. The condition lies dormant or does its damage silently. Unless..." Dr. Cooley paused and glanced at Garrett.

"Unless what?" Garrett's blue eyes had turned frosty.

"Unless you were the carrier."

Garrett bolted from his chair. "How can you suggest that? I was a saint compared to her."

Savannah sobbed aloud as Dr. Cooley looked at Garrett steadily. "It only takes once."

CHAPTER 36

Garrett and Savannah left Dr. Cooley's office, each gripping a prescription, Savannah still clutching Dr. Cooley's handkerchief. Garrett didn't offer to help her into the car but went straight to the front to twist the crank.

How dare Dr. Cooley imply I might have infected Savannah? Everyone knew what she did for a living. Anyway, how do I know she's been faithful to me since we married?

Even as he tried to block out his condemning thoughts, the words her old boss had spoken years ago rang in his ears, "Once a whore, always a whore."

Garrett gritted his teeth as he jumped into the car. "We can't tell anyone what the tests showed."

"What about your parents? And Polly and Jim?" Savannah stared at him through her tears. "Will we lie to them?"

"I don't know. We'll avoid them as best we can." He pulled down on the accelerator.

"Your father is our boss. How will we avoid him? I have Bible study with your mother this evening and you have a meeting with Jim."

Why did she always ask difficult questions? Garrett spun the tires as he backed out of Dr. Cooley's parking area. The silence between them was as frosty as an icy windshield. At least Savannah had stopped crying.

"This morning you said we can't help each other if we aren't honest." Savannah turned to face him. "I think the same is true of other people. They can't help us if we aren't honest with them."

Why was she trying to tell him what they should do? He wouldn't be in this situation if he hadn't married her. Garrett pushed away Dr. Cooley's words that suggested he could have been the carrier. "So what are you saying? We should tell Dorothy and let her broadcast the news to the town so they can all help us?"

Savannah bit her lip and turned away. As Garrett pulled into their parking area, she turned back. "I thought we were going to get through this together. Good news or bad."

♠

A note sat on the small table beside Mother's chair that Polly had missed earlier, intent on getting the children off to school. *Florence, would you call Mr. Cochran's office to make an appointment for me? I need to get his counsel about my accident.*

She set down the basket of wet laundry, plopped into Mother's chair and buried her head in her hands. One more thing to worry about. Would those people really sue Father? The only good thing about the accident was that Lydia hadn't accepted any of her father's invitations since.

Did everyone wake up as she had this morning with her first thought being of every mistake she'd made? Yesterday morning had been even worse.

She'd hurt Jim's feelings by going to the Fair with Will. Then, Will's feelings had been hurt when he saw her in the buggy with Jim and thought Jim was her best friend. Will probably thought she hadn't been honest with him—that's what bothered her most. Why had she even let Jim bring her home? In spite of her efforts to explain, she'd be lucky if either of them ever spoke to her again.

What are you trying to tell me, Father? Yesterday she'd been so busy berating herself, she couldn't focus on Reverend Lawrence's message. Later, no words came when she tried to write in her journal. She needed to get back to spending time with God every day, not just when trouble struck.

Polly stretched her legs and knocked over the laundry basket. She lifted her head, groaned and leaned down to gather the wet clothes. Life never slowed down no matter how disastrous her circumstances.

♠

Somehow Savannah managed to get most of her office work done, although Father Young had given her a puzzled look when he'd spoken to her three times before she heard him. Should she cancel her Monday evening Bible study with Garrett's mother? No, she wasn't going to cancel and she wasn't going to lie.

At noon, instead of going home to grab a sandwich or leftovers, she closed her office door and put her head down on her desk.

The morning in Dr. Cooley's office seemed like a bad dream—if only she could wake up and find it wasn't real. Garrett had acted like he hated her. Of course, he had good reason. Maybe she shouldn't have married him or anyone else who might be affected by her past.

A light tap on her door roused her. She sat up and tried to straighten her hair. "Come in."

Dorothy opened the door. "Are you all right? I just wanted to check on you."

Savannah bit her lip. Nothing good ever came from taking Dorothy into her confidence, no matter how sweet she might appear. "I'm okay. A little tired."

"Maybe you're in the family way. I hear women are often tired in the early days of pregnancy."

"I'm pretty sure I'm not. But thanks for your concern." Savannah stood and pushed away from her desk, turning from Dorothy to hide the tears sliding down her cheeks.

Would this day never end? Somehow, she made it until closing time, fighting back tears. At home, she threw together a light dinner for Garrett, grabbed her Bible and put on a thin coat. She was early for Bible study but she didn't care.

"Aren't you going to eat anything?" Garrett's voice was kinder than it had been earlier.

"I don't think I could keep anything down. I'll be at your parents' house."

"What will you tell them?" His voice was an odd mixture of anger and fear.

"I'll tell them the truth."

♠

Polly dried the last thick white plate and put it in the cupboard. *It's Monday... How could I have forgotten. The day Savannah and Garrett were to get their test results. What kind of a friend am I, thinking only about myself and my problems?*

She tweaked one of Twila's fat brown pigtails before heading for the telephone. "Thanks for helping." She got a nod and a grin in return.

Polly made short work of cranking out the correct number of rings to reach Savannah. No answer. *Of course, they're not home on Monday evenings.* How many times had Savannah invited her to go along to Mildred Young's for Bible study? Surely they wouldn't mind if she came this evening without an invitation.

CHAPTER 37

Garrett drove aimlessly around the country back roads of Jackson Center. He hadn't called Jim to say he wasn't coming. He would have asked about the test results—something Garrett didn't want to talk about, didn't want to think about.

Shall we receive good at the hand of the Lord, and shall we not receive evil? He groaned and pulled over to the side of the road. He'd been so sure he would be the strong one no matter what news Dr. Cooley gave them. Pounding his fist on the dashboard, he bit back the words forming on his lips.

Why God, why? How could you let this happen? We've tried so hard to live lives that are pleasing to you, or at least I have. How do I know what Savannah's been doing when we're not together?

He bowed his head, resting it on the steering wheel. *We'll face this together, Darling. Whether good news or bad.* How easy it had been to say the right words before the ugly truth had been revealed. And how quickly he'd turned on her when Dr. Cooley gave them the diagnosis, even saying he'd been a saint compared to her. How quickly he'd forgotten how much alike they'd been in their pre-Jesus days.

How do you know she isn't still sleeping with other men?

He groaned again and lifted his head to massage his throbbing forehead. *It's been a long time since I've doubted Savannah like I did in the beginning. Please, Father, don't let me give in to that temptation again.*

How like the old Garrett he'd acted today. Maybe he'd fooled the church board into thinking he was ready to be a pastor, but this crisis had revealed the truth. Savannah had said even people who didn't believe in God blamed Him when bad things happened. He was no better than them. But who else was there to blame—except his wife?

Sarah always ran to God instead of blaming Him when something bad happened.

It was obvious Sarah had a depth of relationship with God that far surpassed his. Maybe he should read her diary.

He climbed out of the car and turned the crank. No use avoiding the inevitable. Savannah had said other people couldn't help them if they weren't honest with them. As usual, she was right.

♠

"I'm going to join Mrs. Young and Savannah for Bible study tonight. Twila and Elsie can get themselves ready for bed but I usually read them a Bible story and say their prayers with them."

"I'll take care of it. Have a good time." Her father smiled. "Is that the right thing to say about attending Bible study?"

"Sure, although it might not be such a good time if... Oh, I'm sorry, I'm not supposed to tell anyone." Polly grabbed her sweater from the hook by the door.

Father raised an eyebrow at her secretiveness, but then shrugged and went back to his mining magazine. He wasn't whistling much these days.

She ran down the porch steps and headed up Broad Street. As she neared the Potter place, a Roamer Touring car came to a stop at the end of Walnut Street and turned left. Polly moved to the side of the road and tried not to stare. A familiar face peered at her from the passenger's seat. Lydia Wilds.

No wonder she'd been turning down Father's invitations. She'd found a better offer. Did Father know the company she kept? Polly had no idea who owned this fancy car. Maybe someone from out of town? She wanted to feel bad for her father but couldn't. It would certainly be to his benefit if someone else became Mrs. Wilds' third husband.

In spite of the turmoil in her own life, Polly was in good spirits by the time she reached the Young's. The multi-colored leaves and the nip in the air left no doubt that fall had settled in. Mrs. Young opened the door and welcomed her with a smile. "Savannah, look who's here."

Savannah's smile wasn't as big as Polly had expected. "Are you sure it's okay for me to stay? I've turned you down so many times you're probably surprised to see me."

"I am surprised, but it's all right." Savannah's eyes appeared shiny. Had she been crying?

"After supper, I remembered you were supposed to get your test results at Dr. Cooley's today." When Savannah closed her eyes, Polly rushed on. "But if you'd rather not talk about it, it's okay."

"We were just discussing Dr. Cooley's diagnosis." Mrs. Young touched Savannah's hand. "This is very private information but I know Savannah would want to tell her best friend. You're more like sisters than friends."

Savannah nodded, but said nothing.

"Would you rather I tell her or would you prefer to wait?" Mrs. Young's hand moved from touching to grasping Savannah's.

"You can tell Polly." Savannah's voice was so low Polly could barely understand.

In a voice just above a whisper, Mrs. Young told Polly what Dr. Cooley had said.

"Oh Savannah…" Polly reached both hands toward her friend in a futile effort to express her sorrow. "Oh Savannah…" There didn't seem to be anything else to say. Her petty male friend problems seemed trivial in comparison.

Sobs burst from Savannah's lips. "Polly, you said…" She gasped for breath. "You said God isn't like my mother. But my mother used to get even with me when I did things she didn't like. It feels like God is doing the same thing."

Polly threw Mrs. Young a beseeching look. Savannah's mother-in-law tilted her chin, looking deep into her daughter-in-law's eyes. "Although God forgives us when we repent, Child, there are often consequences from the things we do. The Bible calls that reaping what we sow.

"For example, if someone loses an arm or leg because they did something foolish, being sorry doesn't usually make the limb grow back."

Savannah nodded slowly.

"God will still love you if you blame Him for your diagnosis." Mrs. Young paused. "But it will rob you of His comfort when you need it most."

"I've been reading Sarah's diary again, Polly. It's just like you said, she ran to God instead of blaming Him when something bad happened. If I'm being tested on what I've studied, it looks like I'm failing the test."

"Someone told me that with God, we never really fail a test because He lets us take it over and over until we pass." Polly hugged her friend.

"That's a sure sign God isn't like my mother. With her, it was like a baseball game except instead of *three strikes and you're out,* it was one."

♠

"I'm proud of you, Garrett." Jim ran his fingers over the table and then steepled them in front of him.

"Proud of me? How can you be proud of me when I've failed so miserably?"

"After receiving very bad news today, what did you do? Did you look for answers in a tavern? No, you recognized your failures and your need for a deeper relationship with Jesus. The sorrow you feel for the pain you caused your wife led you here."

Garrett shook his head, and ran his fingers through his rumpled hair. "At least you have to admit the church made a mistake asking me to be their assistant pastor."

Jim picked up a pencil and rolled it between his hands. "That's not for me to decide. That's between you, Savannah and the Lord."

CHAPTER 38

Polly ambled slowly home from Bible study. The wind had picked up, whirling leaves and whipping the skirts of her olive green cotton dress around her. What had begun as a pleasant autumn day had turned stormy, in more ways than one. Eventually Savannah had told them about the unkind words Garrett had directed at her. It brought back memories of the caustic tongue he'd used against Polly when they had courted.

Father, don't let him backslide into the Garrett he used to be. Help him choose to abdicate the throne and be led by your Spirit. Help me, too, Lord. I'm so confused and mixed up.

How she missed her mother at times like these, although she hadn't always appreciated her counsel when she had it. She'd ignored both her parents' insights about Garrett for a long time, insisting that asserting her independence was the only way to become an adult.

Her mother had corrected her so wisely, saying, *It's not by asserting our independence but by learning to be guided by the Holy Spirit and not following our own desires and schemes.* Peace settled around her as Mother's words came alive.

I'm still learning, Father. I have a long way to go. My own desires have been so strong lately. How can I possibly be guided by your Holy Spirit?

As Polly climbed the porch steps, the outline of her father was visible through the window. He had honored her wish not to discuss her friendship with Will Reiser, and she tried not to give her opinion about his friendship with Lydia. Still, was it unwise of them not to listen to each other's counsel? God also used the counsel of others to guide people, didn't He? Should she tell him she'd seen Mrs. Wilds with another man?

Father's head was bent over the newspaper as she entered the house. "Something important in the paper?" She closed the door.

"Lots of war news. So much is happening. I think the end might be near. General Ludendorf had a nervous breakdown, Bulgaria signed an armistice, and even the German government is asking for armistice discussions." Father sighed and handed her the paper. "So much loss of life in battles, as well as from the Spanish Flu. I pray it will be over soon."

"Still no news about Ben receiving orders?" If she were honest, she'd have to admit she wanted the war to end mainly so Ben's life wouldn't be endangered.

"No news. The fighting will continue until an armistice with Germany is signed."

Polly sighed. For the second time that day, her issues with Will, Jim, and Mrs. Wilds seemed petty and small. Her Country was at war and a worldwide flu epidemic was going on. People lost loved ones every day. She folded the newspaper and laid it on the table.

"How was Bible study?"

"Let's just say this evening has been a reminder that a lot of folks have problems much bigger than ours. Good night, Father. Sleep well."

♠

Savannah pushed her chair back from the Young's table, stood and pulled her vivid green jacket from the back of her chair. Polly had left more than an hour ago. She couldn't stay here forever.

Mother Young stood too. "Do you want Father or me to take you home and try to talk to Garrett?"

"No, no. I don't think that's a good idea. He might be angry I told you what happened." Savannah carried her teacup and saucer to the sink. "Thank you for the tea and for explaining sowing and reaping. I don't want to blame God for things I set in motion before I knew Him."

Stretching up on tiptoes, Mother kissed Savannah's cheek. "You've grown a lot as a believer in the past six years. Don't let the enemy or my son tell you any different."

"Thank you. Thank you for believing in me." Savannah hugged Mother's plump shoulders and went out into the night.

In spite of the wind and light drizzle, Savannah's steps lagged.

She and Garrett had exchanged cross words before, but he'd never spoken as hatefully as he had this morning. She pressed her hand against her heart. It was hard not to think of ways to get even, to hurt him back. Her mother had been a master at flinging hateful words around when she was angry.

Holy Spirit, would you comfort me? Would you heal my wounded heart? Forgive me for wanting to blame you this morning. To be honest, I still want to blame you. Help me run to you for comfort instead.

Tears rolled down her cheeks and mixed with the light rain. She stepped back as a car pulled up beside her. Memories of being kidnapped by Mr. Burns surfaced. Then she recognized Garrett's car. He jumped out and came to open her door.

"I called Ma because I was worried. She said you should've been home by now so I came looking for you."

"I—I wasn't in a hurry to get home. I needed some time." Her hand was pressed against her heart again. A self-protective gesture she didn't remember making. She stepped into the car.

When Garrett was seated beside her, he reached for her hand. "I'm sorry for the way I reacted this morning, for the way I treated you. There's no excuse. I was just like the apostle Peter. He said he'd be there for Jesus no matter what, and then when bad things happened, he betrayed Him. I did the same thing to you."

"I…I was afraid to come home. I was afraid you'd treat me the way my mother did. She wanted nothing to do with me because I'd brought shame on her, just like I've brought shame on you." Tears still trickled down Savannah's cheeks.

"We don't know that. Like Dr. Cooley said, I could have been the carrier. We'll never know. I was too quick to throw around blame, and I'm sorry." Garrett let go of Savannah's hand and put the car in gear.

"I thought we were so well-prepared when we went to get the results from the doctor, but I was wrong." Savannah bowed her head and stared at the floor.

"We were prepared to be told we couldn't have children. We weren't prepared to be told we had a disease that would make us feel unclean. Must be how lepers felt in Bible times. They had to go around crying, 'Unclean. Unclean.'" He shifted gears and pulled on the accelerator.

Savannah lifted her head and stared at him. "Do you think we'll ever feel clean again?"

CHAPTER 39

Polly scuffed her Keds through the autumn leaves that covered the sidewalk. The strong winds and heavy rain last night had brought down a new layer. She loved the fact that her new sneakers didn't make a sound. One by one Father had bought each of them a pair of these rubber-soled shoes with canvas tops.

She shifted her bag of groceries from one arm to the other. Although there were plenty of chores to do, the last thing she wanted was to go home. The hours had dragged all week, and the battle to keep her thoughts under control had been fierce. It seemed Friday would never come. *Be anxious in nothing... Be anxious in nothing...* so many things to be anxious about...

Maybe she should stop and see her grandmother or her sister, Maggie. She couldn't talk to them about Garrett and Savannah's personal problems, and she didn't want to talk to them about Will... Polly stopped and stared at the sidewalk. *Why don't I want to talk to them about Will?* She hadn't even told Savannah about him.

Although she'd told Jim from the start that they could only be friends, people had begun to think of them as a couple. They'd been seen riding in Jim's buggy and doing things with Garrett and Savannah. What would people say if she told them about her interest in Will? Besides, Will might never call her again, so what was the use?

Still, after crossing over Main, her feet carried her down Lacock Street where Maggie and her grandmother lived. It seemed like the right thing to do whether or not she wanted to talk about Will. Besides, it had been awhile since she'd visited Grandma Dye. Polly should check on her.

She rapped lightly on the door and went in. The smell of fresh bread reminded her the supply in her bread box was getting low. "Grandma." She wiped her shoes on the rag rug at the door and set down her groceries, then called again. "Grandma, where are you?"

"In here, dear."

Polly followed her grandmother's voice into the sunny living room. "Don't get up, Gram." She hurried to where Gram attempted to push herself from the upholstered settee with walnut-carved frame.

"You're a sight for sore eyes, young lady." Grandma gave her a hug and kissed her cheek. "Was it you that brought the sunshine?"

"Not me, but I'm glad it's shining after all the rain last night." Polly perched on the edge of a chair that matched the settee.

"What are you up to while the youngsters are in school?" Gram pushed her wire-rimmed glasses up, then rubbed her nose.

"Just picking up some groceries at the market. What have you been doing?"

Her grandmother reached for a colorful tin box and pulled out fabric. "I'm embroidering some pillowcases for the church bazaar. My mother always said, 'Idle hands are the devil's workshop.'" She winked at Polly.

"I don't know if I've ever seen you with idle hands, Grammy."

Gram put down her embroidery work and peered at Polly over her glasses. "Speaking of not having idle hands, you're kept busy with things in your household. I don't know what your father would do without you." Gram paused. "Is he still seeing Lydia Wilds?"

Polly cleared her throat. "Not lately." She sat up straighter. "What do you think of Lydia Wilds?"

Her grandmother went into a fit of coughing that brought Polly to her feet. "I'll get you a drink of water." She dashed to the kitchen, grabbed a tumbler from the cupboard and filled it. By the time, she returned to the living room, the coughing had stopped. Grandma slowly and precisely drank the entire glass of water with long pauses in between swallows.

When she finished, she handed the glass to Polly. "Would you get us a little snack from the kitchen, please? There are peanut butter cookies in the apple cookie jar."

As Polly filled a violet-covered plate, she frowned. Had Gram just successfully avoided her question about Mrs. Wilds? Perhaps Polly wasn't the only one who didn't want to discuss certain people.

Returning to the living room, Polly offered her grandmother the plate of cookies. "Gram—"

"How are the girls doing in school? Does Beth still think she wants to be a nurse some day?"

No doubt about it, Gram was avoiding her question. Her avoidance was an answer in itself. Gram never said anything unkind about anyone if she could help it. Sometimes Father said she was a real Pollyanna. Polly strongly suspected she was not the only one who didn't like Mrs. Wilds.

She and Gram talked about the girls until Polly asked another question. "Do you think it's wrong for a Presbyterian and a Catholic to marry?"

Gram"s brow wrinkled. "Why do you ask?"

Polly shrugged. "No reason. Just curious."

Pulling in a long breath, Gram took another bite of her cookie and chewed. "I don't think it's a sin." She swallowed. "I'm no scholar of Catholic affairs but there's talk that the 1917 Code of Canon Law will make things more difficult for non-Catholics who marry Catholics. It took effect in May."

"More difficult how?" Polly squinted at her grandmother.

"I'm not sure. Maybe the non-Catholic has to promise to raise children in the Catholic faith, maybe the Catholic has to promise to try to convert the non-Catholic, or maybe some other promises."

"I don't plan to have children anyway so that wouldn't be a problem." Polly clapped her hand over her mouth.

Her grandmother's brows shot up. "What do you mean, *so that wouldn't be a problem*? What are you not telling me, Polly?"

CHAPTER 40

Garrett finished his paperwork, straightened the office he shared with several other agents, and closed the door. On the way out, he stopped at Savannah's office. "Almost finished?"

Her deep lavender-blue eyes lit when she saw him, and she nodded. He moved on and stepped into his father's office. He had no doubt his mother had told his father about the doctor's diagnosis but it was never mentioned. Garrett wouldn't bring it up and he doubted his father would.

"How are you, Son?"

This was Pa's way of showing he cared without having to get into anything emotional. He nodded. "I'm okay, Pa. Another week behind us."

"Made a decision about the church yet?"

Another issue they hadn't discussed that Ma must have informed Pa about. "No, they want an answer by Sunday so Savannah and I will have to decide soon. We've been praying about it all week."

His father nodded, a pensive expression on his face, but said nothing.

Garrett raised an eyebrow. "You don't have an opinion?" He couldn't believe his father had nothing to say.

"Your mother says I need to be supportive whatever you decide. You're good at selling insurance. I don't know why you'd want to do anything else."

"I'd still sell insurance for a couple years while I'm an assistant pastor."

Savannah came out of her office and slipped her arm through his.

"Have a good weekend." Pa turned back to the papers on his desk.

♠

As Garrett and Savannah lingered over cups of tea and

pumpkin bread after dinner, he brought up the inevitable. "You remember the church wants our decision by Sunday?"

She bowed her head. "I remember."

"What are you thinking? How are you feeling about this? I need to know." Garrett reached across the table to take her hand.

"It's your job offer, so I suppose you should make the decision." Savannah's voice was low.

He shook his head. "No, it's a decision we need to make together. It will affect you too."

She pulled in a deep breath and met his gaze. "To be honest, I don't know how we can say yes. If people find out why we can't have children, can you imagine what would happen?"

"There'd be no reason for them to find out."

"This is a small town, Garrett. It has a huge grapevine. All it takes is one person… Besides, who would want a former prostitute for a pastor's wife?" Two tears slid down Savannah's cheeks. "Wouldn't the church still have to vote on it if we agreed?"

Garrett nodded.

"Some of the people here probably still hate me. They treat me better because of your family, but I don't think they'd accept me as their pastor's wife."

Garrett gazed at the table, then looked at her. "All right, Savannah. We'll tell them no. I won't do anything to put you in the position of being rejected. If God wants me to be a preacher, He'll have to open another door."

♠

Polly hurried to pick up the receiver when the telephone rang on Saturday morning. Joy filled her soul as Will's voice crossed the phone lines. She'd never understood how telephones worked, but she'd never been more thankful.

"It's so good to hear your voice. Where are you?" The quiet on the other end of the line lengthened. "Will, are you there?"

"We need to talk, Lass."

Did anything good ever follow those words? "All right. Where do you want to talk?"

"I have a few days off, so I'm coming home this morning to

visit me mam. If I stop in Sandy Lake, could I pay ya a visit at your house, or do ya have company?"

Polly's ears burned at the implication of his question. "Of course you can come. What time?"

"The train stops in Sandy Lake at eleven o'clock so that should have me at your house by eleven fifteen or so."

"Okay. I'll be waiting."

After they said goodbye, she stared at the telephone. The only thing worse than Will *not* calling was having him use that impersonal tone. He'd had more expression in his voice the first time he'd spoken to her than he did today. Polly dragged herself upstairs to look in the mirror above her dresser. Should she change her clothes, comb her hair? Maybe it didn't matter.

She glanced down at her work dress. It had a dusting of flour from her bread making, so she reached for her second-best one. Most red-headed women didn't wear rose-colored dresses, but Polly had been told it made her cheeks look rosier. She removed her work dress and slipped on the other one, then leaned toward the mirror to pinch her pale cheeks. While she didn't want to appear to be wearing rouge, she wanted a healthy glow.

Twila appeared in the doorway, her sparkling brown eyes not missing a thing. "Where are you going?"

"Nowhere. A…A friend is going to stop in before lunch." Polly picked up her brush and smoothed some fly-away strands of hair.

"A man?"

Her mirror showed her cheeks and neck flushing an even rosier color. Before she could answer, Twila chimed in. "It's the man from the train isn't it?"

CHAPTER 41

"Could you go somewhere else to work on that Buster Brown coloring book, Elsie?" Polly stood at the door of Mother's sitting room. "It's probably better to paint on the table anyway. Less likely to spill. I want to entertain Will in this room."

A scowl crept over Elsie's pretty brow. "Why can't you and Will sit at the table?"

"I'm not sure what he wants to discuss so I'd like a little privacy. You'll understand when you're older." Elsie's immediate reaction told Polly she'd said the wrong thing. Her sister didn't like anyone implying they knew more than she regardless of their age. Her lower lip protruded in an unbecoming pout.

The last shred of Polly's patience fled as a knock on the front door announced Will's arrival. "Just go, Elsie. Do as I say without arguing for once." Without waiting for an answer, she gathered up the coloring book and paints and headed for the front door.

She pulled it open and scanned Will's face seeking to discern his motive in coming.

"Hello, Polly." He glanced at the art supplies in her hand. "Having a painting party, are ya?" The smile in his voice gave her hope. He stamped his feet on the rug by the door to remove the autumn leaves.

"That would be Elsie. She's our artist. Poet, too, sometimes." Polly stepped into the dining room to put Elsie's things on the table.

"A fine one, too, I'll wager, to be sure." Will followed her to favor Elsie with a warm smile as she stomped into the dining room. "Could I have a peek at what you're working on, Elsie?"

After a searching look at Will, perhaps to determine if he was serious, Elsie showed him the autumn scene she was painting with vibrant reds, yellows, and greens.

"'Tis an artist ya are, then, Lass. I couldn't have done as well meself."

Elsie smiled for the first time since Polly had asked her to leave the sitting room. "Thank you. I love the bright colors. Would you like to paint with me? I bet you could do just as well."

Will's smile dimmed. "I'd like to, Little Lass, but me mam is waitin' for me. Maybe some… Not today. But thank you for invitin' me."

The way Will had charmed Elsie out of her bad mood amazed Polly. He must be the Pied Piper of Stoneboro.

"Would you like a cup of tea before we talk?" Polly paused outside the dining room.

"No, thank you. Mam will be wantin' to go to market before lunch."

With an effort, Polly pulled in her lower lip, determined not to display the same sulky attitude her sister had shown. Letting Will precede her to the sitting room, she pulled the door partly closed, motioned for him to sit on the loveseat, and drew up a stool. Before Will's phone call, she would have sat beside him. Now, she didn't know what to think.

She folded her hands in her lap and raised her gaze to his face. He was staring off into space, seemingly lost in another world. *Should I ask him what he wanted to talk about? Do I really want to know?* She couldn't bring herself to say a word, but finally cleared her throat.

Will started, as though he'd forgotten she was there, then raised his eyes to hers. "Oh, Lassie…" He paused and rubbed his slender hands together. "'Tis such a difficult decision."

Polly wrinkled her brow. "What decision? Whether to date a non-Catholic?"

"Nay, that's not me worst stumblin' block. It's somethin' else. As I told ya before, I'm not one to come between two people who have an understandin'."

"You mean me and Reverend Caldwell? I told you…"

"Aye, I know what you said, but still me heart is troubled. I saw his eyes on ya when you were in his buggy. I believe he's in love with ya, Lass. Perhaps you love him too and what ya feel for me is just a passin' fancy."

"But…"

"I can't help but feel I'm intrudin' on his territory. And then there being the fact that he's a preacher. I can't quote things chapter and verse as I'm sure he can from the Holy Bible." Will stared, unseeing, out the window. "If I don't pursue ya, maybe you'll fall in love with him. Our priests don't marry, but I've heard wives are very important to protestant ministers. What a grand preacher's wife ya'd be."

"But Will, Jim and I've been friends for more than a year and…"

"I'm sorry, Lass, me mind's made up." Will walked across the room to the window. "It's barely eatin' or sleptin' I've been all week for wrestlin' with this decision. I have no peace about takin' another man's sweetheart."

A sob escaped Polly's throat. "How many times do I have to tell you, I'm not his sweetheart."

When Will was silent, Polly jumped to her feet. "You met someone else didn't you? That's what it is. Every time I fall for someone, they fall for someone else. Just like Garrett fell in love with Savannah. I should have known your interest in me was too good to be true."

Will started toward her. "No, Lass, no. It's not that way…"

"Garrett pretended to love me while he was secretly seeing other women. I thought you were different but I don't even know you. Maybe every word you've spoken to me has been a lie." Polly pushed the sitting room door open so hard it banged against the wall, then ran out of the room and up the stairs.

Throwing herself on her bed, she sobbed out her frustration and anger. "How could you let this happen again, God? How could you let this happen again?"

♠

Will gazed up the stairs, watching the woman he'd thought for a brief time might be the one he wanted to marry. Is this what people meant when they talked about redheads having terrible tempers? Or was this happening because he'd allowed himself to fall for someone outside the Catholic faith?

Turning away from the steps, he found himself looking into

the faces of two young ladies with wide-eyes. The dark-haired one spoke first. "What did you do to make Polly cry?"

Elsie stomped her foot. "He wouldn't make Polly cry. Don't say things like that about Will."

He had an ally. Squatting beside the girls, Will looked into each of their eyes. "I'm sorry I made Polly cry. Maybe when she has time to think about it, she'll understand."

With a pat on each of their shoulders, Will walked across the living room and opened the door. Maybe his mother had been right. Maybe nothing good ever came of a Catholic courting someone outside the Catholic Church. Why did doing the right thing hurt so bad?

PART 3

CHAPTER 42
May 20, 1920

Bob sat by the table, his head in his hands, as he tried to pray. The only words he could muster were, "Oh God. Oh God."

Occasionally the oil lamp on the table sputtered. It was late and perhaps soon he'd be in total darkness. He couldn't help thinking of the parable of the five foolish virgins whose lamps had gone out. He'd never completely understood that parable but he knew the feeling of having used up all his resources.

The civil case brought against him because of his accident at the Stoneboro Fairgrounds had finally come to trial this week. More than a year and a half had passed since the incident and almost a year since the sheriff had delivered Bob's summons. The waiting had been excruciating while his lawyer hand-carried Bob's answer and the two attorneys took turns filing motions. Every motion was denied.

Listening to the exaggeration and outright lies of Mr. and Mrs. Collins and their witnesses this week had been even more difficult than the months of waiting. His attorney would wrap up his case tomorrow. Then the jury would decide. If they didn't rule in his favor, the damages could ruin him.

In addition, his mother, always a steadying force in his life, had passed away a month ago. She had been so much like Margaret that losing her was like losing his wife all over again. How much could a man bear?

Footsteps coming up the porch stairs startled him. Who would be visiting at this time of night? He walked to the window, trying to distinguish the features of the person coming across the porch. Lydia. He had stopped trying to court her when her involvement with Byron

Chesterfield became common knowledge. How could he compete with the wealthy investor from Franklin?

Why was Lydia here—at 10:00 at night? His pulse quickened. He had missed her.

Bob opened the door before she knocked to avoid disturbing the children. "Lydia. Is everything all right?"

"Oh Bob, I've been so worried about you. Talk is all over town about the lawsuit and the huge damages wanted. What does Mr. Cochran think will happen?"

Lydia closed the door and stepped closer to Bob. Her lily of the valley perfume brought back memories he'd tried to forget. He closed his eyes. What had she asked him? Oh, the lawsuit. "T. C. says it's too soon to know. We'll have to wait for the jury's verdict."

"Can we sit down?" Lydia took his hand and headed for the davenport. "Since I was with you at the Fair the night of the accident, I thought maybe I could help."

Bob's brows raised in a puzzled frown. "But you weren't with me when the accident happened."

Lydia sat down, leaving only a small space between her and the arm of the daven for him to fit into. He was torn between wanting to be near her and wanting to ask questions about Mr. Chesterfield. "Lydia, what about Mr. Chester—"

"I could have been standing near by. I could have seen what happened even if I wasn't in the car." She tugged on his hand, pulling him down beside her. After Bob wriggled into the space, she snuggled against him. He had no choice but to put his arm around her.

He tried again. "What about Mr.— Wait, what are you saying? Are you saying you saw the accident?"

Her cheeks flushed. "I said I *could* have seen what happened. No one would know if I did or not. I could testify."

"I can't let you do that. That's perjury. You could get in serious trouble."

"You have a lot to lose, Bob. I just want to help."

The lamp sputtered and died, leaving them in complete darkness. When Bob moved to get up, Lydia reached out to pull his head toward her. Her perfume fogged his brain as his lips met hers.

♠

Polly rolled out of bed and grabbed her robe off the chair. Sleep hadn't come easily tonight. Unless she was imagining things, the front door had opened and closed a few minutes ago, followed by bits and pieces of conversation. In spite of that, not a speck of light crept up the stairs as she went into the hall.

After a few steps, she found the railing and inched her way down the stairs. Maybe she'd been mistaken about the noises. Complete silence greeted her as she reached the lower landing and stepped into the living room. She sniffed. Where had she smelled this scent before?

Was there one shadowy figure or two sitting on the davenport? She blinked as her eyes adjusted, and then sniffed again. Lily of the valley… Of course, the fragrance that had been in the house after Lydia was here a few years ago. How could Polly have forgotten?

She took another step toward the daven. "Father?"

The shadows separated and one of them leaped up. "Florence, what are you doing up?"

"A better question, why are you sitting here in the dark with Mrs. Wilds?"

"We were talking and the lamp went out." Her father headed for the kitchen. "I'll go refill it."

The silence after her father left was oppressive. Polly cleared her throat and searched for something to say. Why beat around the bush? "What are you doing here, Mrs. Wilds?"

"I've been so worried about your father. I wanted to find out if I could help."

"Almost a year since the original complaint was filed, and now you want to help?" Polly couldn't keep the skepticism from her voice.

"I knew he had a good attorney. Mr. Cochran is the best. But even so, now that the case is wrapping up tomorrow, no one seems certain of the outcome." Mrs. Wilds sat up a bit straighter and smoothed her hair. "It could be very bad for your family if he loses."

Why did Mrs. Wilds care about the outcome of Father's case? Polly's gut instinct was that this woman only cared about things that affected her.

"I understand Mr. Chesterfield is a man of influence." Polly squinted, trying to see Mrs. Wilds' reaction to the man's name. "Did you think he could help Father?"

"I don't know what makes you think I have a connection with Mr. Chesterfield." Mrs. Wilds' voice had turned frosty.

"You must be the only one in Sandy Lake who doesn't think you have a connection. It's common knowledge. Unless..." There was a pregnant pause. "Unless the reason you're here is because he's broken his connection with you."

CHAPTER 43

Savannah stirred and reached for Garrett as she did when she woke every morning. She found only bedclothes where his body should have been. This had happened more and more frequently of late. She pushed up on one elbow and rubbed her eyes. Perhaps it was time to check on him, make sure he was all right. The restlessness she'd detected in him for several months had increased.

She got out of bed, padded to the doorway, and peered into the living area. Garrett had mentioned the possibility of finding a bigger place, perhaps buying a house, but based on Dr. Cooley's diagnosis she didn't see the need.

Her husband sat in the corner of the loveseat, head bowed over a book, bronze-gold hair shining in the light from the kerosene lamp.

Stepping in his direction, she cleared her throat so as not to startle him. "Good morning, handsome husband. What are you reading?"

Garrett raised his head, his mouth tilting in a smile. "Good morning, beautiful wife. I guess you found me out. I'm reading Sarah's diary." He held up the faded book.

"I noticed it was missing from my bedside table. I've been thinking I need to get it back to Polly. She hasn't been herself since… Well, for a long time. Maybe it's the court case." Savannah bent and kissed Garrett's lips, then dropped down beside him. "What prompted you to read the diary?"

"When I responded so poorly to Dr. Cooley's news about our," he swallowed, "our condition, I grew convicted of my need for a deeper walk with the Lord. The Holy Spirit kept reminding me what you'd said about Sarah's responses when bad things happened."

He glanced at his wife. "It took me more than a year to follow through. After all the years I've studied the Bible with Jim, I didn't think I needed to read an old diary. Pride, I guess."

Savannah reached for his hand. "Is it helping you?"

"I keep coming back to her words early in the diary after her baby died." Garrett flipped back through the fragile pages. *Lord, to whom else will we go? If I turn against God, to whom will I turn for comfort and strength to get through the days ahead?"*

"Your mother and Polly have helped me see what a good, wise Heavenly Father we have." Savannah smiled. "He doesn't promise we won't go through hard things, He just promises to go through them with us."

Garrett nodded. "In many ways, Sarah's faith was so simple and childlike. And yet she battled fear and overprotected her remaining children. She was human."

Quiet and peace permeated the air. Then Garrett shifted so he could see her face. "I need to tell you something." He bit his lip. "Every day my sense of God's call on my life is stronger. His words are like a flame inside me. Three times earlier this week, I came across the verse in Romans ten where it says, *How can they hear without someone preaching to them*?" Garrett's voice trembled with emotion.

The pounding of Savannah's heart was so loud she could barely hear Garrett's words. What was God asking of them?

"I'm so aware of my faults and my flaws—I'm human just like Sarah, but God is calling me to preach, flaws and all."

"Where do you think He wants you to preach?" Savannah forced the words through dry lips.

"I told Him if he wanted me to preach, He'd have to open another door. So I'm waiting to see what door He opens. I just know when it happens, we have to be ready to walk through." He drew Savannah close and pressed his lips against her hair. "Jim told me a long time ago he wanted God to tell me Himself if He had other work for me to do. I didn't believe He would but I can't run from it anymore."

♠

A knock on the door took Polly by surprise on Friday morning. The children were almost ready for school and she wanted to go with Father to the last day of his court case. She opened the door and could hardly resist rolling her eyes. For goodness sake, what was Mrs. Wilds doing here again?

"Has your father already left for Mercer?"

"He's still here. Out feeding the animals." Polly didn't open the screen door or invite Mrs. Wilds to come in. "I'm trying to get the children off to school."

"Could I come in and wait? I promise not to get in your way. I need to talk to your father. "

Polly sighed and stepped back so the woman could enter. "You might as well sit down." She pointed at the davenport, then returned to shoo the girls out of the dining room to get their coats.

When the children came into the living room, Mrs. Wilds sprang to her feet with the biggest smile Polly had ever seen her wear. "Good morning, Twila and Evie."

Elsie's brows drew together. "Elsie, not Evie."

"Oh, of course. Is there anything I can do to help you get ready for school?" Mrs. Wilds hovered around the girls like a hummingbird buzzing around fragrant flowers.

"We don't need any help. We're big enough to take care of ourselves." Elsie would not soon forget being called by the wrong name, nor being treated like a child.

"We don't need any help but thank you for offering." Twila smiled as though trying to make up for her sister's brusque tone.

"Beth, George, it's time to go." Polly peeked up the stairs to see Beth heading down. What a young lady she had become. She and George would graduate at the end of the next school year.

The back door opened and closed. Father had returned. How would he respond to Mrs. Wilds' early morning visit? Polly didn't have long to wait. Acting as though she were a frequent visitor, Mrs. Wilds ran out to the kitchen calling, "Good morning, Bob. I want to go to the courthouse with you."

♠

Bob sat in the courtroom, with Lydia and Polly seated behind him, while T. C. made his closing argument. The faces of the jurors gave nothing away. He couldn't tell if they were impressed with his attorney's remarks or not. At last the judge dismissed them to make their decision. It was time for the courthouse to close, so his attorney told him he might as well go home. There was no way of knowing how long the jurors would deliberate. He would be notified when they reached a decision.

When Bob turned to leave the courtroom, Lydia slipped her hand through his arm and matched her steps to his. He glanced at Florence who walked behind them. Was that a quick roll of her eyes? Would his daughter never get over her dislike of the woman beside him? Didn't she understand he'd never find anyone who could compare to her mother?

CHAPTER 44

The evening dragged on with no word that a decision had been reached. This couldn't be good. Twice Bob called T. C., only to be told the jurors were still out. Twila and Elsie tiptoed around him where he slumped in Mother's chair, and Beth and George had disappeared to their rooms soon after supper. Even Florence had made herself scarce. Perhaps she was in the sitting room.

Bob stood and began to pace back and forth. How he missed his wife's wise counsel, at a time like this, and his mother's prayers. He tried to pray but no words came. What would they do if they lost the case? Would he have to sell the house and the mines to come up with the funds to pay the Collins' demands? Where would they live?

When he plopped down on the davenport, the fragrance of lily of the valley wafted into his nostrils. Leaning his head against the back of the daven, he closed his eyes and breathed in. Lydia. She and Mr. Chesterfield must have parted ways or she wouldn't have come to him last night.

He stood and pushed open the sitting room door where Florence played a quiet game with Elsie and Twila. "I'm going to talk to Lydia. She'll be wondering if the jurors have made a decision."

Florence raised her head. "Why don't you call her instead? What if Mr. Cochran calls while you're gone?"

Bob hesitated, then shook his head. "I can't sit here waiting another minute. You can call me at Lydia's if you hear from T.C. I'll leave her telephone number."

He tossed a slip of paper with Lydia's number on the table as he trotted through the living room, grabbed his light jacket and left the house. The moon and some twinkling stars filled the sky but he had no interest in them. *The heavens declare the glory of God; the skies proclaim the work of his hands.*

Margaret had loved to walk with him and enjoy the stars, wondering aloud how anyone could doubt God's existence. What had happened to his faith during the past year? Was it so fragile that it couldn't survive a court case and the loss of his mother? Even Florence had stopped encouraging him to trust God.

He suspected the change in her had to do with Will Reiser disappearing from her life as quickly as he had appeared. Or perhaps it had to do with the ending of her friendship with Reverend Caldwell. When he tried to talk to her about Will or the pastor, he could sense walls being erected, shutting him out.

Lights shone from Lydia's windows, penetrating the darkness. One bright spot in his world. Having her in his arms again last night had been such a balm to his soul. He picked up the pace, almost running as he neared her house.

♠

A car backfired, and Polly went to the window. Was that Garrett's car? Difficult to see in the darkness. She sprinted to the door in time to see Savannah getting out on the passenger's side and heading up the steps.

Polly opened the door and called, "Savannah. Is everything all right?"

"We're okay. Do you have time to talk?"

"I do. Is Garrett coming in?" Polly peered around Savannah.

"He's going to talk to his cousin, Irv, for a bit if he can catch him before he leaves the Mill." Savannah waved to Garrett and closed the door.

"Are you sure everything is okay between you and Garrett?" Polly motioned for Savannah to follow her and headed for the sitting room.

"We're fine. We miss having you and Jim—"

"Savannah—"

"I know, I know." Savannah patted Polly's shoulder. "You said you can't give him false hope. But we still miss those evenings."

Polly sighed and stepped into the sitting room. "Elsie and Twila, put away your game, then run upstairs and get ready for bed. When you're finished, ask Beth if she'll read your bedtime story and say prayers with you."

Elsie frowned. "I can read to Twila…"

"I can read as well as you can." Twila jerked her head toward Elsie, flipping her dark braids over one shoulder.

"But I'm almost thirteen—"

Holding up her hand, Polly stared at her sisters. "Stop. You can each read a story and say your prayers together. Do I need to ask Beth to check on you? She's doing her school work upstairs."

"No," they chorused. Feet dragging, they put away their game and trudged toward the steps.

Plopping on the loveseat, Polly patted the place beside her. "Have a seat. What's in your bag?"

Savannah sat down, pulled Sarah's diary from the small paper bag she carried, and held it out to Polly. "I'm sorry we've kept this book so long. There's no excuse. Garrett just finished reading it."

Polly made no move to take the diary. "It doesn't matter. I've already read it." Her tone was flat and her eyes dull.

Wrinkling her forehead, Savannah gaped at Polly. "But you were so happy the diary didn't burn in the fire. I thought you'd be excited to get it back."

Not meeting Savannah's eyes, Polly stared at the floor without speaking.

"What's wrong, Polly? You haven't been yourself for a long time, long before your grandma Dye passed. You're almost melancholy."

When Polly still didn't speak, Savannah tilted Polly's chin in her direction. "Are you angry with me? You used to be my best friend, like a sister but..." She shrugged. "You don't seem to want to talk to me about anything important anymore."

Polly buried her head in her hands, then peeked at Savannah between her fingers. "It's not you. I don't want to talk to anyone. There's nothing anyone can do."

"About what?" She pried Polly's fingers gently away and looked into her eyes.

"Didn't Jim tell you anything?"

"Polly, have I just fallen down a rabbit hole? I have no idea what you're talking about."

Polly stood. "I'll go make you a cup of tea—"

Savannah grabbed her hand. "I don't want a cup of tea. Sit down and tell me what's going on."

"It's such a long story and you'll think I'm foolish. My problems are so small compared to yours." She tried to cover her face again, but Savannah wouldn't let go of her hand.

"Start at the beginning, Polly. Stop stalling."

Savannah knew her well. Polly sat up straight and turned to face her friend. "I should have told you a long time ago."

CHAPTER 45

Early Saturday morning, the telephone jangled a clamorous summons before the sun was up. Polly rolled over when her father's footsteps on the stairs told her he would quiet the noisy intruder. Then her eyelids popped open. The jury decision… The call that never came last night. When her father had finally returned from Lydia's, they'd given up and gone to bed.

What would this day hold? She leaped up, grabbed her robe, and ran down the stairs as her father hung up. His face was wreathed in smiles. "The jury ruled in our favor. We don't have to pay the settlement. I can't wait to tell Lydia."

Polly's joy dimmed a bit with that statement, but then she straightened. She wouldn't allow Lydia Wilds to steal her delight at the good results of the lawsuit. She grabbed her father and gave him a huge hug. "Thank you, Lord. Thank you, thank you." How long had it been since she spontaneously prayed?

"Yes, thank you, Lord." Father took the stairs two at a time as he ran upstairs to get dressed.

Polly curled up in Mother's chair with her legs tucked under her. Her talk with Savannah had done her more good last night than she could ever have imagined. Perhaps that was the reason James the brother of Jesus had said, "Confess your faults one to another and pray for one another that you may be healed."

In a way Polly had been right. There was nothing Savannah could do about Polly's situation. Still, telling her about that short, bittersweet time with Will had emptied her of so much pain and anger. It had also brought down the walls Polly had erected to protect herself from more pain. She had cried in Savannah's arms until she had no more tears.

She picked up Sarah's diary and stroked the faded cover. "Forgive me, Lord, for turning my back on you and everything you've taught me. Thank you for not giving up on me and for receiving me with open arms when I ran back to you last night."

After opening the diary, she flipped a few pages. *The Lord gives and the Lord takes away. Blessed be the name of the Lord.* How angry she'd been at Sarah the first time she'd read those words. How sure she'd been that God had failed Sarah just as He'd failed her.

"No matter how much I liked Will, I don't want him to court me unless that's what you want, Father. I'm choosing to trust you for my future. And I still have children to raise."

♠

Polly had just stepped back into the house after hanging up her Monday laundry when the telephone rang. She put down her empty basket and said, "Hello… Oh, hello Savannah. Thanks again for coming to my rescue on Friday night."

Savannah laughed. "You've come to my rescue often enough. It was my turn."

"That's what friends are for. What can I do for you today?"

Silence greeted Polly's question. "Savannah, are you still there?"

"I'm here, but I don't think you're going to like what I have to say."

"Oh dear." Polly clutched the receiver. "That sounds ominous. What is it?"

"Jim wants to talk to you and me and Garrett this eve—"

"Savannah—"

"Hear me out, Polly. He said it's not a social call, and it's very important that you be there too."

"But isn't this the evening he and Garrett usually have Bible study?"

"It is, but he wants to meet with us at our apartment instead."

Polly closed her eyes. *What shall I do, Father? I'll do whatever you say.* Peace flowed through her as she considered her answer. "All right. I'll come."

"You will?" Surprise tinged Savannah's tone.

"I will. What time?"

"Do you want to come for supper?"

Chewing her lip, Polly wrinkled her forehead. "It's awfully short notice for you to make dinner for us. How about dessert?"

"That sounds good. Let's say six-thirty?"

"Okay. And Savannah, I'll bring our horse and buggy."

♠

Polly clucked to Jasper and held lightly to the reins. What in the world did Jim want to talk to the three of them about? After her disastrous conversation with Will, she had told Jim and Savannah people were getting the wrong idea about their relationship. Savannah hadn't given up easily but Jim had never called her again. She missed his friendship but it was hard not to blame him for how things had ended with Will. If Jim hadn't insisted on being her friend, maybe…

"Whoa, Jasper." She pulled hard on the reins. Breathing a sigh of relief, she hopped out of the buggy. She'd purposely come early to avoid talking to Jim alone. After hurrying to the apartment door, she gave a light tap and ran up the stairs. "Hello Savannah. Hi Garrett."

"Hi Polly. Come on in. There's been a bit of a change of plans." Savannah hugged her.

"What's that?" Polly was out of breath from her sprint up the steps.

Garrett joined them, light jackets for him and Savannah in hand. "Delilah's gone lame for some reason. Jim asked if we could come to his apartment in Jackson Center. I was late getting home from work or we could have started sooner."

They all herded down the stairs and piled into his car. To her surprise, Polly found herself flooded with memories of all the times she'd ridden in Garrett's car while they were courting. Vivid pictures of how intimate they'd been caused warmth to flood her cheeks. *Oh Lord, how foolish we were. Thank you for your forgiveness. Please, wash away all those memories.*

In the quiet moments that followed, Polly suddenly understood that if shame nearly overwhelmed her at the things she and Garrett had done, how much more would Savannah battle shame because of her former lifestyle. *Free her, Father, from the guilt and shame. Remind her she's a new creature in Christ.*

Garrett turned a little so Polly and Savannah could both hear his question. "What do you suppose Jim wants to talk to us about?"

"I was going to ask you. I haven't seen him for months." Polly paused. "I don't know why it's important for me to be there."

Quiet reigned again during the rest of the ride to Jackson Center, each one perhaps preoccupied with questions that could only be answered by Jim.

When he opened the door to his apartment and greeted them, Jim's expression gave nothing away.

CHAPTER 46

Polly had never been at Jim's apartment. The main living area was sparsely furnished with only the bare essentials—a worn dark blue couch beside a faded brown armchair. Across the room was a small old-fashioned table with two chairs and a woodstove that probably served both for cooking and heating. The income of a circuit-riding preacher probably didn't allow for luxuries.

"Please sit down." Jim motioned to the couch and armchair, then pulled out one of the chairs at the table for himself. "Thank you for coming at such short notice."

Polly dropped into the armchair. "Will Delilah be okay? What happened to her?"

"I think she picked up a pebble in her right hoof. I'll have to take a look at it when I have better light in the morning."

"So…" Garrett scooted to the edge of his seat on the couch. "What did you want to talk to us about?"

Jim grinned, looking more like his old self. "I'm fine. Thanks for asking. How are you doing?"

Garrett chuckled. "I'm sorry, I guess that was a little abrupt. I'm not good at chitchat when curiosity is getting the best of me."

With a nod, Jim steepled his fingers on the table. "I won't keep you in suspense. I've been called to be the pastor of an interdenominational church in Akron, Ohio."

Surely she must be wearing the same stunned expression as Garrett and Savannah. Regardless of the fact that she and Jim were no longer close, she'd assumed he'd always be around.

"You can't go." The expression on Garrett's face had gone from stunned to stubborn. "We need you here."

Jim raised an eyebrow. "Surely you know me well enough to understand that I can't stay if God calls me elsewhere."

Garrett groaned. "So you believe this is what God wants you to do?"

"He's called me to Akron, just as surely as He called me here years ago. I wanted the three of you to be among the first to know for several reasons." Jim tilted his chair back on two legs. "As you know, I've been more or less an independent circuit-riding preacher. However, as I've told some of the pastors in this area that I'm leaving, they've gathered together to form a new alliance that will call and help support the person who takes my place."

What possible reason could Jim have for wanting her here tonight? Polly hadn't even been a good friend to him for more than a year. She chewed her lip and waited.

Jim brought his chair down on all four legs with a thud. "You're the person I'm recommending for the job, Garrett."

For a moment, no one moved. Then Savannah reached to take Garrett's hand. "Tell him what you told me on Friday."

In a low voice that gained strength as he talked, Garrett shared his sense that God was indeed calling him to preach, that he'd been waiting to see what door God opened. "I just didn't think it would happen at the same time we're losing you, Jim. I always thought you'd be here to provide support."

"Support can become an unhealthy crutch when it's time for you to stand on your own. I believe that time has come. The alliance of pastors will also be there to provide guidance and encouragement." He turned to Savannah. "How do you feel about this, Savannah?"

"I'm still concerned about how people will feel about the circuit riding pastor being married to a former prostitute." Savannah lifted her gaze to meet Jim's.

"*Former* is the key word. I told the alliance pastors your story. Turns out many of them already knew. They believe your transformation is a huge testimony of God's grace. Also, the expectations for you will be somewhat different than the expectations for a pastor's wife in a denominational church."

Savannah bit her lip and tried to smile as Garrett patted her hand. "This may be the door we've been waiting for. We'll pray."

Polly squirmed in her seat. She still had no idea how any of this concerned her. As though reading her thoughts, Jim turned toward her. "I know you're wondering what this has to do with you."

She nodded and a few strands of fly-away hair fell on her forehead.

"My feelings were hurt when you said people were getting the wrong idea about us, when you refused to continue our friendship. Later, the Lord convicted me that my attitude was self-centered." Jim rubbed his hands together. "I suspected that one person getting the wrong idea about us had caused you a lot of heartache."

Polly dropped her gaze to the worn rag rug in front of her chair. Finally, she raised her head and nodded again. "Yes." Her answer was barely a whisper.

"I'm so sorry. What can I do to correct Will's wrong idea?"

"It's too late. It started out with a misconception, but I made a lot of wild accusations. Will never called me again." A tear slid down Polly's flushed cheek.

Jim pulled a clean handkerchief from his pocket and came over to press it into Polly's hand. "Maybe it's not too late if this man is the one God has chosen for you. God says nothing is too difficult for Him. Is Will seeing someone else?"

"I don't know. He lives in Stoneboro but boards in Franklin where he works for the railroad."

Jim squatted in front of her. "If you would do me the honor of trusting me with his full name and address, I'll do my best to correct whatever misconception he may have had. I'll also tell him that I'm moving."

Polly stopped blowing her nose and stared at him. "You'd do that for me, after I treated you so badly?"

Jim nodded. "You were acting out of your pain."

"That doesn't excuse me from cutting you out of my life, refusing even to be your friend."

"I think being around me would have been too strong a reminder of the damage our friendship had caused. I've forgiven you long since." Jim walked to the table, and picked up a pencil and paper which he handed to Polly. "I can't make any promises but if you give me the information, I'll do my best to undo the damage I did."

Polly sighed and looked at Savannah. "Do you really think it will do any good?"

CHAPTER 47

Will gazed out the window as the train whistle blew and wheels scraped across the tracks, preparing to stop in Sandy Lake. He drew long breaths as he always did to minimize the pain that threatened to steal the air from his lungs at this stop. *Will it ever stop hurting, Lord?*

It was hard to imagine he could still be missing a woman he barely knew after all these months. Here on this platform is where she'd captured his heart. He'd never believed in love at first sight and told himself repeatedly it couldn't be love. His mother fretted because of his lack of appetite. She wanted him to visit Doc Cooley but what would he tell him? That he was acting like a lovesick teenager?

Resolutely Will closed his eyes, attempting to shut out his memories. Sunday would be Decoration Day. There'd likely be big plans afoot this year since veterans would be honored not only from the Civil War but also from the Great War. He'd heard some towns were observing Memorial Day on Monday, since it fell on a Sunday this year.

Many families were still grieving the death of loved ones, while others, like Polly's family, would rejoice for loved ones returned unharmed. Someone told him her brother, Ben, living with his Aunt Flo and Uncle George since his return, was now employed as a grocery clerk in Sandy Lake.

The train whistle shrilled once more, and as always, Will marveled that his mother and Polly lived such a short distance apart. It might as well be a hundred miles as few opportunities as there'd been for their paths to cross in the past year. Of course, the fact that he worked and boarded in Franklin contributed to that.

He stood, collected his knapsack, and hustled off the train, pasting a smile on his lips. His mother would be waiting, and he needed to practice looking happy. Otherwise, she might call Doc Cooley herself.

When he stepped from the train, he paused, amazed at the crowds of people swarming down the road toward the lake. He'd forgotten the beach opened the Saturday of Memorial Day weekend. Growing up, he'd counted the days until he could go swimming. Were any of his nieces or nephews in that herd?

Someone eager to get off the train rammed him none too gently from behind. Will hurried across the platform and strode up Franklin Street. His mother always insisted on waiting to eat lunch with him when he visited. She lived alone in her house on Chestnut Street when he was in Franklin, although two of his brothers lived nearby.

His long legs ate up the distance, and he turned onto Chestnut Street as some of his nieces and nephews barreled around the corner clutching towels and swimming suits. "Whoa there, is it in a hurry ya are then?" He reached to tousle sixteen-year-old Dasie's dark hair, but she evaded him with a good-natured smile.

"Don't mess up my hair, Uncle Will."

"Won't ya be messing it up in the lake?"

She grinned. "Un huh, but I want to look good when I get there."

"Someone special ya be wantin' to impress?"

Dasie glanced at her brother and two cousins, then shook her head. "No one special."

Before he could say more, she narrowed her lovely brown eyes. "What about you, Uncle Will? Anyone special you're wanting to impress?"

Her younger brother, Russell, responded without a pause. "You know everyone says Uncle Will is going to be a bachelor."

Will stared at his thirteen-year-old nephew. "And what would ya be knowin' about being a bachelor?"

"It's someone who doesn't have a wife. That's what I'm going to be."

Russell's cousin, George, also thirteen, added, "Who needs girls anyway? Always bossing a fellow around."

Opting not to comment on that, Will stepped around the group. "You'll be havin' plenty of time to figure that out. Just enjoy swimmin' and bein' kids."

They chorused their goodbyes and, with a lot of good-natured pushing and shoving, took off down the sidewalk. Will headed for home. So folks assumed he planned to be a bachelor, did they? Not hard to understand, him being unmarried at thirty-two. Until he met Polly, he might have agreed with them. And now? Well, being a bachelor might be a good option if he couldn't have Polly.

He ran up the porch steps and pushed open the door. "Mam, I'm home." Without a doubt, Mam was cooking coddle. The fragrance of sausage and bacon blended in the air. He followed his nose to the kitchen where his mother was getting up from the kitchen table, a sharp knife in her hand.

She hugged him with one arm, shielding him from the knife. "Welcome home, Son."

"Thank you. What would you be doin' with that knife?"

Tilting her head toward the table, she gestured to a stack of mail. "Openin' the mail."

"Of course, what was I thinkin'? Your favorite letter opener. Anything interesting?"

"Not much today. Nothing from our family in Ireland."

If folks back home knew how his mother longed for news of home, they'd correspond more than they did. "I'm sorry, Mam."

She shrugged and wiped a film of sweat from her upper lip. It was unseasonably warm for so early in the summer. "Is it hungry ya are?"

Will evaded the question. Had he been really hungry since the day he walked out of Polly's house? "The coddle smells good. Would you be wantin' me to set the table?"

"You could be gettin' out the silverware and fillin' the tumblers, and I'll dish up the soup."

In a few minutes they were seated across from each other. They bowed their heads and said a short table grace Will learned as a child. When he lifted a spoonful of coddle, praying he'd be able to eat enough to satisfy Mam, she pushed back from the table.

"It's so forgetful I'm becomin'." She took a few steps away from the table and pulled an envelope off the windowsill where she sometimes kept his mail. "Were you expectin' a letter?"

He shook his head. "Nay. Not so far as I can remember."

"Well this is addressed to you." He reached for the letter but she held it out of reach. "I curbed me curiosity. Ya know what they say about curiosity and the cat."

Will grinned.

"Do we know any Caldwell's?" His mother peered at him.

"Caldwell… The name has a familiar ring…" He leaped to his feet, upsetting his chair and snatching the letter. Could it be? But why would Reverend Caldwell write to him?

CHAPTER 48

Will righted his chair and dropped down on it. Could he excuse himself to go read the letter? He glanced at the steaming bowl of coddle, then tucked the envelope in his pocket. "It'll not be anythin' that won't wait until we've eaten, I'm sure. Wouldn't want our coddle to get cold."

His mother picked up her spoon without taking her eyes off the missive in his pocket. He quickly loaded his spoon and shoved it into his mouth to buy some time before having to answer the questions he knew would come.

"What was it that startled ya so about that letter?" Mam held her still-empty spoon over her bowl.

Chewing until the sausage, bacon and potatoes were mere mush in his mouth, Will desperately searched for an explanation that would satisfy her curiosity without giving too much information. He cleared his throat and took a swallow of water. "I once met someone by the name of Caldwell but I can't imagine why he'd write to me."

He loaded his spoon again and emptied its contents into his mouth.

"Where did ya meet this Caldwell?" Mam took a spoonful of coddle at last.

The truth was always the best policy. "At the Stoneboro Fair."

She chewed and swallowed, her brow wrinkled in a frown. "And ya have no idea why he'd write to you?"

"None." That was the truth. "I met some of your grandchildren goin' to the lake on my way here. Brings back memories for sure of when I was their age."

Mam's eyes sparkled at the mention of her grandchildren. This became the focus of conversation and there were no more questions about the letter. Now if he could only find a way to disappear long enough to read it after lunch.

Swallowing his last bite, Will gathered his bowl and his mother's to carry to the sink. "I'll be takin' me knapsack upstairs so we won't be fallin' over it."

"Don't forget to read your letter." His mother's eyes focused again on his pocket.

Will nodded and beat a hasty retreat, grabbing his knapsack and running up the stairs. Dropping down on his bed, he pulled out the object of interest and held it in front of him. He observed again the neat printing of his name and address. How would Reverend Caldwell have known his address?

He slid his index finger under the seal, trying unsuccessfully to open it without ripping the envelope. Where was Mam's knife when he needed it? At last he took a deep breath, drew out the folded sheet of paper, and opened it. The letter was printed in the same neat hand as the envelope.

Dear Will,

I'm sure you're surprised to get a letter from me since we only met twice—neither time under the best of circumstances.

I've come to realize my friendship with Polly Dye was misconstrued and was the cause of you two parting ways. Let me assure you that from the beginning, Polly made clear we could only be friends because of the promise she made to her mother on her deathbed to help raise the children. However, after seeing her interest in you, I suspect the reasons were deeper than that.

This letter should have been written months ago, but I admit I held out hope that someday Polly's feelings for me would change, even though she'd broken off our friendship. That never happened. Now I've received a call to pastor a church in Akron, which I know is God's plan, and I'll be moving there soon.

After confirming my suspicions about the reason you and Polly weren't seeing each other, I asked her for your address so I could convey this message. I'm amazed at the integrity you've shown, making a hard decision in order to do what you believed was right. I pray God's blessing on you and Polly if it's His plan for you to be together.

Sincerely,
Jim Caldwell

Will read the letter twice, unable to believe this man's kindness in writing to him even when his own heart must be aching.

"Will, are ya ready to take me to market?" Mam's voice broke into his reverie.

"Comin', Mam." He smoothed his fingers over the words he'd read, then folded the missive and tucked it beneath the long underwear in his bureau.

As soon as he reached the bottom of the stairs, his mother called from the kitchen. "So who's this Caldwell the letter was from?"

"A minister I met a time or two."

Mam appeared in the doorway. "Why would ya be needing a minister when you have a priest to talk to?"

"It's nothing for ya to worry your head about, Mam. He wasn't givin' me religious counsel. Do ya have your marketin' list?"

His mother sniffed and gazed at him for a long time before reaching into the pocket of her dark blue dress and pulling out her list.

♠

Garrett and Savannah sat across from each other at the dining room table. They'd finished their lunch, but lingered over cups of steaming tea. She gazed at her husband, thankful for God's healing since the day they'd learned about the disease they both carried. Their marriage was stronger than before and Dr. Cooley's latest tests showed that his merbromin treatments were effective.

Her husband reached across the table and took her hand. "We've been praying about my call to be a circuit riding preacher all week. Are we ready to give Jim an answer?"

"I don't think there's any doubt this is God's will, so how can we say anything but 'yes.' Savannah squeezed his hand.

With two quick nods, Garrett reached to take her other hand and bowed his head. "Father, we believe this is your answer to my request for an open door if you want me to preach, so we'll tell Jim yes. The rest is up to you and the alliance of pastors."

With a firm shove, Savannah pushed away the fear of people rejecting her if they learned of her past or of the reason they couldn't have children. If it happened, they would face it together—hopefully having learned from their last test.

CHAPTER 49

Polly and all the Dye family who lived at home trooped into the sanctuary on Sunday morning with five minutes to spare. Somehow they'd all managed to get ready on time even before Maggie, Ben and Robert left home. Would Ben show up now that he was living with Aunt Flo? She missed having him at home but he had his own room there.

Catching a glimpse of her brother, Polly made a beeline for the pew where he sat. There should be room for all of them. She leaned down and whispered in Ben's ear, "Scoot over, we want to sit with you."

He beamed a smile her way, stood, and walked to the opposite end of the bench. Polly followed and seated herself beside him. "I'm so happy you're back. Sometimes I can't believe you're real."

Ben shrugged, as though it was no big deal, but his eyes told a different story. He was glad to be back.

I'm so thankful the war ended before he had to go into battle. What effect would the fighting and killing have had on his gentle spirit? She shuddered.

A sharp elbow in her side preceded George hissing in her ear. "Look who's preaching today."

She'd been too busy delighting in Ben's presence to notice who walked to the pulpit. Jim stood before them, hands clasped behind his back. She hadn't expected to see him again before he left or to be this happy if she did. He'd been a good friend and she would miss him.

"Good morning. Today is a very special day as we celebrate the many brave lives that were given for our freedom. We hope you'll join in the parade at ten o'clock at the Catholic cemetery tomorrow morning where Father John Craig will give an address. Following that, Doctor Robert Green will give a message at the Oak Hill cemetery. Let's bow our heads and give thanks for the sacrifice of these brave men."

Polly stared at Jim. If only she'd treated him better. If only she'd valued his friendship. Another sharp elbow in her ribs prompted her to bow her head, but even with her eyes closed, Jim's past messages bombarded her. She had learned so much from him. How could she have forgotten what a huge role he'd played in her growth in Christ?

Do we dare to believe it is not in spite of God's unchanging love for us but because of it that He doesn't always immediately remove our pain? That message had been based on the account of Jesus not going to Mary and Martha immediately when He learned of Lazarus's illness. Believing the truth Jim spoke that day had been a turning point in her life.

"What's wrong with you? The prayer is over." George's tone revealed his frayed patience at her strange behavior.

She opened her eyes and smiled at him, while mouthing the words, "Sorry."

On her other side, Ben, always sensitive to her feelings, smiled at her. "No harm done."

From the other end of the pew, Father frowned and held a finger to his lips. Polly sat straighter, determined to listen, but still found bits and pieces of conversations with Jim, Garrett and Savannah washing over her. How grateful she was for all the happy times they'd shared.

At last Jim closed his Bible and smiled at the congregation. "Thank you for all the opportunities you've given me to break the bread of life with you. Thanks also for all the good meals and conversations we've shared over the years. What a blessing you've been.

"It's with mixed feelings that I tell you I've answered a call to be the pastor of the Bread of Life Church, an interdenominational congregation in Akron. While I know this is God's plan, I will miss you all. Pray for me as I travel down this new road and I will continue to keep you in my prayers."

Ben looked at Polly. "Did you know?"

She nodded, but no words came. A tear slid down her cheek. Why had she wasted all the opportunities to learn from this man?

♠

"Mam, are ya coming with me to the Decoration Day observance? We need to leave soon." Will stood and headed for the kitchen.

Even though Mam had conceded to go to his brother, John's, house for a picnic today, she'd been in the kitchen preparing food all morning. It would take many trips to carry the food across the street. At least she hadn't asked any more questions about his letter.

Mam appeared in the doorway, taking off her apron and wiping the sweat from her brow. "I'm coming. Just let me tidy up a bit." She hustled up the stairs as best she could. Steps weren't as easy for her as they used to be.

"I'll be out gettin' the buggy ready. Come as soon as ya can."

Will strode out the back door and went into the small barn that gave shelter to Sally, their roan mare. He stroked her velvety nose, making gentle noises. Although he wasn't a farmer, he loved animals. He hitched up Sally and settled on the plain seat that matched the no frills buggy. Mam had never seen the need to replace it as the years passed after Da's death. What would Da have thought of him courting Polly? Would he have agreed with Mam?

At last Mam exited the house and they were on their way. The weather was beautiful and boded well for the picnic that afternoon. Mam patted his arm. "I heard there's a dance at Hines Hall tonight. Why don't you invite Susie O'Toole? She's such a nice girl."

Will bit his lip. Mam meant Susie was *a nice Catholic girl.* "Sally's nice but me thinks she isn't right for me."

Before his mother could comment, he changed the subject. "The newspaper said the graves of the dead soldiers of both the late war and those of the Civil war will be decorated. A solemn occasion it will be."

Mam nodded. "A solemn occasion, indeed."

He breathed a sigh of relief as they entered the Catholic cemetery and joined a line of cars, interspersed with some horse-driven carriages. He helped Mam out of the buggy near the platform that had been erected and found a spot where he could tie Sally to a fencepost. Patting her nose once more, he glanced at a car that pulled over in front of their horse. He didn't recognize it. When the back door opened and an auburn-haired woman got out, his pulse quickened.

He couldn't see her face, so he took a few steps in her direction. Another woman stepped out of the passenger's side, turned and spoke to the lady who might be Polly.

Striding forward, he touched the auburn-haired woman's shoulder. "Polly?"

She turned and seemed to have been struck dumb, staring at him as one might stare at a ghost.

"Polly…" He said her name again, although this time there was no question about her identity.

"Will… Is it… Is it really you?"

CHAPTER 50

Will took the hand Polly reached in his direction, restraining himself from bending to kiss it as he wanted to do. A sheen in her green eyes told him tears lingered there.

"I can't believe it's really you, Will. Some days it seemed like I had dreamed you."

"Oh Lass." Will's voice croaked and he cleared his throat. "I've missed you so. How many times I've dreamed of you and awakened to find you only a dream."

The man who'd gotten out of the car Polly came in moved toward him. Will smiled in his direction, reluctant to let go of Polly's hand. "I'm sorry. Will Reiser is my name. It's pleased I am to meet you."

As the gentleman stretched out his hand, Will gently released Polly's and reached out to him.

"I'm Garrett Young and this is my wife, Savannah. We're pleased to meet you, too. I believe Father Craig's address is about to begin. Would you like to join us?"

Will stepped back, reality returning. "I'm sorry, me mam is waitin' up near the platform." Springing Polly on his mother without warning might not turn out well, but he couldn't just leave without knowing he'd see her again.

He held out a hand to Polly once more. "It's so happy I'd be…" Where could he invite her to go? Will began again. "It's so happy I'd be if—" the dance, the dance at Hines Hall… "…if you'd allow me to take you to the dance at Hines Hall tonight. I believe it's to benefit the American Legion."

What did it matter who the dance was to benefit? What an idiot, stumbling over his own words in his fear she would say no, or disappear again.

Polly took the hand he held out. "I'd love to go with you. What time?"

"Would seven o'clock be too early?" He clung to her fingers.

"Seven o'clock would be fine. I'll be ready."

♠

Polly walked away with Savannah and Garrett, taking a couple of deep breaths to calm herself. When they were out of hearing, she turned to them. "Do you suppose Jim wrote to Will? Do you think that's what changed his mind about courting me?"

"Jim didn't mention it, so I don't know if he wrote to Will or not. You can ask Will tonight." Garrett smiled.

"I could've asked Jim when he preached at our church Sunday, but it didn't seem like the right time." Across the crowd, Polly caught a glimpse of Will standing next to his mother.

She'd been so excited to see him, she'd forgotten his mother's less than enthusiastic welcome when they'd met after the Stoneboro Fair. Even though Will knew her father from the mines, it wasn't likely he'd be thrilled either.

Concentrating on Father Craig's Memorial Day address was impossible while worries nibbled at her. The pain of being separated from Will all these months had caused her to forget all the differences that existed. Before Gram died last month, she'd said the Catholic Church began enforcing a new law that could make things difficult for marriage between Catholics and Protestants. It was too late to ask her more questions. What if the differences in their religions became insurmountable?

A long sigh escaped her lips. When Savannah glanced at her, Polly spoke the same words she'd said to her father months ago. "I just want to have this one magical evening with Will."

At last the Memorial Day observances were over. The Dye family enjoyed a picnic at Aunt Flo's house with everyone contributing their share, trying to ignore the absence of their beloved grandmother. At last, Polly was free to go home to get ready for the dance.

What to wear? She pulled the pale green dress she'd ironed on Monday from its hook. What were people wearing to dances these days? Too late to fret about that. She freshened up with a little water from the pitcher on her bureau and sprinkled on a bit of rosewater.

Almost time for Will to arrive. Father didn't know he was

coming. *I'd better be downstairs to greet him.* Skipping down the steps, she entered the living room.

"My, you look lovely, Shortie." Her father smiled as he called her by a pet name he hadn't used lately. "Where are you going?"

"Will is taking me to Hines Hall for the dance."

Her father stilled and bit his lip. "I…see. It's been quite awhile since you've seen him, hasn't it?"

"I met him today at the Memorial Day observance and he invited me."

The clatter of horses' hooves heralded Will's arrival. Polly sprinted to the door, hoping to avoid an encounter between him and her father. She hesitated as her father spoke.

"Florence, a lady always waits for a gentleman to come to the door."

Will had already leaped from the buggy and was taking the concrete steps to the porch two at a time. She needed to honor her father's words.

When Will caught a glimpse of her in the doorway, his smile was like the sun coming out on a cloudy day. "Hello, Lass. 'Tis fetchin' you look in that pale green dress."

Did Will hear her father snort at his words? As she opened the screen door and stepped out, she beamed at him. "Thank you. It's my favorite dress."

Will caught the screen door before it closed. "It's wantin' I am to come in and say hello to your father."

She stepped back into the house as Will strode to her father's chair, hand outstretched. "Good evening, Mr. Dye. Mighty nice it is to be seein' ya again. How are things at the mine?"

Father stood and shook Will's hand, although his smile didn't hold the warmth Will's did. "We're doing all right but concerned about possible strikes. I was sorry to lose you. How are things at the railroad?"

"It's busy they are, sir. The work is steady."

As they stood side by side, Polly couldn't help but compare the two men. Will, tall and lean but strong, in his cotton seersucker shirt and summer-weight trousers and her father, lean and just a tad shorter, in dark blue shirt and trousers of sturdy material. Each so special in his own way.

Her father cleared his throat, never a good sign. "Will, I don't want to be speaking out of—"

Polly reached for Will's hand. "We'd better be going before the dance floor gets too crowded."

"But…" Will resisted her tug and glanced at her father.

"Make sure the girls don't stay up too late. They have school in the morning." Polly smiled at her father as Will finally yielded to her gentle tugs and followed her out the door.

They had escaped her father's lecture this time, but she was sure it wouldn't be the last.

CHAPTER 51

Will caught up to Polly and captured her hand as she hustled down the porch steps. "It's in a frightful hurry ya are, Lassie. I'm thinking your da had something he wanted to say."

Polly shrugged and stepped into the buggy. He didn't know her father the way she did. "I was afraid Father would say something that would spoil the evening." She waited until Will sprinted around to the other side and settled beside her. "I don't want anything to ruin our time together."

With a cluck to Sally and a light tug on the reins, Will took Polly's hand in his again, interlacing their fingers. "No one will be ruinin' our evening unless we allow them." His voice was so soft Polly could barely hear him. "I'm sorry I allowed a misunderstandin' to wreck our friendship in the past. Seems like a lifetime we've wasted."

As they stopped at the end of Broad Street, he gazed at her. She allowed herself to get lost in his eyes by the light of the full moon and edged closer on the narrow seat. "I'm sorry for all the crazy things I said. I must have been out of my mind. Really, I didn't think I'd ever hear from you again."

He slapped the reins lightly and clasped Polly's hand tighter. "I'm sorry I caused you so much pain, Lassie."

"What changed your mind after all these months?"

"Many's the time I wanted to call ya or write to ya. I wasted many a sheet of paper with letters I never finished." Will tugged on the reins to guide Sally down the road toward Stoneboro. "Me problem was I had no way of knowin' if you and Reverend Caldwell were courtin'. Who could I ask such a personal question?"

"You could have asked me." Polly tried to tug her hand from Will's, frustration warming her cheeks. He clung to her hand.

"Don't be angry with me, Lass. I was tryin' to do the right thing, to be the man me father would have been proud of, even though he's passed."

Polly stopped struggling, the pleading note in his voice her undoing.

"When I received Reverend Caldwell's letter sayin' God was movin' him, I knew I was released from the promise I'd made me self never to pursue another man's sweetheart."

"But I wasn't his sweet—"

"There was no convincin' me of it before I read his letter. There's no doubt *he's* a man his father would be proud of."

"He's a good man, just not the right one for me."

A smile tugged at the corners of Will's mouth. The same words he'd used with his mother on Monday when she brought up the O'Toole girl.

Will guided the mare into a far corner of Hines Hall parking area. He left a generous amount of space between them and the other cars, horses and buggies. Sally munched contentedly on a patch of grass as Will released Polly's hand and gathered her close. Then he leaned back so he could see her eyes. "And who might the right one be, Lass?"

Polly touched his cheek and leaned into his embrace, not breaking their gaze. "I think, perhaps, it might be you."

As their lips met, Polly's eyes closed, clinging to the promise in his eyes.

♠

The evening flew by filled with laughter, dancing, and tasty refreshments provided by the American Legion. Once again it was as though Will's presence had lifted her burdens and made her young, carefree and lighthearted. She spoke to old classmates she hadn't seen socially in a long time, many of them married.

Polly didn't regret the years she'd invested in raising her younger brothers and sisters but why had she completely abandoned her social life? As Will whirled her around the dance floor, she glimpsed the face of a young man who had invited her to a dance years ago. There had been no magical lifting of her responsibilities with him. Instead, he had seemed immature with interests completely different from hers. They had nothing in common. She had asked him to take her home early to avoid prolonging the misery.

Only with Will did she become a person able to enjoy the things she used to fancy, young enough to have a good time, while still being a mother to the children as well. She had been right that first evening at the Fair—it was magical.

After they finished a rousing fox trot, Will wiped his forehead with a clean handkerchief. "Shall we get some punch and step outside for a few minutes to cool off?"

"Sure. Now that prohibition is being enforced, we won't have to wonder if someone spiked the punch, will we?" Polly chuckled. She had never been much of a drinker so it didn't take much alcohol to make her silly.

"Not everyone will abide by the law, of course, but surely no one would risk it in this public settin'." Will tucked her hand through the crook in his arm and escorted her to the refreshment table.

In front of them, Mrs. Wilds' daughter, Colleen, and Peter Avery, who had fought in the Great War, were dipping punch, barely able to keep their eyes off each other. They must have become a couple since Peter returned. They seemed to be making up for lost time as she'd heard many returned soldiers were. Even after their cups were filled, they continued to stand by the punch bowl as though moving away might break the spell.

At last, Will stepped closer. "Beggin' your pardon, but could ya be moving along then?"

Without a word of apology, Peter slid his arm around Colleen, and they moved away as though they were one person. Will winked at Polly and dipped a cup of the red beverage for her, then one for himself. Drinks in hand, they went into the cool evening.

Polly glanced at other couples who'd come out to cool off or perhaps, in some cases, to have a nip at a hidden bottle. "Are any of your family here this evening?"

"I haven't seen them. I thought perhaps some of me nieces and nephews might come but most of them were still at the family picnic when I left."

She glanced at him. "Did you tell your mother where you were going?"

"Mam knew."

"Did she know you were going with me?"

Will sighed.

"You didn't tell her, did you?"

"I saw no reason to be lookin' for trouble. With all our big, rowdy family at John's, I was able to slip away without her askin'. She didn't ask and I didn't tell."

A loud screeching of tires claimed Polly's attention. Mr. Chesterfield's Roamer Touring car swung by them as it exited the parking lot. Mr. Chesterfield was definitely in the passenger's seat but who was driving his car?

CHAPTER 52

Polly grabbed her market basket, bounded into the sunshine and headed downtown. Today was Friday, not only the end of the week but the last day of school before summer vacation. She should enjoy it while she could. She loved her sisters and brothers but there was always a little grieving when school ended. Gardening, canning, sewing new clothes to replace the ones nearly outgrown, settling arguments… Life was different in the summer.

All week she had debated whether to tell Father she might have seen Mrs. Wilds with Mr. Chesterton. In the end, Polly held her tongue because she couldn't be one hundred percent sure it was her. Besides if she didn't want him to lecture her about Will, perhaps she should keep mum about Mrs. Wilds. She couldn't be too angry at Will for not telling his mother he was taking her to the dance. After all, Polly had tried her best to avoid having Will meet up with her father.

Life can be so confusing, Lord. At my age, one would think I should have things figured out.

Her stomach growled reminding her it was almost noon. Perhaps she could stop and visit Savannah on her lunch break. Polly hadn't spoken with her friend since the Memorial Day observance on Monday. Savannah would be full of questions and Polly had some of her own. She pushed open the outer door into the Furniture/Undertaker's building and then the inner one to the insurance office. Dorothy stood and picked up her coffee cup as Polly entered.

"Hi Dorothy. Is Savannah here?"

"She should be going to lunch in a few minutes. I heard you and Will were at the dance at Hines Hall on Monday evening."

Polly bit her lip to keep from laughing. Savannah didn't call Dorothy the town crier without reason. She might as well follow her lead. "That's right. We saw Colleen Wilds and Peter Avery there together too."

"You mean to say you didn't know about them? They've been

seeing each other hot and heavy since Peter came home after the war. I thought everyone knew that." Dorothy lowered her voice and stepped closer to Polly. "I think I overheard Colleen telling her brother that Peter is going to give her an engagement ring soon."

"Is that right? Interesting." Polly tapped her toe. She shouldn't encourage Dorothy but this might be relevant information. "Do you know when they plan to marry?"

Dorothy's mouth drooped. "No, I couldn't get close enough to hear everything they said."

"What are you doing, Polly?"

Savannah had come in and Polly had the grace to blush as her friend's tone chastised her for egging Dorothy on. "I wasn't gossiping. Just playing detective. Sometimes it's important to have the latest information."

With a shake of her head, Savannah rolled her eyes. "Want to eat a sandwich with me? I made some chicken salad last night and Garrett won't be home for lunch." She paused, took a deep breath, and turned to Dorothy. "Would you like to come, too?"

"Not today. I'm meeting my mother at the market to help her get a few groceries."

Polly avoided Savannah's eyes, not wanting her relief to be too obvious. She didn't mind using Dorothy when she needed information but she didn't want to give her more fodder for the rumor mill by eating lunch with her.

As soon as they were out of hearing, Savannah grabbed Polly's arm. "Tell me everything. How was your date with Will? Was it as magical as the first one?"

Tilting her head, Polly smiled at her friend. "It was every bit as magical. The way he makes me feel is… indescribable. Just listening to his voice soothes me and transports me to—oh this sounds so corny…"

"No, tell me." Savannah stopped at her apartment door and clasped her hands.

"Well, I guess the best way to describe it is, he transports me to never-never land. For so many years, my whole life has been about being a housewife and mother without a husband. I didn't know I could still feel young and carefree. But I do when I'm with Will."

"Oh Polly, I'm so happy for you. If only…" Savannah turned, opened the door and motioned Polly to precede her.

Polly didn't move. "If only what?"

Her friend moved around her and started up the steps. "Nothing. I shouldn't have brought it up."

"You were going to say if only Will wasn't Catholic, weren't you?" Polly followed her.

Savannah reached the top of the steps and turned to Polly. "I don't mind Will being Catholic. Of all people, I have no reason to throw stones at anyone. But your father and Will's mother… This will be hard for them."

The silence echoed as Savannah went to the refrigerator to pull out the salad and Polly grabbed plates from the cupboard. Then together they said, "Let's talk about something else."

Savannah chuckled. "Good idea. I have a question for you. Why did you say you were playing detective when you asked Dorothy about Mrs. Wilds' daughter and Peter?"

"You'll probably say I have an overactive imagination. If Peter and Colleen are getting married soon, Mrs. Wilds' search for a husband might be getting more serious. She'll need someone to support her if Colleen gets married."

A frown wrinkled Savannah's brow but Polly burst out before she could speak. "Now I have a question for you. Has Garrett talked to the alliance of pastors who are hiring Jim's replacement yet?"

"Okay, we can change the subject." Savannah grinned. "On Sunday evening the pastors and their wives will have a dinner for us at the Jackson Center Presbyterian Church." Savannah spread mayonnaise on two slices of bread, then added the fragrant chicken mixture. "Afterward, the pastors and Garrett will talk while I help the wives clean up."

"How do you feel about that?" Polly squinted at her friend, then fixed her own sandwich.

After a moment of silence, Savannah shrugged. "I have to admit I'm scared. The pastors have already told Jim they're okay with my past, but I doubt if anyone consulted their wives."

CHAPTER 53

Polly stopped at the market after lunch at Savannah's, then turned down Lacock Street to visit Maggie. After today, Twila and Elsie would want to accompany her on every visit. A lump rose in her throat as she passed her grandparents' house. It sat empty now that Grandpa had moved in with Aunt Flo. How she missed Gram's sweet smile and wise ways.

Her sadness disappeared when Maggie opened her door holding one-year-old Leah. Her four-year-old brother, Eugene, raced up behind them.

"I'm so glad to see you." Her sister swung the door wide. "I miss you even more since Gram is gone."

Polly swept Eugene into her arms for a quick kiss before putting the wriggling little boy down. He grabbed her hand to drag her to his toy box, not satisfied until she plopped down on the floor. Immediately, he pushed a truck toward her with appropriate sound effects.

"Eugene, maybe Polly wants to visit with me. Don't make so much noise." Maggie set Leah on the floor. She crawled into Polly's lap and snuggled against her. Leah's giggles rang out as Polly tickled under her double chin.

Maggie leaned forward and raised her voice to be heard over the screeches of the children. "So how was the dance? Leah, not so loud."

"It was fun. Took ten years off my life, like I was young and carefree again. Ouch, Eugene. You ran over my foot."

"Be careful, Eugene." Maggie used her stern mother voice. "Did Will say what changed his mind about courting you?"

"You'll never believe it. A letter from Reverend Caldwell telling him we weren't courting. I wanted to be angry because I told him a year and a half ago that Jim and I weren't courting. Think of all the time we wasted... But I didn't want to waste more time being angry."

Maggie asked question after question, wanting to hear more details about Polly's evening than she was ready to share. Finally, Polly changed the subject. "Guess what? I saw Mr. Chesterfield leaving Hines Hall in his car, and Mrs. Wilds might have been driving." Polly glanced at her sister. "Do you think I should tell Father?"

Rolling her eyes, Maggie shook her head. "For goodness sake, Polly. Leave Father and Mrs. Wilds alone. They're grown ups. Just because Mother asked you to help raise the children doesn't mean you're in charge of Father's love life."

The long sigh that escaped Polly's lips drew Leah's attention, and she patted Polly's cheek.

"You know what I think?" Maggie stared at her. She spoke her mind much more freely since becoming a mother. She would tell Polly whether she wanted to hear or not.

"I think you should get married and have children of your own, and let Father marry someone to help him finish raising the children. I'm glad you finally have a beau."

Polly bit her lip. "For one thing, I don't want children of my own. I've already raised enough children."

"But you love Leah and Eugene."

"I do love them." Polly kissed Leah's cheek. "But I can give them back to you when it's time to go home. That's not the same as having children of my own."

"Didn't you tell me Will is Catholic?" Maggie lifted an eyebrow. "Does he know you don't want to have children?"

Polly plunked Leah on the floor and scrambled to her feet as the baby let out an unhappy wail. "Mother didn't leave you in charge of my love life either, Mag. Will and I barely know each other." How long could she use that excuse? "It's time for me to head for home."

With a few quick steps, Maggie picked up Leah and hugged Polly. "I'm sorry. I shouldn't be so bossy. I'll try to stay out of your business but you need to stay out of Father's."

"Why couldn't he pick someone like Mother?"

"I'm not crazy about Mrs. Wilds either, but I doubt you'd be happy no matter who he chose. That's why you need to… Sorry, there I go again." Maggie stepped back a few paces.

"Maybe you're right. I don't like Mrs. Wilds and I don't trust her, but I can't make Father's decisions.

♠

Garrett held the car door for Savannah. The color of her dress matched her eyes perfectly. There was no doubt about it, his wife was still the most beautiful woman he'd ever known. She leaned out to kiss his cheek before he closed the door.

After cranking the car to life, he jumped in and gazed at her. "Are we ready for this?"

"I'm afraid to say yes. Last time we thought we were ready for something, we got the shock of our lives and failed miserably." Savannah opened and closed her handbag several times before meeting his eyes.

"You're right. Let's ask God for His grace to pass this test." They bowed their heads. "Heavenly Father, thank you for this opportunity. If replacing Jim is something you want me to do, give us favor with the alliance of pastors. Open doors and give us grace to bring much glory to your name today. Amen."

He shifted into reverse and turned his head to be sure the coast was clear as he backed out of their parking space. As he did, Savannah's face came into view as she repeatedly nibbled her lower lip. "What's troubling you?"

She stopped nibbling. "I…I'm a little worried about being alone with the pastors' wives after dinner tonight. Jim said the men weren't opposed to me but…"

"You're afraid the wives will be unkind?"

Savannah nodded. "You can't really blame them for thinking I'm not an ideal pastor's wife."

"I'm not too concerned about what they think." Garrett glanced at her. "I'm just concerned about how they treat you."

♠

To Savannah, it seemed the trip to Jackson Center flew by. Her stomach churned as they pulled into the parking lot. No one had ever treated her unkindly here before but everything had changed now that

Garrett was being considered for this position. *Help me not to put up walls, Lord, or assume folks won't like me.*

When they arrived, Jim met them at the car. He opened Savannah's door and walked with them to the church. He would introduce them to the alliance pastors and their wives to make his recommendation official. The heavenly smell of roast beef greeted them as they opened the church doors and descended the steps to the basement. Soon they were surrounded by beaming men and women making them welcome. Her head throbbed as she tried to remember names.

"This is Reverend Greely and his wife, Roberta." Jim gestured to the last couple to come in. Savannah stretched her hand toward Mrs. Greely who was suddenly very busy untying her bonnet. Savannah's hand dropped to her side as the woman bustled to the coat rack. Pastor Greely greeted her and Garrett warmly, shaking their hands and saying how happy he was to meet them.

When he moved on, Garrett took her hand and Jim moved closer to her. "Don't let Mrs. Greely upset you. She can be a bit—" Jim paused. "Well, a bit prickly, but remember the words of Jesus. "Don't be overcome by evil but overcome evil with good."

Reverend Greely moved to the head of the table. "The ladies tell me dinner is ready. Let's gather round and have a blessing."

Jim glanced at Garrett and Savannah. "Reverend Greely is the chairman of the alliance."

CHAPTER 54

Savannah sampled the strawberries and pushed her cheesecake around on her plate. How could she eat when her stomach wouldn't stop churning? She didn't want to hurt anyone's feelings by not finishing her dessert and forced herself to swallow a bite.

Reverend Greely was on his feet. "I want to thank the ladies for the delicious meal. I'm sure no one will go away hungry."

Is his wife staring at me? Did she notice my half-eaten meal the servers carried away? She sat up straighter. *Stop it. Don't imagine things.*

Pastor Greely cleared his throat. "If we've all finished, I'd like to ask all the pastors to convene to the classroom at the top of the stairs to proceed with our business of the evening."

After much scraping of chairs on the concrete floor, the men herded up the steps, except for Garrett who wavered beside Savannah. "Will you be all right?"

She stood and tried to rearrange her face into some semblance of a smile and squeezed his hand. "I'll be fine. Don't allow worry about me to interfere with your interview."

"I'll try not to." With a final squeeze of her fingers, he was gone.

Starting at the end of the table nearest her, Savannah began scraping and stacking dessert plates, then carried them to the sink. One jolly, heavyset woman whose name she couldn't remember took them and began to rinse.

"What else can I do?" Savannah desperately wanted to keep her hands busy.

"Why don't you grab that green and blue dish towel and dry some of the dishes after I wash them."

Quick to comply, Savannah smiled at the friendly lady. "I'm sorry I can't remember your name. I think it started with a B?"

The woman laughed. "Right you are. I'm Bertha. We hate to

lose Reverend Caldwell, but we're so glad you're here. There aren't many pastors willing to continue the circuit riding tradition."

"We're happy to be here. Garrett has been sensing God calling him to preach, so perhaps this is His plan."

"Don't be too sure about that. young lady." Mrs. Greely stood behind her, lips pressed into a straight line. "The alliance hasn't decided yet."

"I'm sorry. Of course, we have to wait for their decision. I didn't mean to imply…"

"Of course you didn't." Bertha cast a baleful glance in Mrs. Greely's direction. "Everyone I've spoken to has a positive opinion of your husband so I don't believe you're being premature in thinking this could be God's plan. Reverend Caldwell's recommendation means a lot."

Mrs. Greely continued to hover behind Savannah tapping her toe. "We'll see."

♠

Polly slipped out of the house without being seen by Twila and Elsie, and headed down Broad Street. She needed a breath of fresh air. In spite of the beautiful weather, time had dragged all weekend without Will. He hadn't been given any days off because of his three-day weekend over Memorial Day. Less than a week since she'd seen him, but it seemed like forever.

The year and a half they'd been apart had been the longest of her life, and she regretted every moment they'd lost. She longed to dispense with their courtship and go straight to marriage. Heat rose in her cheeks as she allowed herself to imagine being married to Will.

Does Will know you don't want to have children? She covered her cars as Maggic's words plagued her. How did one broach a subject like that? *Oh, by the way, I don't want to have children.* She envied Father. If he remarried, no one would expect *him* to have more children at his age.

Polly passed Mrs. Wild's house, turned right before reaching the small bridge, and trudged to the stream as dusk gathered. After plopping down beside it, she tossed pebbles into the flowing brook, one by one.

Just because Mother asked you to help raise the children doesn't mean you're in charge of Father's love life. It had been a mistake to take a walk with nothing to distract her from Maggie's words. Still maybe she needed to listen.

It was true that Mother hadn't asked her to manage Father's love life... Was Maggie right? Did she need to leave Father and Mrs. Wilds alone? She could go along with Maggie's suggestion about getting married herself if she wouldn't need to leave Elsie and Twila or have children of her own.

Father... The word hung in the air. *Heavenly Father... I'm so confused. Maggie's good at telling me what to do, and I'm good at telling Father. And of course, my father and Will's mother seem to think they know what's best for Will and me. How in the world am I supposed to know your plan? To be honest, I'd just like to run away and marry Will but then I'm afraid Father would marry Mrs. Wilds. Maggie would say that's none of my business. How does my promise to Mother fit into all this?*

Polly stood and headed for the road. It was getting dark and Father would be concerned if she didn't get home soon. When she reached Broad Street and turned left, she glanced up the narrow dirt lane that ran between Mrs. Wilds' house and the stream. Parked almost out of sight was Mr. Chesterfield's car. As Polly's eyes adjusted to the dim light, the outline of a man and a woman became visible, engaged in an intimate embrace.

After leaning in to make sure it wasn't Colleen and Peter, Polly stepped back onto the street. *Oh Father, what shall I do?*

As if in answer to her prayer, a conversation surfaced that she'd had with her father about Garrett cheating on her. After Polly discovered her father had known, she asked him why he hadn't told her. His answer had been succinct. "Because I didn't think you'd believe me until you saw it with your own eyes. You were so determined not to see his faults, I felt it best to let you find out for yourself."

Why is it, Father, we can see things so clearly in the lives of others but are unable to see them in our own? God had given her wisdom and guidance through her father's reply many years earlier.

Difficult as it was, she would keep quiet and pray her father would find out for himself the truth about Mrs. Wilds before it was too late.

CHAPTER 55

Polly's eyes smiled at her from the mirror as she prepared for her evening with Will. He was working daylight shift this weekend and had invited her to ride the train to Franklin to meet him. They'd been courting for two months and he'd managed to get home every week until now.

She slipped her new jade green dress over her head. Will had liked her mint green dress. Would he like this one as much? He told her often in his adorable Irish accent that she was beautiful no matter what she wore. She blushed at the memory.

Tonight they needed to talk about the issues they'd been avoiding—the differences in their faith, whether Will's mother knew they were courting, and the delicate question of whether or not they would have a family.

No more putting this off. You can't use the excuse any more that you and Will hardly know each other.

Polly's gaze returned to the mirror. She tried to force her cheek muscles into a sober, pre-discussion expression, but her sparkling eyes gave her away. Who could be sober at a time like this? She rarely had a reason to ride the train to Franklin so that would be an adventure in itself.

Skipping down the stairs, she arrived at the bottom out of breath. Her father sat in Mother's chair doing nothing, staring straight ahead. It was such a rare sight that Polly screeched to a stop in front of him. He'd missed supper and didn't seem interested in eating.

Instinctively, she stooped beside him. "Father, what's wrong? Did the miners go on strike?" He had fretted all through July about the threat of strikes at many mines in Western Pennsylvania.

Father blinked as though coming back to the present with a start. "No, nothing like that. I stopped on the way home to ask Lydia to have dinner with me. She has plans with Byron Chesterfield.

Apparently, she never stopped seeing him completely."

Polly swallowed. "I've seen her with him a number of times." She took a deep breath. "I didn't think you'd believe me if I told you."

He gazed at her for a moment. "Maybe not."

"Do you think Mrs. Wilds is in love with him?"

After a long pause, Father shrugged. "I don't know." He glanced at Polly's dress. "You're all dressed up. Where are you going?"

"I'm riding the train to Franklin to meet Will. He's working day turn this weekend." Polly started for the door, expecting a negative comment. When none came, she glanced back at him. Several times this summer, he'd tried to speak to her about the problems in Protestant/Catholic marriages. Each time she'd evaded the issue

He stared at his work-worn hands, then looked at Polly. "Are you in love with Will?"

Surprise stole her breath. It was the first time Father had mentioned love to her. She drew in a gulp of air. "I am. I've never felt like this about anyone."

He nodded. "Then I won't stand in your way."

Her jaw dropped. "What changed your mind?"

"If you pass up this chance for love, you might never have a second chance." He cleared his throat.

"Thank you, Father." Was Father thinking of himself and Mrs. Wilds when he said those words? What could she say to him? "I'm sorry you're disappointed about your relationship with Mrs. Wilds. It was hard for me when I found out the truth about Garrett even though he wasn't the right one for me."

"I didn't say Lydia wasn't the right one for me. It's just that apparently she doesn't think I'm the right one for her."

Polly tried to restrain a heavy sigh. So Father still might marry Mrs. Wilds if he had the chance. She bit her lip and opened the door. "Good night, Father."

♠

As Polly stepped onto the train to Franklin, she relived the moment she and Will had met here almost two years ago. She'd been a goner ever since he caught her when she'd almost fallen. His lilting voice was music to her ears. And Father said he wouldn't stand in her way. She gave herself over completely to a rose-colored daydream.

By the time the train reached the Franklin station, having a serious discussion with Will wasn't anywhere on the horizon. He beamed at her from the platform and she couldn't wait to join him.

When she reached the sliding doors of the train, he was standing as close as he could to them. He stepped in front of her and lifted her over the threshold as he had the first time they'd met. An impatient push from behind warned Polly that other passengers weren't interested in their romantic moment. Stepping away from the doors, they headed across the platform and down the stairs.

"It's a surprise I'm havin' for ya." Will smiled. Instead of walking toward the sidewalk, he moved toward the parking area and stopped behind a dark green Model T. "Past time it's been for me to purchase an automobile so I won't be always havin' to depend on the train for transportation to Sandy Lake."

The car wasn't luxurious but she was impressed. "That's wonderful, Will. So much more convenient for you."

"Shall we take it for a spin? You'll be my first passenger." Will opened the door for Polly.

"First I want to see the railroad yard where you work."

Will raised an eyebrow. "'Tisn't much to see. Dirty, noisy…trains comin' and goin'."

"I want you to show me what you do."

"If that's what you want then, Lass. But we don't need to drive." He closed the door, took Polly's hand and walked with her to the railroad yard. As he explained the scope of his job, she cringed.

"So if the air brakes fail, you have to climb on top of the train while it's moving, then run and jump from one freight car to the next to apply the brakes manually? What about when there's ice and snow on those cars?"

"Whatever the weather, it's part of me job to run from car to car as fast as I can to apply the brakes. Someone has to do it."

"But that's dangerous. You could get hurt or killed." Polly shivered.

Will pulled her close. "Every job has its dangers, Love. But it's in me blood and it's what I'm lovin' to do."

It was the first time he'd called her "Love," but in the same breathe, he'd told her he loved this dangerous job. She glared at the noisy, smelly engines and train cars that competed with her for Will's affection.

Tilting her chin, Will gazed into her eyes. "Come now, let's not be lettin' me job spoil our time together." He walked quickly away from the trains, drawing her back to his car.

She settled onto the leather seat as Will cranked the engine and then jumped in beside her. "Have you eaten, Lass?"

"I had to get dinner for the children so I ate too. We hadn't talked about eating."

"Maybe later an ice cream cone would hit the spot. There's a shop in town where we can get cones." Will backed out of the parking area.

"That sounds good on a warm night. Where did you learn to drive?"

"A couple of me buddies have cars. They've been lettin' me practice so I wouldn't be a greenhorn me first time to drive ya around." Will winked at her, a smile tugging at the corners of his mouth.

Polly smoothed her dress and returned his smile, trying to push away the image of Will running on top of icy railroad cars. "Where are we going?"

"We'll be driving to an area where we can park and walk by the river. I've never been havin' anyone to walk with me, but me buddies told me about it." Will raised the level of their speed as they left the city limits.

"Thank you for planning this. I love to walk or sit by the water." Polly's spirits lifted.

After a few more turns, Will swung into a small parking area and shut off the car. "What is it you're thinkin' of Miss Nellie?"

"Miss Nellie?"

"That's the name I've been givin' the car. Does it seem fittin' to you, Lass?"

Polly smiled. "Just so long as Miss Nellie doesn't try to steal your heart away, I won't have a beef with her."

Will jumped out and came around to open Polly's door. Instead of helping her down, he leaned in to kiss her lips. "It's longin' I've been to do that since last time I saw ya. No one else will be stealin' me heart because it only belongs to you." He put both hands around her waist, eased her to the edge of the seat, and swung her around to face him. After leaning in for another long kiss, he lifted her to the ground.

The only thing that mattered was being with Will. Anything she had intended to discuss would have to wait for another day.

CHAPTER 56

A week later, Will cranked his Model T, sprang into the driver's seat and headed for Stoneboro. Mam would be surprised. For years, he'd saved every penny he earned except what he gave to help her with living expenses. Now for the first time, he had someone with whom to share his life and his enjoyment of things money could buy.

This car wasn't the only thing Mam would be surprised about. Up until now he'd managed to hide the fact that he was courting Polly. He'd told himself he didn't want to cause Mam unnecessary worry if the relationship didn't last. The truth was he hated conflict worse than almost anything, but he couldn't wait any longer. He had to prepare Mam for what was coming. He groaned. Why couldn't he have fallen for Susie O'Toole? His mother would have been so pleased.

For most of his life, Will had tried his best to please her, especially since his father died twenty years ago. How would she respond to him going against her wishes? *I'm not a child. My entire life can't be lived to please Mam. Grown-up decisions must be made. I love Polly and I won't let anything come between us if I can help it.*

There were things he and Polly needed to discuss. But first, he needed to tell Mam. All the way to Stoneboro, he practiced different approaches.

I have some news for ya, Mam. Maybe you should sit down. No, No, not good to start out on a negative note.

Mam, you remember Polly Dye, don't ya? I've been courtin' her all summer... No use to draw attention to the fact he'd hidden this from her.

Ya know how ya used to always tell me I needed to find a good wife... A non-Catholic would not fit that description in Mam's opinion.

All his attempts seemed weak, even with no rebuttal. He couldn't appreciate the beauty of the ride as he anticipated his mother's displeasure.

Two years ago, he and Polly had spent time together for the

first time at the Stoneboro Fair. They would celebrate that anniversary next month. The Franklin newspaper said all those desiring aeroplane rides could get free passes at the Fair's Sandy Lake gate. Also, the first stage performances with lights would be held on Tuesday and Wednesday. Both sounded like activities Polly would love so he'd already asked to have those days off.

Too soon, he turned onto Chestnut Street. Almost home. He pulled up in front of the house, got out of the car, and dragged his knapsack toward him. Then he trudged toward the house, postponing the inevitable as long as he could. The front door opened and Mam stepped out. "William, whose car is that? It'll be making enough noise to wake the dead."

Just one of Mam's complaints about cars. "It's mine, Mam. Want to go for a ride?"

"Not likely." His mother snorted. "It's perfectly good legs and a horse I have to take me where I'm needin' to go."

"All right. Would ya be wantin' me to fetch any groceries for ya before I come in?" Will was stalling, plain and simple. "

"You know I like to do me own marketin'. Let's be eatin' the colcannon bakin' in me oven first." As his mother bustled into the house with Will trailing behind, the fragrance of cabbage and onion increased.

A few minutes later, Will grinned into his steaming bowl of colcannon. Perhaps if it were Hallowe'en, slipping a wedding ring charm into his bowl might have provided a good lead in for his discussion with Mam about Polly. It was a tradition from the old country that finding a charm in one's colcannon on Hallowe'en could predict one's future.

Mam glanced at him after their shared table grace. "What is it you'd be laughin' about then?"

"Just wonderin' if I'd be findin' a wedding ring charm in me bowl." Will stirred his food and winked at her.

"Have ya already forgotten 'twas unmarried women, not men, whose marriage could be predicted by findin' that charm in their bowls?"

"That hardly seems fair, does it now?"

"An Irish man can be asking a lass to marry him anytime he wants. But an unmarried woman needs the charm in her bowl so a man will ask her." His mother spoke so seriously, he raised an eyebrow.

"You wouldn't be believin' that would ya, Mam? You won't be findin' that in the Holy Bible."

Mam shrugged. Best to leave that discussion alone. Will cleared his throat. He had to get the words out. "Speakin' of women findin' charms in their colcannon, I've been hoping one comely unmarried lady might be finding a weddin' charm in her bowl some time soon."

She choked and put down her spoon, coughing and raising her tumbler to her lips to take a long drink.

"Talk to me, Mam. Are you okay?"

His mother nodded, giving him a level glance as she set down her glass. "It's misunderstandin' ya I must have been. I thought ya said—"

"I said I've been hopin' one unmarried lady might be findin' a wedding charm in her bowl some time soon, so to speak. I fancy her and it's wantin' to marry her I am.

"Marry her?" She began to cough again.

Will squirmed, waiting for the spasm to pass.

"Did you change your mind about Susie O'Toole? I'm believin' she'd be the perfect wife if it's a wife you're wantin'." His mother fanned herself with her hand.

"It isn't Susie." Heat rose up his neck. "I've been courtin' Polly Dye and I want to marry her."

She dropped her chin to her chest. "You might just as well say you're courtin' trouble, son."

"Why? Have ya been hearin' bad reports about Polly?" Will kept his tone level and reasonable, although his insides quaked.

"I've heard only good about the girl. How she's been spendin' her life helpin' her father raise—" A light came on in Mam's eyes. "Son, you can't take her away from the little sisters she's helpin' her father raise. That wouldn't be right, askin' her to break the promise she made to her mam."

Will frowned. "How did you know about... Never mind. It's

never I'd be askin' her to break her promise to her mam."

CHAPTER 57

Polly stood and wiped sweat from her forehead before picking another ripe tomato. She scrubbed it on her dark blue work dress and bit into it. Flavor and juice burst all through her mouth. They had plenty of tomatoes and her mother had always said, "Don't muzzle the ox."

She took another bite. Summer had passed in a happy haze, and school would start next week. After the girls helped hang out laundry this morning, Polly gave them the rest of the day off. They wanted to get in a little more swimming before vacation ended. Although work in the garden and all that went with it kept her and her siblings busy, she always made time for Will. They'd gone for long walks and rides in his Mam's buggy and his car. They'd also danced at Hines Hall and eaten at Aunt Adda's restaurant.

There was only one fly in the ointment. She suspected Will still hadn't told his mother they were courting. Sooner or later someone else would tell her. Would he be strong enough to continue courting Polly if his mother pressured him to end it? Family was so important to him.

When are you and Will going to discuss your feelings about having a family? Polly cringed. So maybe there was more than one fly in the ointment... How could she talk to Will about whether they would have a family when his mother didn't even know they were courting?

♠

Garrett climbed the stairs to their apartment where Savannah was cooking dinner. He sniffed appreciatively. Fried chicken must be on the menu. His mother had taught her well. He went straight to the kitchen to drop a kiss on her lips as he always did.

"Any mail today?" This had been his standard greeting all summer as they waited to hear from the alliance.

"I forgot to check. I did talk to Jim while you were out this afternoon." Savannah turned the sizzling pieces of chicken. "He said Reverend Greely told him they've been interviewing other candidates and will make a decision soon. I didn't know they had other candidates."

Dropping his keys on the counter, Garrett ran his fingers through his hair. "I didn't know either. Jim is moving after Labor Day—a week from today. They'll have to decide soon."

When he bent to place another kiss on Savannah's cheek, he tasted salt. "Are you crying, Honey? What's wrong?"

"We've been tiptoeing around this all summer. We both know I'm the reason you haven't been hired yet, even with Jim's recommendation." Another tear rolled down her cheek.

Garrett drew her close. "Don't forget Scripture says God opens and no one can shut, and He shuts and no one can open. If I'm meant to have this position, no one will be able to stop me."

"But Mrs. Greely—"

"Not even Mrs. Greely. God says there's nothing too difficult for—"

The telephone rang. He paused, and picked up the receiver. "Hello… Oh hello, Reverend Greely."

He smiled at Savannah as he listened. "We haven't sat down to eat yet. Savannah is busy making the best fried chicken ever." Garrett motioned for her to come over so they could both listen.

Reverend Greely's voice boomed in their ears. "We're happy to tell you that the alliance of pastors wants to hire you as our circuit riding preacher beginning after Labor Day. Are you still interested?"

"I am. We've been praying all summer for God's will." Garrett held the receiver farther from his ear.

The head of the alliance cleared his throat. "Since this is your first time serving as a pastor, we'd like to hire you on a trial basis for the first year."

"Okay. That's understandable, Pastor."

"I'll send you a letter confirming our conversation and the compensation we're offering. I'm sure you understand the salary won't be large since each of the churches have many other expenses in their budgets. However, you'll also receive a love offering each time you preach."

Before Garrett could respond, Mrs. Greely's shrill voice in the background made some comment about the compensation being more than enough.

Garrett coughed and tightened his grip on the receiver. "That won't be a problem. My wife and I plan to continue working for my father for the present."

"That's probably wise. You should receive my letter—"

Another comment from Mrs. Greely vibrated over the line. It was obvious Reverend Greely covered the receiver to muffle her words before ending the conversation. "It's been nice talking to you. My letter should arrive in a few days."

"Thanks for calling. Good bye." Garrett hung up, his blue eyes sparkling. "What did I tell you, Savannah? Not even Mrs. Greely can stop what God has ordained."

"Maybe not but she can make life miserable for us."

"God says if our ways please Him, He'll make even our enemies to be at peace with us. We'll pray that God will turn Mrs. Greely into a friend." He hugged Savannah.

"I can't believe all the Scripture that comes out of your mouth these days. All your years of studying with Jim and reading God's Word is paying off." Savannah sniffed. "Oh dear, my chicken..." She dashed to the kitchen and began removing well-browned chicken from the iron skillet.

"I'll set the table so we won't be late for your Bible study with Ma and my last study with Jim." Garrett headed for the cupboard.

A half hour later, they were ready to leave. "I'll take you to Ma's. Then I want you to stay there until I get back from Jackson Center to pick you up. Is Polly coming tonight?"

Savannah started down the stairs. "I think so. She's been joining us all summer. It's been so good."

♠

Polly was climbing the porch steps when Garrett and Savannah arrived at the Young's. She waved at Garrett and waited for Savannah to join her before knocking gently on the screen door. Mildred Young answered the door with her usual ready smile. Soon they were seated at the kitchen table with glasses of iced tea and their Bibles.

"Does anyone have any news they'd like to share before we start?" Mildred glanced around the table.

"We had a telephone call from Reverend Greely before supper." Savannah went on to relay the conversation. "I have to admit, I'm still scared. It's obvious Mrs. Greely doesn't like us—well, doesn't like me."

Battling an urge to give her opinion of that woman, Polly took a few deep breaths and squeezed Savannah's hand instead. "If she causes trouble, be sure to do what Sarah did when she experienced trials. Run *to* God instead of blaming Him."

Savannah nodded. "I need to remember that. Although *my* response in this situation would probably be to blame myself. If only I could go back and make better choices."

"Sometimes the hardest person to forgive is yourself." Mildred got up to pour more tea.

Sighing, Savannah bowed her head and stared at the table, then suddenly sat upright. "Here's some information you might want to hear, Polly. I don't usually repeat Dorothy's gossip, but this could be important. She said Colleen Wilds and Peter Avery are getting married in October. They plan to marry in Cleveland and begin their married life there."

"Wow…" Polly's eyebrows shot up. "That is big news."

Savannah frowned. "Is your father still seeing Mrs. Wilds?"

"He was. Then two weeks ago, he discovered she's still seeing Mr. Chesterfield. He was pretty discouraged."

"Well, here's the other news." Savannah glanced at Mildred. "I hope this isn't idle gossip. Dorothy said Byron Chesterfield gave Mrs. Wilds an engagement ring Friday."

Polly's jaw dropped. "When are they getting married?"

"They haven't set a date."

♠

Garrett sat quietly as Jim prayed for him at the end of their meeting. Then he prayed for Jim. How could he ever thank this man for all he'd done for him?

When their prayers ended, Jim tapped his fingers on the table and raised his eyes to meet Garrett's. "I have a favor to ask."

"Anything. I can never repay you for all you've done. Other than the Lord and my parents, no one has ever believed in me and invested in me as much as you have. What can I do for you?"

Continuing to tap his fingers, Jim sighed. "It's a lot to ask, given the circumstances."

Garrett frowned. "I told you, anything you need. Just tell me what it is."

"I've been visiting George Burns in jail every week since he was convicted of kidnapping Savannah. He hasn't made a commitment to the Lord yet, but he's so close. I don't know who else to ask. Would you be willing to visit him after I leave?"

CHAPTER 58

"Garrett, you haven't been yourself since your meeting with Jim on Monday night. Are you upset about him leaving or are you worried about your new position?" Savannah glanced at her husband strolling beside her. They had gone for a walk to enjoy the cooler temperatures now that the sun had set.

He ran his fingers through his hair, a gesture he had begun over the past year. It was quite uncharacteristic of his former image that didn't allow one hair out of place. She liked the new, more casual look.

"I haven't wanted to tell you." Garrett sighed.

"Tell me what? You can tell me anything." Savannah reached for his hand.

"Jim had a favor to ask of me when we met."

"After all he's done for us, I can't imagine anything he could ask that you wouldn't want to do." She lifted the tendrils of hair that had escaped from her upswept hairstyle to allow her neck to catch the breeze.

"That's what I said until I heard what he wanted."

Savannah dropped his hand, stopped walking and stared at him, eyebrows puckered in a frown. "What in the world did he ask?"

Garrett paused to face her. "Jim wants me to visit George Burns in jail after he leaves. He thinks he's close to receiving Christ."

"But of course, you have to do it, Garrett. You're a pastor now."

"After what he did to you? How can I visit him in jail after what he put you through?" Garrett began walking again at a much brisker clip. "There must be someone else who can go."

Savannah caught up with Garrett and tugged at his arm until he stopped. "We've never talked about it, but I forgave Mr. Burns long ago. God says if I want to be forgiven, I need to forgive. My past is so sinful, I can't afford to withhold forgiveness from anyone."

"It's much easier to forgive people for what they've done to me than for what they've done to someone I love." Garrett's eyes begged her to understand.

She nodded. "Even so, I don't think there are any exceptions that allow us not to forgive those who've hurt our loved ones. Not even for God. Jesus asked God to forgive the ones who crucified Him, God's beloved Son."

"But I'm not God."

Savannah was silent for a moment. "Didn't Pastor Jim say the same Spirit that raised Christ Jesus from the dead lives in us? We're not God, but His Spirit lives in us to enable us to do things we couldn't do otherwise."

Garrett drew her close and kissed her forehead before taking her hand and walking on. "Who's the preacher here, anyway? Seems like you're doing a pretty good job of quoting Scripture too. What a great pastor's wife you'll make."

"You may be the only one who thinks so. When do you need to give Jim an answer about visiting Mr. Burns?"

"Tomorrow. I'm helping him pack." He glanced at his wife. "Would you like to invite Jim for dinner afterward? I should probably have mentioned it to you sooner."

"Of course. It's the least we can do."

"The alliance is having a farewell picnic for him on Labor Day. He said we could come, but I think it's best just to let him have this last opportunity with them alone." He raised an eyebrow. "What do you think?"

"I agree. They'll see plenty of us in the days to come."

♠

Garrett glanced around Jim's apartment. It hadn't taken long to pack his few belongings. The apartment had been "furnished" if you could call the few pieces *furnishings*. He admired his friend's ability to be content with so little. Would he and Savannah have been willing to move into this small apartment to obey God's call?

He couldn't answer. Although his father wasn't thrilled about what they were doing, he was willing to let them continue working for him, reducing their hours as necessary in the days ahead.

Jim stepped out of the bedroom where he'd packed a few personal items. "Ready?"

"I'm ready. Do you want to ride to Sandy Lake in my car? I'll be happy to bring you back later."

"No, I think I'll ride Delilah. She hasn't had much attention lately. I'll meet you there."

Raising a hand, Garrett saluted before he strode to his car. Maybe Jim's salary at the Bread of Life Church would allow his friend to purchase a car, although he'd never mentioned wanting one.

As he cranked his car and leapt into the driver's seat, he couldn't believe his Monday evenings with Jim were ending. How many times had he made this journey over the past six or seven years? It never occurred to him that he wouldn't go on meeting with Jim for the rest of his life. To whom would he turn with his questions, doubts, and fears? Something like panic rose in him. He took deep breaths. Jim had said support could become an unhealthy crutch when it was time for a person to stand on his own. But was he ready to stand on his own?

At last he pulled into the parking area behind their apartment. The smell of roast beef reached his nostrils as soon as he opened the door. Savannah had outdone herself with dinner tonight, knowing this might be her last chance to cook for Jim. He helped her put the finishing touches on the meal as they waited. Pushing his own concerns aside, he determined to focus on Jim during his farewell meal.

Easy, lively conversation filled the dining room after Jim arrived until silence fell. Garrett glanced at his friend whose face was inscrutable. "What is it, Jim? Something bothering you?"

Jim shook his head. "I'll miss the fellowship we've had, and I'm missing Polly tonight even though she hasn't been with us in some time."

Savannah glanced at him. "Maybe I should have invited her—"

"No, no." Jim waved a hand. "That wouldn't have been a good idea." His smile drooped a little. "I wouldn't want anyone to get the wrong idea again."

"Perhaps God has someone special for you at the Bread of Life church." Savannah touched his arm lightly.

"Maybe He does." Jim straightened in his chair. "Garrett, have you had a chance to think about my request?"

"I have. I admit it hasn't been an easy decision. The only answer I can give is that if God will enable me to forgive Burns for what he did to my wife, I'll do it."

"I can't ask for more than that." Jim stood and Garrett followed suit.

"I don't know how to thank you, Jim. *Thank you* just isn't enough." Garrett embraced his best friend. Tears shone in Jim's eyes, and although he opened his mouth several times, no words came.

In spite of all Garrett learned from him, would he be able to fulfill God's call without the help of this man on whom he'd leaned for so many years?

CHAPTER 59

"I know you girls want to go the fair tonight but this is a special night for Will and me. Sort of an anniversary." Polly squatted beside the davenport where her little sisters sat like statues.

Elsie scowled. "An anniversary? You aren't married."

"There are different kinds of anniversaries. It's the anniversary of when we met. Do you remember?"

"Course we remember." Elsie rolled her eyes. "It's when you got all mushy about Will after you almost fell and he caught you."

"We like Will, too." Twila's voice had a bit of a whine to it. "Why can't we go with you?"

"Maybe tomorrow night you can go if Will says it's okay." She'd never have dared suggest that the girls go along when she and Garrett were courting, but Will seemed to genuinely like Twila and Elsie.

Her brother, George, thundered down the stairs and into the living room, so dashing and debonair. "Father said I could use the automobile this evening to go to the Fair." He seemed to grow a few inches as he relayed the information.

"Take us with you. Take us with you." Twila and Elsie outdid each other begging their brother.

They were no match for George's desire to have the car to himself. "Not tonight. A couple of my buddies are going with me."

Father strode into the living room. "Be careful, George. Remember what happened to me at the Stoneboro Fair."

"I've been driving much longer than you had been at that time. Don't worry about me." With a flip of his hand, George left.

He had barely departed with a couple of loud backfires, when another automobile pulled in beside the house. Father smiled at Polly. "Your chariot awaits."

She patted her sisters' heads and started for the door, then glanced back. "Where's Beth? What's she doing tonight?"

"I believe she's going to ride the train to Stoneboro with some of her friends." Father opened the screen door for Will. "Come in. Come in. That's quite a nice jalopy you have there."

"Father, it's much better than a jalopy." Polly rushed to put a hand on Will's arm.

"It's not new, for sure, but it gets me where I need to go." Will glanced at his car. "What do you think me Da would think of it?"

"I'm sure he'd be mighty proud of it and of you." Father gave Will a hearty slap on the shoulder. "I've never heard one bad word spoken about you."

Will blushed "Thank you, sir."

Polly stifled an urge to hug her father. Such a change in his attitude. He'd been telling the truth when he said he wouldn't stand in her way if she loved Will.

"Are you ready, Lass?" The love in Will's eyes as he reached for her hand increased her pulse.

"I'm ready."

After Will cranked the car and they were settled, he paused before pulling down on the accelerator. A puzzled frown puckered his brow. "Your father... What happened? It's been seemin' like... Well, the last few times he's acted as if—as if he were glad to see me." Will put the car in motion.

Since Will hadn't clearly stated his intentions, Polly hadn't told him about her father's change of heart. Warmth crept up her neck into her cheeks. "Father told me a few weeks ago that if I love you, he won't stand in my way."

"Oh Lass, that means everything to me. We're both adults but it would mean the world to have his blessing. Now if only me mam—"

"Does she know we're courting?" The question burst out of Polly's mouth.

"She knows. Early in August I was tellin' her. She knows me intentions."

"What did she say, Will?"

He shook his head. "I'd rather not be sayin', Lass. Just give her time to get used to the idea."

"I don't want to come between you and your mother."

"I love me mam but it's me who won't be lettin' her come between us, Lass. I learned a hard lesson from losin' ya once."

Polly brushed away a tear. She didn't want Will's mother to be unhappy but his words mirrored what she'd been thinking. The love they had for each other was worth fighting for.

While they waited in the long line leading into the fairground's Sandy Lake entrance, Will reached for her hand. "One more thing we're needin' to discuss, Lassie." Will's tender voice brought tears to her eyes again. "Reverend Caldwell were tellin' me in his letter about your promise to your mam on her deathbed."

Polly nodded. Her lips trembled. She'd never told Will about that promise for fear of what it might mean to their relationship.

"I'm making ya a promise we'll be findin' a way to keep your promise to your mam. I'm believin' God will make a way."

Sobs escaped Polly's lips as she covered her face with her hands. Tears rolled down her cheeks, and she pulled a handkerchief from her sleeve to wipe her eyes. "Oh Will, do you really believe He'll make a way?"

"I do, Lass, that I do." He reached to tenderly wipe a tear from her cheek. Then he pulled up to the ticket booth. "I'll be wantin' two of those free passes for an aeroplane ride the News Herald were advertising', if ya please."

"Oh Will." Polly clapped her hand over her mouth to muffle her squeals of joy "I heard there'd be aeroplanes but I didn't know the rides would be free. How did you know I'd want to do this?"

Will winked at her. "I'm knowin' ya much better than ya think, Lass. Love does that, ya know."

After parking near the aeroplanes, they got in line. "Hold our place. I have a wee errand to run." Will disappeared in the direction of the planes and returned a few minutes later.

When Polly questioned him, he just grinned. "It's spoilin' surprises ya'd be by askin' questions. Ya'll be findin' out soon enough."

When their turn came, to Polly's surprise, only she and Will were ushered into the plane. With a jovial smile, the pilot shook his head at the next in line. "Only two on this ride. It'll be your turn soon."

Polly had dreamed of the day she would soar so high that people and buildings were mere specks, and the ride was everything she had imagined. Hanging onto Will's fingers, her gaze never left the scene outside their window until he withdrew his hand. She turned to find him on one knee reaching into his pocket. When he pulled out a ring box, her heart hammered against her ribs.

"Lass, there's no way I could ever be tellin' ya how much I love ya. I'm so poor at makin' speeches. But if you would do me the honor of marryin' me, ya'd make me the happiest man in the world."

He opened the velvet box to display a sparkling diamond ring.

"But Will, what about your mother?"

"We won't be gettin' married tomorrow, but it's marryin' ya she knows I want. Say ya will, Lass."

"Oh, Will. Nothing would make me happier. If you're willing to trust God to make a way for me to keep my promise to my mother, and work out any problems with yours, then my answer is yes, yes, yes. I love you so much."

He slipped the ring on her finger, drew her close, and sealed the moment with a kiss. His gaze, so tender and filled with promise, spoke volumes to calm her doubts and fears. No further words were needed.

EPILOGUE

December 4, 1920

Polly smoothed her hand over the yellow and green wedding ring quilt Savannah and Mildred Young had pieced and quilted as a wedding gift.

"Do you remember the day we moved into this house, Polly?" Beth had slipped so quietly into the back bedroom which had been their parents, Polly hadn't noticed. "I told you maybe this room could be yours because of the splashes of your favorite colors—yellow and green—in the wallpaper."

"I remember. Who would have believed that more than twenty years later, my husband and I would share this room? So generous of Father to allow us to live here."

"We all wanted to do everything we could so you can marry Will and still keep your promise to Mother." Beth hugged her.

Marry Will… In a few hours, Will would be her husband… Polly wanted to pinch herself to make sure it was real.

"Are you disappointed you can't be married in this house as Savannah and Garrett were?" Beth's fingers glided over Polly's simple but lovely white satin gown.

"A little, but Will and I want to make this as easy for his mother as we can. Being married by a priest in the Catholic Church they attend will soothe some of her fears."

Beth nodded. "I can see your reasoning, although some of our family may not be so accepting." She picked up a brush to smooth Polly's auburn hair, pulled high on her head with a few fly-away strands framing her face. "You and Will talked to Father Craig, didn't you?"

"We did. It was a little unsettling." Polly wound a curl around her finger. "So much I don't understand, but we've chosen to focus on the things we agree on in our faith, rather than the things that might divide us."

"Does Will know you don't want to have a family?"

A smile lifted the corners of Polly's mouth. "I decided if he's willing to help me keep my promise to Mother, I'm willing to have a family should God bless us with children."

"Girls, it's time to go." Father's voice echoed in the stairway.

"You go ahead, Polly. I'll check on Twila and Elsie, and we'll join you in a few minutes." Beth strode out of the bedroom, heels tapping lightly through the nursery and into the hall. A rap on George's door reached Polly's ears.

Polly gazed at the girl in the mirror and whispered, "Good bye, Polly Dye. Next time I see you, you'll be a married woman."

♠

Polly gripped her father's arm as Twila and Elsie wound their way down the aisle of the St. Columkille Roman Catholic Church, dropping rose petals as they went. Savannah and Beth, one in green and one in yellow, waited in front of Polly and Father. Father Craig and Will stood at the altar with his attendants. Keenly aware of the empty pew where Mother would have sat, gratitude filled her heart that Will's mother had agreed to come.

Give me your love for her, Father. It can't be easy to have her son marry a Protestant. Comfort her, Lord.

After Savannah and Beth started down the aisle, Polly and her father waited a few beats, then followed. The empty church seemed to echo around them in spite of the lovely organ music. For a moment Polly regretted their decision to limit the wedding to participants and parents. It had seemed best because of the varied responses of their family members.

As they approached the altar, her gaze met Will's love-filled eyes. The man she loved waited to make vows with her to be true to each other and to love and honor each other all the days of their lives. Whatever challenges lay ahead, whatever twists and bends they might find in the road, they would keep their eyes fixed on Jesus, the Author and the Finisher of their faith. They would allow Him to write their story.

After her father placed her hand in Will's, Father Craig voiced the first question that preceded their vows. "William and Florence, have you come here freely and without reservation to give yourselves to each other in marriage?"

The warmth of their love and the love of God surrounded and consumed Polly as they answered in unison, "We have."

AUTHOR'S NOTE

Robert Dye (Bob/Father) was one of the appraisers for a property owned by a woman whom he later took to a cottage on French Creek, owned by his parents, James and Charlotte Dye. His parents and his brother, Peter, and his family were also there. The woman's name and the names of everyone connected to her have been changed. (Mr. Chesterfield is a fictitious character.)

James (J. R.) and Adda Dye, Robert Dye's brother and his wife, had a restaurant in Sandy Lake for a number of years.

Benjamin Dye registered for the draft on June 5, 1917, and was later drafted. His name is on the War Memorial in Sandy Lake but it is unknown where he served.

Polly (Florence) Dye of Sandy Lake, Pennsylvania, and William Reiser from Stoneboro, Pennsylvania, were married by Father Craig on December 4, 1920. He was Catholic and she was Presbyterian. It is not known where they met or whether they lived with Polly's family after the wedding, although the newspaper account said they would be "at home in Sandy Lake" following their wedding trip. William and his mother, Mary, lived in a house on Chestnut Street in Stoneboro which is still owned by descendents of Mary Reiser.

The Stoneboro Fair did not take place on Labor Day weekend during this book's timeline as it has now for many years. The New York Central Railroad gave special rates in 1918 for people traveling to the Fair on their trains. The Fair was not held in the evenings in 1918 because there was no electricity yet, but I've chosen to use poetic license here. Robert Dye had a car accident on the Stoneboro Fair grounds in 1918 and a civil suit was brought against him. The timeline and the results of the suit are as given in the book. Free tickets for aeroplane rides were given out at the Sandy Lake Fair entrance in 1920.

Please refer to the author's notes in books one and two for a listing of those characters based on real people and those which are fictitious. As I've said before, the characters I've created (whether fictitious or based on real people), the conclusions I've drawn, and the story I've written are a work of fiction.

We lived on Beech Street in Stoneboro, Pennsylvania, many years ago, and I loved researching Chestnut Street and the Reiser family in Stoneboro. For those who aren't familiar with the area, Stoneboro is only two miles from Sandy Lake. Both are part of the Lakeview area we love—the place we raised our family and where our children attended school. The place we called home.

About the Author

Daisy Beiler Townsend has been writing and publishing in magazines and periodicals such as Guideposts, The Upper Room and the Secret Place for almost forty years.

In earlier years, she and her husband, Donn, wrote more than 100 songs and had a family music ministry and Christian Nursery School. Later, Daisy pursued certification as a pastoral counselor with the NCCA and ordination with the NCCC with whom she served for many years. Daisy and Donn were also missionaries to Japan with One Mission Society, with whom they are still affiliated, and led the Japan Prayer Initiative.

Researching the history of their home in Sandy Lake, PA, in 1998 led to beginning a historical novel inspired by the lives of former residents of their home in the late 19th and early 20th centuries. In 2014, Daisy published her first book, Homespun Faith, an autobiographical devotional, and then completed the first book in the Sarah's Legacy series in 2017, the second in 2019.

Daisy and Donn live in Pennsylvania and have three children and six grandchildren. Visit Daisy on Facebook, Twitter, Instagram or www.homespunfaith.com.

www.ingramcontent.com/pod-product-compliance
Lightning Source LLC
Chambersburg PA
CBHW030736110726
47900CB00008B/2328